*Always dedicated
and my gorgeous grandc...... ....be
number of grandchildren has grown to eight with the
birth of gorgeous Edie-Rose. Thank you all for your
wonderful support and encouragement. LUA*

*Special thanks to Gary Dunn based at Paglesham. His
enthusiasm and knowledge of the waterways around
Paglesham has been fantastic.*

*Special thanks to Allan Sargent for
brainstorming with me.*

*I would also like to give recognition to the fantastic
work of the RSPB on Wallasea Island for their Wild
Coast project that features in the novel.*

THE GODFATHERS OF LONDON

SECOND IN THE SINGHING DETECTIVE SERIES

M.C. DUTTON

Matador
9 Priory Business Park
Kibworth Beauchamp
Leicestershire LE8 0RX, UK
Tel: (+44) 116 279 2299
Fax: (+44) 116 279 2277
Email: books@troubador.co.uk
Web: www.troubador.co.uk/matador

ISBN 978 1783061 655

British Library Cataloguing in Publication Data.
A catalogue record for this book is available from the British Library.

Typeset in StempelGaramond Roman by Troubador Publishing Ltd
Printed and bound in the UK by TJ International, Padstow, Cornwall

Matador is an imprint of Troubador Publishing Ltd

THE GODFATHERS OF LONDON

Also by this author:

THE DEVIL'S TEARS
SILENT NIGHT
THE SINGHING DETECTIVE (Jaswinder Singh 1)

CHAPTER ONE
A dish best served cold

'John, John, John,' he said to himself almost absentmindedly whilst gently swirling his whiskey in a glass choked full of ice. Previously most of his evenings had been full of laughter and adoration, but since the court case they had been silent, with only the constant staccato of chinking ice to keep him company.

He had spent the month recuperating. The court case had worn him out somewhat. The questions had been specific and awkward, and the attention from the public distasteful and unsophisticated. As a professor who lectured in English Literature, specialising in poetry, he considered himself a bard who wrote a few worthy, meaningful and (he hoped) legendary verses to be preserved in the annals of time. His female students always loved to sit with him as he recited his poetry for their pleasure. He found this excited them and although never openly acknowledged, it was his best seductive line. Now all the students were kept away from him, and this depressed him. He needed to feel the warmth of love and adoration; he needed someone to caress, someone to be taken willingly to bed and loved expertly and intensely. He wanted the enthusiasm and refreshment of youth between his sheets.

Laura had been a mistake, he conceded. He had the pick of umpteen girls, better looking and more willing than Laura. He still couldn't figure out why he'd wanted her so much. She had been dowdy: a pretty girl, he forced himself to admit, but she dressed a little too ordinarily for him. He liked his girls in tight jeans with skimpy tops that just covered delicious places he wanted to explore. Laura had been like one of those clumsy puppies that want to love you but don't know how. She had followed him around, hanging on his every word. It seemed to him that wherever he was he would turn and bump into a pair of adoring eyes just following him around the room. If he needed a pen, a tissue, anything, she rushed up and offered it. He was used to being adored but this was something else. He'd often mused that if he told her to jump off the top of the building, she would have done it for him. It was a heady and addictive pleasure that consumed him. He knew she was a virgin and it became his goal to take her virginity as his own.

Thinking back, he wondered how he could have been so taken in by her. He knew it wasn't an egotistical thing. She had cast a spell on him. He was, after all, only a man and she was using all her womanly guile to ensnare him, but she was the devil incarnate. She was never going to give away her virginity willingly; he'd tried, and she had stopped him. Everyone knew an inflamed man couldn't have his passion quashed. She was goading him and teasing him, and it had driven him mad.

That night had been difficult. He knew for certain she wanted to be taken. Some women were like that; they couldn't say yes but they didn't mean no. He took her virginity in a flurry of spittle and screams, with an urgency that ripped her clothes and left bite marks on her beautifully budding tits and neck. It was wonderful and glorious. He loved the fight but she wasn't strong; she whimpered and screamed, and this made him thrust harder. He climaxed magnificently and shouted in pleasure. This had been the best he'd ever had.

She lay still, silently crying. At first he was surprised, then angry. What the fuck was she crying for? She'd been taken by the best lover in the land. She would never find another so exciting and so proficient. Yet she accused him of rape. He sat up, shocked and amazed at such an assumption. He had no need to rape anyone, he told her; he could have at least ten women at any time just by clicking his fingers – and he flicked them in her face, angry now. He could see she was scared, and this made him even angrier. When he asked what she was going to do, she said she wanted to go home to her parents; she wanted her mum. He could see she would tell all, and it wouldn't be the truth. He hadn't raped her! It was a game she had been playing; he knew these games.

She got up and arranged her clothes, crying louder and telling him he had no right to do what he did. He was scared and angry, and they argued violently. He still didn't know what made him pick up the bronze statue of Wordsworth that sat close by, but when she said fiercely that she would tell the police what he'd done, he picked up the heavy statue and hit her across the back of the head. She fell across the bed – and he could see she was dead.

It had been a terrible time for him. He hadn't meant to kill her. He wasn't that sort of man and he was upset that she had died. She wouldn't listen to him and this had made him so angry he'd done something he didn't think he was capable of. It took him an hour of shaking before he could pull himself together and dispose of the body. He still shuddered at the thought. He'd wrapped her in bedding and carried her to his car. It was late, she was heavy, and he grunted and groaned with the effort. But no one was around and he took her to Hainault.

He knew he'd done wrong but it wasn't his fault. If only she had listened to him and been honest with him, they would never have been in that situation. He'd told the court they were lovers, and that she'd been a very energetic lover, which accounted for the internal bruising and that on her thighs. He had to protect himself; no one would understand, so he permitted himself to lie a little. He couldn't admit to killing her. It was a kind of accident; he would never have picked up the statue if she'd been more sophisticated, and just talked to him instead of screaming and threatening him. The jury found him not guilty and he was grateful for that. At the moment he was on garden leave but he expected to be reinstated as a lecturer when everything had calmed down a bit. For the moment he just idled away his time in alcoholic contemplation – until he got his calling.

The knock on his door at 11 p.m. was unexpected and interesting. He hoped that one of his girly students had decided to ignore the ban and seek him out. Full of sexual anticipation, he went to the door: it was a shaft of brightness in a dark hour. He opened the door with an expectant smile that drained from his face when he saw four men there, standing very close to the threshold. The man in front was smiling, asking brightly if he was John Carpenter. But the smile didn't reach his eyes, which were sizing him up coldly. The two strangers at the back kept glancing behind them, seeming quite edgy and anxious, while the third man just stared at him in a manner that made the hairs on the back of his neck stand up. Guardedly, he asked why they wanted him.

Their answer was swift and deadly. Of course they knew who he was; they had watched him for days. In seconds the door was closed and he was marched back into his flat, and roughly thrown to the floor. The acid down his throat stopped the screams and the last thing he saw before it took his sight was the face of his attacker frowning intently as he carefully squirted the contents of the bottle – the burning, painful, life-destroying liquid – into each of his eyes. Never again would he feel anything other than the exquisitely deep intense pain created by the acid as it burned through his voicebox and then the corneas of his eyes. It was the start of a fear and panic that seemed impossible for a human being to live through.

A heavy object, a club hammer, crashed down on his shoulders, breaking them in one blow. The pain was so intense it took his breath away, and then the hammer fell with force onto his arms, breaking them. The pain reached an intensity that caused him to black out. He didn't feel his legs being broken. Now limp and lifeless, he was lifted unconscious out of the flat and into the waiting car. The journey took them to Epping Forest. No one spoke for the whole journey. The men were used to these sorts of jobs but the very specific instructions they'd received had taken them by surprise. No one had ever requested something this gruesome before and it wasn't pleasant.

They had to carry him some distance into the forest. The instructions had specified a particular area. They crashed through the forest, shining large torches to find their way. It took just one of them to carry him; he was slight and limp, able to be thrown over a shoulder and carried with ease. They found the spot, where a white sheet hung from a tree. Dropping him onto the ground, they took down the white sheet. As instructed, they waited until he became conscious. It took some time and they paced up and down, anxious to leave. Four cigarettes later, they noticed him stir.

He looked pathetic; trying to make a noise but nothing happening; his arms and legs didn't belong to him and nothing moved. It was dark but he was blind. As instructed one of the men leaned over him and said, 'You are in the middle of Epping Forest. No one will find you for days. You are blind, you can't shout, your arms and legs are broken and you can't move. All you can do is listen and feel. When we have gone, the animals will come out and find you and it is hoped you will rot in hell. With that, they all left, glad to be going back to the car, and off to get a stiff drink.

He lay there, suspended between hell and madness. A crack of a twig, a rustle of a leaf: he heard it all. The first touch, the first bite, the first hairy creature he felt, caused a chasm of fear that could not be breached. He wished he could die and be out of it but his senses kept him wide awake and alert. He wanted out of this hellhole but his body was on crisis alert and would not let him rest. He felt every little bite that tore through him as his flesh was ripped into. It took three days for him to die, by which time insanity had invaded his mind with a fear of everything living. He died in an intensity of pain and a suicidal depression of fear and forgotten-ness. He died knowing no one loved him and he was alone.

CHAPTER TWO
Recap

Jazz had been back at Ilford Police Station just two months when Laura was murdered. He should never have been given the case. After Bam Bam's trial for the murder of DC Tony Sepple, and the gangland murders, Jazz was given leave to recuperate. In other words, the police psychiatrist had recommended he went away to rehab for his budding breakdown and the drink problem that had grown up. He was in rehab for six months and actually enjoyed it. He was somewhere in the Cotswolds, and the peace, walks and company did him a power of good. When he returned to Ilford, to De Vere Gardens and Mrs Chodda, he was fitter and leaner, with no drink problem. Again, he thought he wouldn't stay there too long but for the moment it did him okay, and he had warmed to Mrs Chodda and her ways. He found his room just the way he'd left it, except that Mrs Chodda had gone in and cleaned everything for him.

His team as it was had moved on. He heard that Sharon was now 'shacked up' with a DS in Lewisham and had moved to the station there. The big difference was no Bob as Custody Sergeant. Jazz took great pleasure in being at his trial and seeing him get twelve years. Hopefully his time in prison would be painful.

Bob had pretended to be Jazz's friend at the police station, but all the time he had been working for Bam Bam, one of the local gang leaders. Jazz had confided in Bob as a fellow officer and friend, telling him things about his investigation that he would never tell another officer, and all the time Bob was passing everything on to Bam Bam. Jazz still felt the immense anger rising as he remembered that it was Bob who was responsible for the death of a fellow officer. A crime that should have seen him hung. Oh no, he certainly wasn't at all ashamed about what he had organised. Jazz had some very useful contacts and he'd arranged for Bob to be given a prison welcome when he arrived. He had heard that after an indecent amount of time in prison Bob was found in the hospital wing with enough cracked and broken bones to keep him in agony for quite some time. Jazz hoped he would never walk again. No, he definitely didn't feel any shame in arranging this. He was proud of it! He did it for Tony.

Now Bam Bam was a different matter. This big, fat, evil bastard was well looked after in prison and closely guarded by the cons and guards. Bam Bam had contacts on the inside and couldn't be touched, Jazz knew this, but he had killed DC Tony Sepple and that meant that Bam Bam would have to die. Jazz could wait. There would come a time when he would get his revenge for Tony's death and all the treachery.

Again, he expected his team to be new Detective Constables. No one wanted to work with him. As was said none too quietly, he had now got two DC's killed. They conveniently forgot to mention to the new team that it wasn't Jazz's fault, but all to do with Bob the Custody Sergeant and Bam Bam who were now behind bars.

First of all he had to report to Detective Chief Inspector Radley, who had been on the telly again recently. He had become the blue-eyed boy in the Met Police and the press loved him. He got full credit for breaking 'The Holy Trinity' and seemed to be enjoying the fame. No one had mentioned Jazz in this, but he didn't care. He hated the press anyway. They just caused trouble and poked their noses into areas that were better left undisturbed.

Jazz had many anti-press stories but it was when the body of Laura was found that his full hatred of the press exploded. The press camped outside her parents' house for weeks. Laura's mother Amanda, whose nerves were very near collapse, was only just saved from an overdose. All the noise and the prying and the flash of cameras had whipped her up into a frenzy and one day she was munching tablets like they'd gone out of fashion when her mother found her. She made her sick them up and she got over it but the press had made a bad situation worse. When the ambulance arrived to take Amanda to hospital the frenzy outside was like a pack of wolves trying to get at the carcass. They fought and pushed to get 'the picture'. Jazz knew they would have been happier if Amanda had died: better story line. He grimaced in disgust at the memory.

He knocked on DCI Radley's door and entered.

Nothing much had changed in the office except for the huge pictures of Radley taken by the press association. The six smiling pictures showed Radley shaking hands with the Commissioner, with the Mayor of London, with members of some community group, and with various others. Jazz's eyes were drawn to a commemorative plaque for DC Tony Sepple, placed near the town hall in Ilford. His mother was shaking hands with DCI Radley in what looked like a very formal way. Jazz still felt responsible for Tony's death. He knew it wasn't his fault but – and he beat himself up every time when he thought about it – he should have made Tony report more to him that day and he would never have been in that position. The thought he could be alive if things had been different was gut-wrenchingly choking.

DCI Radley watched Jazz look at the pictures and, after a suitable minute, told him to take a seat. Of course there had been a debrief after Jazz was rescued, but as DCI Radley had put it he had been 'a babbling wreck at the time'. It had taken a lot of work to keep him going until the trial, which took a year to get to the Central Criminal Courts at the Old Bailey. When justice was done and all had been found guilty and put away for a very long time, Jazz was allowed to go away and get his treatment. He'd been away at the Metropolitan Treatment Centre in Sussex where they helped him get fitter in mind and body and now he was ready for work. It had taken six months of intensive therapy but it seemed to have worked. Jazz hadn't had a drink for six months – but now he was back, the itchy thirst at the back of his throat had appeared again.

DCI Radley wanted him back. He was a good officer with a lightning mind. His contacts in the area were phenomenal. When cleaned up, he was an officer that could be trusted. DCI Radley needed to read him the riot act and get him to understand that from now on he did things by the book. He wanted no more undercover work without permission. Radley warned him that not many officers wanted to work with him. They all thought he was jinxed, which made Jazz smile. 'Pricks,' he muttered 'Officers have no gut feelings these days, sir. Life is tough out there and you have to know what you are dealing with.' DCI Radley didn't want to hear any of that. He wanted Jazz to know that his new team obviously knew what had happened before and it was up to him to instil confidence in them. Jazz waited expectantly to hear who was in his new team. He was told clearly and firmly that he had one officer in his team, a new Detective Constable with no actual experience who had previously been a beat officer and had risen through the ranks. Jazz looked at DCI Radley incredulously. 'One officer? How the fuuu–' He stopped short and started again. 'How is that a team Sir? No one else has such a small team! Where did the term "team" come into this?' DCI Radley shrugged. Rebelliously Jazz added, 'I did it before! I can run a small team and still get the results.' Leaning towards his DCI, he said provocatively, 'The Holy Trinity was mine, remember Sir?' He stared darkly at DCI Radley. The silence was ominous.

DCI Radley was going to settle this. He broke the silence briskly. 'I know it was your work that got the Holy Trinity jailed. Everyone in the station knows it's down to your excellent work. I was the one who called you back from Manchester, you knew that. I saw something in you I needed here. I'd read your record, I knew how you worked. You were the only officer I could trust. I knew something was rotten in Ilford nick, and I needed a ferret like you to go in and bring him out. You did, you uncovered Bob. Bam Bam was a bonus and we are rid of him on our patch. You will, in time, receive a medal for your work but at the moment it's too soon. The shock of what's happened in this town is still reverberating and we don't want any trouble from the gangs, who have been very unsettled by the killings and the jailing of their respected leaders.'

Jazz opened his mouth to reply but actually didn't know what to say. He sure as hell didn't expect to hear such kind words.

DCI Radley took the silence as his cue to proceed. 'I'm a good guy, Jazz. I want us to have the best policed sector in the Met. I need your help to do it and I don't want your face plastered over the newspapers; I want you as anonymous as possible.' He looked at Jazz and added unnecessarily, 'Just try not to get your man killed this time, okay?'

Jazz was dismissed with a wave of the hand and he left not quite knowing what to make of it all, smarting at the comment. Two men were killed working on his team. He still asked himself every day if he could have done something differently to have stopped it happening, and every time he came to the conclusion that yes, he could have done something. It weighed heavily on his shoulders. He was learning through counselling to stop beating himself up, accept what had happened and move on. Disgusted at being slighted in this way and knowing he would be the laughing stock of the police station, he went off to find *his team.*

He had been here before but this time he was truly nervous. 'Bloody hell,' he thought. 'The little newbie is going to be shit scared I'm going to get him killed. Not a good way to gain his trust.' He walked the length of the corridor thinking of DC Tony Sepple and fervently telling himself that this time his Detective would work closely with him. What he didn't admit to himself was that he was going to give his new DC all the baby jobs, like stolen bicycles, shed burglaries and showing old ladies how to protect their homes with locks on doors and windows. No one would die on his watch!

CHAPTER THREE
Here we go again

Striding into the main CID office, he found an officer sitting nervously waiting for him. He was glad Sharon had moved to another region. It would have been difficult to work with her. He remembered the drunken night of lovemaking. It wasn't passion; neither of them had the energy for that. But he had broken a vow he'd always made: never to mix business with pleasure. Sharon had been good at her job and he would miss her for that.

The young man looked up as Jazz walked over to him. It was obvious in his face: he was young, eager and obviously intimidated by all the gossip about Jazz that had been wildly exaggerated by many in the CID office. Jazz felt old, looking at the officer's barely shaved face. Smiling, trying to look friendly, he gave the usual routine about how he had come back from Manchester into a viper's den and how he'd cleared the Holy Trinity from the East End. He added that his best friend had turned out to be a grass for Bam Bam, and that he was now banged up. He hoped the officer would work hard for and with him.

The young man seemed quiet; he reminded Jazz of DC Tony Sepple, and this made him feel uneasy. He wore the same type of smart suit and tie and he was wearing cufflinks, for Christ's sake! His handshake was firm and confident. He introduced himself as DC Ashiv Kumar. 'But most people call me Ash.' He'd worked at Plaistow Police Station for the past four years, had studied hard to be a Detective Constable and had passed the first time just over a month ago.

Jazz thought this one had a fair bit of confidence; if he was as good as he was confident, then Jazz might be able to work with him. But he couldn't shake the feeling that, although Ashiv Kumar might be useful, he would never trust him.

Again, here he was with no decent jobs to look at. Jazz felt a disquieting sense of déjà vu. This was how his last team had started and he didn't want it finishing the same way. No one had a desk anymore in Ilford Police Station. It was all now 'hot desking', which Jazz thought was a pile of pants. He liked his own space and he took over a desk in a corner of the open planned office, making sure Ash took the one beside him. The desk cabinet had a key in it and Jazz made sure the drawers were locked before putting the key in his pocket. This was his place now. Every officer had a small locker in which to keep case papers, in a bank of lockers at the end of the office. It wasn't the way Jazz would work, and he would argue their case as and when. For now, he suggested Ash went to the canteen for some lunch and return ready for work. He himself was going off to the IBO room to find some work. He would find a safe job for Ash of looking for pedal bikes stolen from some eleven-year-olds, whilst he tried to get something more meaty for himself. It was at this time that the call came through that Laura Kent was missing. She was found dead and the search began for her killer.

It wasn't hard work; John Carpenter was the murderer. It took a year for the case to go to trial. It was a done deal as far as Jazz was concerned, even though Carpenter protested his innocence. Jazz spent a year helping Laura's family get ready for the trial. It felt personal and he had got involved.

CHAPTER FOUR
Madness: it's all in the mind

Hugging herself, she repeated the same statement she had made for the past year. Everyone around her cringed at having to hear it again. They loved her and cared about her, but they could do nothing. The statement couldn't be rationalised or chewed over. It was swallowed whole and everyone choked on it. It was just one of those things that could only be listened to, not commented on.

Everyone wanted to make things better, to say something positive, to make her feel good about herself, but there was nothing they could say. The statement fell on deaf ears; it was too horrible to see her like this and they would rather be somewhere else than hear it again. How many times in a lifetime can you hear the same statement over and over again? The frustration of not being able to put it right, to make the person feel better, was too much. Only close family were still around. Friends and acquaintances had made excuses, preferring to avoid her rather than hear it again.

'She left the house thinking I hated her. She called me jealous. She died not knowing I loved every hair on her head. Why did I tell her to get out and never to come back. Why did I do that?' It was a question no one could answer. Some had foolishly tried to sooth her with platitudes of 'She knew you loved her' and similar comments but they were furiously shouted down. With eyes sparking she would turn on the unfortunate person and tell them they knew nothing. The words she spat were so harsh, they cowered back to their seats. The insane and pervading hatred boiling inside her was contained, for the most part, within a quiet demeanour that was tightly held in place; but they knew she was on the edge and could explode hatred over anyone at any time. The tension in the room was so thick it could be tasted. Everyone tiptoed around her and she felt like an island, remote and alone in a sea of faces.

The trial had finished last month and today was the anniversary of her death. He had got away with it. They found him not guilty. Those filthy, evil words could not be said in her hearing. Again, she asked those sitting in her front room: 'why did I tell her to get out and never come back? Why did I do it?' Imploringly, she searched the sea of anguished faces in front of her for an answer. No one gave her one. They just looked at her and hoped she would sit down. Her mother, a seventy-five-year-old who felt worn down by the grief and worry of the past year, got stiffly out of one of the dining chairs lined along the wall and walked over to comfort her.

The room had been arranged for visitors. All the chairs were placed in a line. She had room to seat eleven people. Only a few managed to arrive. Her mother, Grace, Auntie Edith who was Grace's sister, Tom's Auntie Janice, and Isabella, her niece, who brought little

Kyle – just one year old, and a pleasant distraction for those seated in the room.

The grieving Amanda was the mother of Laura, a beautiful girl who would have been twenty-three years old this year. James was Amanda's husband and Laura's father. Laura had been a strong-willed girl who flounced a lot. She would flounce into the house and if things didn't go her way she would flick her hair and flounce out again. It was just a phase she was going through. It had caused Amanda a lot of arguments with Laura. Amanda never liked flouncing.

The argument on that fateful day was about Laura seeing John Carpenter again. Amanda knew John Carpenter from the college where she worked as an office administrator. He was a lecturer who had an eye for young women. John was fifty-one, and he looked an ageing mess: a weedy little creep with jeans so tight they looked painted onto his skinny legs. His wavy hair, worn to his shoulders, was going grey and he had a perma-tan that would have suited an aging rock star. What Laura saw in him, Amanda never knew. Of course she knew that students fall easily for their tutors but her Laura wasn't a stupid little girl; Amanda had told her what lecturers could be like often enough. She'd told Laura many times that John Carpenter was only after her for one thing, that she could find a nice young man to go out with who was more her age. Laura would dismiss such comments and flounce out of the house. She was so young, so beautiful, so intelligent – and her mother knew she was wasted on Carpenter.

It was just one of those arguments where you say

things you don't mean. She had told Laura to get out and never come back. Laura had goaded her mother and told her how John was just the kind of man she needed. She'd shouted and stormed around, saying that her mother knew nothing about love, and nothing about her and how she felt. The final straw had been her look of contempt and the words she spat at her mother: 'You're just jealous of me.' That was the last sentence Amanda would ever hear from Laura. She asked herself time and time again over the year, 'Was she jealous of Laura?' She wasn't; she loved her and wanted her to live a full and wonderful life. Now she would never see her again, nor see her happily married, nor see her beautiful grandchildren. Amanda couldn't bear to think ahead; it was all too much.

It was a couple of days later when frantic Amanda and James had pestered the police umpteen times. Their daughter was missing and she would never go away without telling them. They told the police about John Carpenter, and James went round to see him in the halls of residence. John Carpenter had reassured James that Laura had been to see him and left at 10 p.m. to go home. He had said he was really worried and asked to be kept informed.

Her body was found in Hainault Country Park in a glade, lying on the ground as if she hadn't a care in the world. Her hair was arranged, her arms folded, and she looked peaceful. She was naked with her modesty covered in leaves. The pathologist said she'd been hit over the head with a blunt instrument. The violent redness at the back of her head was hidden until she was moved. Her skull was shattered. At the time it was said that someone would have to be very strong to do so much damage. The pathologist said skulls are stronger than most people think. Amanda identified the body. She wouldn't let anyone else do it. She had to know for certain it was Laura. She sat still on a seat provided for her just looking at Laura until she was quietly moved because it was getting late. Her quiet despair had started then, and grew with each day.

Cuddling Amanda, her mother Grace looked around for James. She didn't want to be unfair, because he must be grieving too, but where the hell was that man? He was never here to support Amanda. He had sodded off to his shed again, she surmised. The bloody shed should be burned to the ground and then perhaps he would do something for his wife. Grace could feel herself tense up and she knew that was no good for Amanda. Grace was worn down by the grief. It had been her gorgeous, beautiful granddaughter who had been murdered, but no one recognised that. Everyone was too busy comforting Amanda and trying to keep her from going totally mad. They all sat quietly waiting for DS Singh to arrive. He promised to tell them what had happened to John Carpenter when he was released.

James looked up from his silence at the sound of someone knocking on his shed door. Distractedly, he opened the door.

Jazz knew that was where he would find James. He hadn't seen James since the end of the trial and in that time he seemed to have aged considerably. James was fifty-five: a man in his prime, some would say, but today he looked like an old man. His hair looked greyer and thinner and he seemed to have developed a stoop. He looked as if he had given up on life. The laughter lines around his eyes and mouth, from better times, were now etched so deep, all you could see was pain. He'd been a proud man. At six feet tall he had carried himself with a confidence that now seemed unbelievable. He almost shuffled when he moved back to his chair in the shed.

Jazz and James had come to know each other well over the past year, and they greeted each other with easy nods of the head. Everything had been said after the trial: the anger, the recriminations that the police could have done more. The bloody jury made up of stupid halfwits that had ruined their lives by saying Carpenter wasn't guilty, and the judge who should be shot for allowing him to go free. James had expended all his hatred in Jazz's direction; now he felt cold. He knew he couldn't get justice, but he wanted revenge.

Jazz had worked with the family for a year. It was his team that had investigated Laura's murder. John Carpenter was the murderer. They knew this. His semen had been found inside Laura. She was bruised between the legs and on her arms. The sex had been forced and from the bruising inside her vagina it all pointed to rape. Jazz remembered interviewing John Carpenter. He found him a sanctimonious little prick who had a great opinion of himself. He'd said that the girls he tutored were always chasing him; he called Laura a silly little girl like many others who pestered him. He had smiled during the interview and said it was all part of the problems of being a charismatic lecturer. Jazz wanted to smash his perma-tan face up into the wall and give him a good kicking. He knew he was the murderer.

Gathering all the evidence to get him to court took a while. John Carpenter had a group of girls that were infatuated with him and Laura was one of them. Jazz found out from the Head of the College that John Carpenter was being investigated, and that he was about to be called to a meeting to discuss his close association with students. The question was always why would he rape and murder Laura. It didn't make sense; it seemed as if he could have any girl he wanted. What was found out but could not be proved beyond reasonable doubt was that Laura was most probably a virgin when she was raped. Jazz wanted her mother to know that, in this day and age, it was unusual to be a virgin at twenty-two, so all Amanda's worries had been unfounded until the fateful night.

What John Carpenter had said in court was something no mother or father should hear about their child. He told everyone loudly and clearly that Laura loved rough sex and she couldn't get enough of him. The bruising was just how she liked it. He went into details about what she did to him and how he made her climax, seeming to relish the discomfort of Laura's parents and family. He promised the jury that he would never harm a hair on her head, and that he loved and respected her – and the jury bought it.

What Jazz deducted had happened was that Laura had hung around John Carpenter, professing love and adoration and making his ego even bigger. She was a beautiful girl and a virgin to boot; she had told Carpenter this. The challenge was to take her but she wouldn't be taken, no matter how great the persuasion or promise.

She'd never had a boyfriend before and seemed very innocent, perhaps because of her upbringing. Jazz believed that Laura had frustrated Carpenter to the point where he just took her. She would have screamed and struggled; the bruising on the legs and arms showed this. When Carpenter had finished he knew she couldn't go home. She would have been crying and shaking and frightened. The stupid bitch would tell everyone and his life would be over. A man with such a huge ego would have no alternative but to get rid of her.

Cold-bloodedly, he must have made her sit down, perhaps on sheets he could burn before he hit her hard with something heavy. He'd taken her clothes and the possible sheets, and burned them in the furnace at the college. The investigation found his fingerprints in the boiler room. Of course he had an explanation for this – that he'd recently cleared out lots of old papers from ex-students and, to ensure confidentiality of their work, he burned them in the furnace. The caretaker spoke up for him, saying he was there when Carpenter burned all the papers. The caretaker also confirmed he wasn't in the boiler room on the night Laura was murdered. Carpenter must have taken her in the dead of night to his car and dumped her. She had been laid out quite poetically which, for an English Literature lecturer, seemed appropriate. When police forensics examined his rooms, odd flecks of her blood were found, but Carpenter explained that could have been from the rough sex. The jury had obviously found this plausible.

The verdict of 'not guilty' was too much for Amanda and James to bear. They left the court devastated by such a decision. John Carpenter must have felt invincible; he walked slowly out of the court smiling and shaking the hands of his team of lawyers. He looked at Jazz and smirked. He hated Jazz. Their paths had crossed many times during the investigation and there was no love lost between them. Jazz knew he was a rapist and a murderer.

So Jazz was here now, to inform the family that John Carpenter was unfortunately living not far from them. He had left his rooms at the University, having lost his role as lecturer. There was no way they could keep him on with his talk of rough sex with one of the students. He had been stupid. His ego had made him boast about his prowess as a lover. Now he realised he should have kept quiet.

Jazz didn't want the family to bump into him on the street. James probably wouldn't do him any harm, but Amanda was close to madness and capable of anything, and besides he just didn't want her to suffer any more. It was also his way of saying goodbye to the family he had been in close contact with for a year. He liked them all. They were a decent, hardworking family and this incident had ruined their lives.

He asked James to leave the sanctuary of his shed and come indoors with him. Nodding, James followed Jazz into the house and into the front room with all those chairs lined up. As they walked into the room Amanda looked up and followed Jazz with her eyes. He said a respectful hello to the grandma, who looked greyer than he remembered, and went to sit by Amanda. Most of the family sat a few chairs away from her; she seemed to prefer it that way. James took a chair near

Amanda and they both sat there expectantly, waiting for Jazz to tell them something. They hoped he would tell them that John Carpenter was dead, killed in a horrible, tortuous way, but that wasn't going to happen.

Jazz was there just to finish off the case. Every visit to Amanda and James made him feel as if he was beating his head against a brick wall. There was nothing he could do to help them, and it gave him a sick headache every time he left them. His visits gave them a bit of reprise in their thick, dark and useless days; they liked him, although he would never know that. They were past any emotions that were sociable. His job was to tell them that John Carpenter was still living in the area. The fact that he had lost his job caused the minutest glimmer of interest. James wanted to know where he lived so they would never see him again. Jazz couldn't give him the address but said it was in the vicinity of Parsloes Park in Dagenham, which was far enough away from Chadwell Heath where they lived. 'Thank you,' nodded James. But Amanda sat not saying anything. The usual platitudes about being glad to have helped and to have worked with them didn't seem appropriate to Jazz, so he got up and left, giving a parting hug to Amanda and a handshake for James. He looked at Grandma and gave her a long hug; clearly the woman was holding in every emotion to help Amanda.

He left the house frustrated that he couldn't have done more. He was The Jazz Singher, with a reputation for solving cases, and he could do fuck-all for them. He hated John Carpenter with a passion for what he had done. He had raped and murdered a beautiful, innocent girl; he had made her out to be a slut in court and dashed any hope her parents might have of getting over this. He had left them with nothing. He had ruined so many lives. Jazz was determined to keep an eye on him; if he so much as farted in the wrong place he was going to have him. It wasn't going to be long before he was talking to the family again about John Carpenter's murder.

CHAPTER FIVE
Furry, filth and fuss

The IBO room, which takes in all the 999 calls and calls from other officers out on beat, was quite dead. There was nothing much happening out there at the moment. A big football match was on this afternoon and it was thought that most of the East End were busy storing up beer cans and crisps for the match. The pubs were full but no trouble yet. Jazz was bored and itching to get his hands on something of interest. He went back to his desk to wait for his weekly meeting with DC Ashiv Kumar.

Over the year Ash had worked quietly and consistently, and Jazz thought he might have found someone he could work with, although trust was still an issue. He saw Ash regularly to get updates on the jobs assigned him. He had noted that as time went on Ash had got more pleading in their meetings. He was sick of finding stolen bicycles! He kept asking to work closer with Jazz on some of his jobs. He wanted to help with the murder enquiry for Laura but Jazz would have none of it. He didn't want Ash involved in anything that might smack of publicity or danger; he wanted him safe and unknown. He didn't realise he was mollycoddling Ash.

He said loudly and often that, although they were a small team, their record for solving crimes was higher that anyone else. Darkly Ash suggested that finding stolen bikes and shoplifters on CCTV was not crime-solving to be proud of. In a pompous tone, reminding himself oddly of DCI Radley, Jazz told Ash that every crime was important and solving those crimes meant that their patch was safer and the public would feel safer and prouder of their police force. Realising how he sounded, he made his excuses and slipped away muttering, a tad embarrassed: something about a meeting. 'Keep up the good work,' he told Ash.

Jazz quickly leaned forward when his phone rang, hoping it was a juicy crime to solve. It was the front desk. 'It's Mary again. She heard you were back and she has something of interest to tell you. But she'll only tell you in person if you go to her house.' The message was relayed with a hint of mischief. Everyone in the station knew of Mary O'Connor and no one wanted to touch her with a barge pole.

Jazz knew Mary of old. She had a 'thing' for him. He wondered why he seemed to attract all the eccentrics of London. He wanted an Angelina Jolie type to fancy him and call him regularly to her house, but oh no, he gets Musty Mary. To be fair, she wasn't that bad an old dear. It was the cats that got to him: crawling over him, meowing in his face and smelling of stale fish. He would add smelly mutts to his list of fans, he thought ruefully. But Mary had given him some useful information in the past, and if she said she had something of interest to tell him then that was good enough. With nothing better to do he figured now was a good time to visit Musty Mary. He made his way to Parsloes Avenue in Dagenham to find out what she had to offer.

If he didn't know her address he could have guessed where she lived. Mary had a little two-bedroom council house beside the Parsloes Park fields. It was an adequate size for a small family but far too small for her family of cats. She had a small front garden neatly fenced off and it was full of cats sunning themselves. The front door was open and led straight into the lounge; these sorts of houses were called parlour houses, because they had no hallway. Jazz tiptoed his way past the resting felines, noting at least four of them looked pregnant, as they laid spread-eagled across the path to the front door. He stepped over them carefully. They stared indolently at this trespasser. They were kings and queens of Mary's house and would not tolerate any disrespect. He knew one wrong move and they would jump up caterwauling and spitting as their claws tried to find flesh to scratch. Past experience told him that these prima donnas were fickle and one minute he was the best thing since sliced bread and the next they would become creatures possessed in an effort to maim and injury him. Timidly, he called out Mary's name, keeping one eye on the cats.

Hearing a noise, he looked towards the parlour lounge ahead. The vision of loveliness ahead of him was draped with fur. Musty Mary had a cat lying around her neck, and one on her arm. Both cats looked at him with total disdain. The only things glinting with pleasure were Musty Mary's eyes at the sight of Jazz. 'Hello darlin', come in. You look lovely and oh so tasty in that shirt.' He wondered if she was taking the mickey but by the way she swanned up to him, giving him her version of a look of sultry sexiness, he feared she was serious. How did she ever make any money as a prostitute? Her look was dirty, her style was tatty and she smelled. 'Sit down darlin', and I'll make you a cup of tea.'

Jazz thanked her and refused point blank, stating that he'd just had a cuppa and was fine. The last time he was here he'd got milk out of her fridge and found a dead kitten in a see-through plastic bag on the fridge shelf. Apparently one of the cats had given birth to a still-born kitten. Mary had stated airily that when she had some spare time she would bury the little mite in the garden. In the meantime, it sat in her fridge with her food and milk. Jazz shuddered at the thought.

She went off to make herself a cup of tea and left four cats guarding Jazz. He sat uncomfortably as they fought for pride of place on his lap. With every snarl, warning caterwaul, and pacing around his lap and the arm of his chair, he ducked, ready for the four of them to jump upon each other and in the melee scratch and bite his face and hands. He tried to just push them off him but they turned as one on him, biting and lashing out with sharpened talons. So he just waited tensely and patiently for Mary's return. Only with her cheerful cry of 'Off you go my little darlin's,' did the cats jump down and disappear.

For a second, left alone with Musty Mary with that glint in her watery eye, Jazz thought he would rather have the cats. He took a good look at Mary. She had declined over the months. She never looked that good but the drugs, the filth, and the laziness had turned her from a shabby, tatty cheap fuck to a dirty, slobby desperate fuck. He realised he was staring and, to break the ice, asked how business was going. She shrugged in disdain. 'Nah, not good. Most of my customers seemed to have gorn. I think it's this double-dip recession that's to blame.'

Jazz nearly choked at the words of wisdom from the nicotine-stained lips of Mary. 'Mary Mitchell, where did you get those words from?' It was no time to crack a joke; she was serious. Truth be told, her customers had left her because she was the last piece of meat a blind and desperate man would go for. There was now a lot of competition in the area for a cheap fuck with all the '*Stanics*' that were now working in the East End. Romanians, Lithuanians, etc. She looked sheepish, which amazed Jazz. 'I met this fella who is something in the City.' By now Jazz was holding his chin to stop his jaw dropping. What sort of man would be interested in Musty Mary, let alone a normal or clean man?

It transpired that Mary had met a caretaker – well, a toilet cleaner – for one of the big buildings in Canary Wharf. He was Polish, lonely and homesick. He was a cat-lover and had struck up a friendship with Mary. By the sounds of it they were a pair of lost souls that had come together. He lived in Rainham Road South, which was close enough to visit. Jazz was actually quite pleased for her. He liked her and she was just trying to survive.

The smell was beginning to bother him and he wanted to go as soon as possible so he came straight to the point. 'Well, Mary, why have you summonsed me here?'

She liked the way he said that; he always made her feel important. Most people just pushed past her as if she was nothing; even potential clients did that these days. Mr Singh never did that. Again that coy look appeared. Tilting her head towards him, she said in a whimsical way, 'I may have something interesting to tell you, Mr Singh.' He sat up, interested. Mary never wasted his time.

The coyness left her and she sat down beside him. With a sense of urgency, she pulled out a newspaper from behind the grubby cushion. Jazz grimaced as she brushed a splodge of brown off the paper; he hoped it was cat food. 'Look at that, Mr Singh,' she said, pushing the paper towards his face. He pushed it away and asked her what was he supposed to look at. An article on the front page told of a man found dead in Barking Creek, with his throat cut.

Jazz knew of this case. He wished it had been his, but the murder squad got it and Tom Black had been on the case. What the public didn't know was the victim, Mr Barry Jessop, an insurance broker in the City, had been killed in what was believed to be a gangland murder. In the East End of London it wasn't unusual to see a gang killing, but to have your throat cut and your tongue pulled down and out through the slit leaving it hanging down your neck like a tie was very unusual. Abroad it was well known as a Columbian gangland murder, but it was a rarity in England and had never been seen by Jazz or DS Tom Black. The pictures of the deceased were on every Met police officer's Aware computer. It was still the most talked about case, and the pictures were regularly scrutinised by all officers who were fascinated by such an unusual murder. DS Tom Black was still working on the case and getting nowhere.

Musty Mary could see Jazz was interested. 'I've got some juicy information for you on this, if you want to know it,' she said, going all coy again. He wanted to ask how on earth she had any information on a case like this. Musty Mary was not Pussy Galore or any kind of femme fatale who would have access to anything this big or interesting. Usually she had information on street-corner drugs, street robberies, fencing, etc: low-life stuff, but always useful. She licked her lips in anticipation of his question, waiting eyeball to eyeball for his reaction. 'Okay, Mary, what do you know on this case?' It was as if a starting gun had been fired. She jumped up and tried to close the front door. The angry screech of a marmalade tomcat made her apologise and shoo the offended creature out. The door now closed, she almost ran back and sat on the settee. In a rush of whispers she told him everything she knew.

'Yen, that's not his full name, but it's full of z's and j's and I can't pronounce it properly, Mr Singh. Well, he's my friend and he works in the toilets in Canary Wharf. He was working late one night. He was actually in a cubicle about to have a fag when in comes Mr Jessop. He had the door closed but Yen said he knew it was him because he always worked late and he always went to the lav before he went home. He could smell his aftershave, which was very strong. Yen thought he stunk of B.O. and that's why he wore such strong aftershave. I said it never got rid of the smell of B.O. but Yen said it did.'

Jazz was getting impatient, he could see Musty Mary was going off track. 'Okay, Mary, what happened then? I presume something did.'

She looked impressed. 'Hey, you are so right, Mr Singh, something did happen then.'

'And?' said Jazz encouragingly.

'And the men came in. Yen thought he heard lots of them. He could hear scuffling and pushing and Mr Jessop crying out. Yen said it sounded like they punched him and he gave a funny sound and he thinks he fell to the floor.' Musty Mary was getting into this and she could see Mr Singh was hanging on her every word. She liked that.

'Yen said he was scared to breathe, he could hear them talking to Mr Jessop. By now it sounded like they had taped up Mr Jessop's mouth because he sounded all muffled. Now this is the bit, Mr Singh, that made me think. Yen said the man said to Mr Jessop that they were taking him back to the place where he had *deflated his vitamins.* Now I just laughed when Yen said that to me but his English ain't the best it could be and I thought about it, especially when I saw this in the papers. The dates are about right for when they found Mr Jessop. Yen said they left with Mr Jessop. It was about twenty minutes before Yen left the cubicle, he was too scared to come out in case the men were around but they had gone. I think it's possible that what that man said to Mr Jessop was, '*they were taking him back to where he had defrauded his victims.*' It makes more sense than deflated his vitamins, don't you think, Mr Singh?' Triumphant and proud of herself, Musty Mary lit a fag in celebration of her cleverness. She added, 'I could be your sidekick, Mr Singh.' He avoided answering that.

Deep in thought he remembered something about Jessop being accused of fraud by taking money from a group of people on a housing estate. They had clubbed together to fund a club for all the residents. It was hoped it would be a community centre that could house a youth club, OAP club and a mother and toddler group. Jessop had been accused of taking their money to invest and keeping it. It had gone to court and been thrown out on a technicality. The residents of the Gascoigne Estate weren't used to investing money and Jessop had come recommended and worked in the City. The housing association had raised £20,000. It had taken some Lottery money and four years of hard work, tears and time-consuming fundraising. Jessop had promised to double their money in an indecent amount of time and they looked forward to organising the next stage of building the community centre. The papers had slated him but the courts let him off. There didn't seem much justice in that. The housing association had all but disbanded in debt; disillusioned by the injustice, and now dysfunctional, the well-oiled team of enthusiastic amateurs had gone their own way, leaving a bad taste in everyone's mouth.

Musty Mary waited patiently whilst Jazz thought. She could see she had his interest and her hands shook with excitement.

'So why haven't you contacted the police and told them this?' asked Jazz.

Mary smiled coyly and said she had only told him

because he was always nice to her. 'Well, Mr Singh, is this good stuff I've given you?'

Jazz nodded and smiled. There was much to think about and his mind was going ten to the dozen when he was yanked out of his thoughts by a deep-throated warning wail that he recognised as one of the cats. He needed to get out before trouble started. Promising he would be back later, he left a disappointed Musty Mary who had rather hoped he would stay a little longer.

He was glad of the fresh air. He stuck out his tongue and pulled off stray cat hairs. He would meet up with Tom Black from the Murder Squad, to talk through what he had just been told. He knew for a fact that anyone who had worked on the housing association had nothing to do with the murder. Everyone and anyone who had anything to do with the Housing Association had been checked out. He remembered how it had taken a squad of police officers and more overtime than the Met could afford to prove everyone had a cast-iron alibi. All had surprisingly good alibis but one had the best alibi: the chairman of the housing association had been with the Chief Superintendent at a charity function, for Christ's sake! They were all good, hardworking people and Jazz was glad they all could prove where they'd been. Another piece in the jigsaw puzzle was needed and perhaps Musty Mary had that piece.

It was the start of a good day, and Jazz felt good. Stale cases were often revived by a smidgeon of new information. He made his way back to the CID office in Ilford Police Station after receiving a call from DI

Jack Hardy, a stuck-up candy-arsed knob of the first order who needed his help. A DI requested his help? He smirked at the thought. They must be fucking desperate.

CHAPTER SIX
Fairy light fest

Back at Ilford Police Station Jazz headed for DI Jack Hardy's office. He had phoned Tom Black on his way back and was told he was out on a job. They arranged to meet later for a chat.

DI Jack Hardy, he of the grey suit brigade. With grey hair, grey suit and no sense of humour detectable in his lined face, his greeting was more of a grunt than a greeting. To be fair, over the years Jack Hardy had seen the worst side of life in the East End. He was the first officer on the scene of a gruesome murder when he was an IPLDP (a raw police officer). Life's cruel and disgusting crimes seemed to have torn through him and now he was a disbelieving, dried up, disillusioned officer who saw evil in everyone.

Gold was worth a fortune at the moment along with lead, which was being stolen from anywhere and everywhere. It turned out that Jazz was needed because of his ethnicity. The recent crimes on the streets had been the stealing of gold jewellery from Asian women. Jazz had to admit that an Asian woman of standing went out with more bling than a Christmas tree. Gold jewellery was an important part of Asian life. When you married the bride was covered in gold jewellery from the groom's family: nose chains, necklaces, earrings, bracelets galore, and rings. To be fair, when an Asian woman went out she didn't wear all of it but she did wear the bracelets, rings and of course necklaces. It was traditional.

DI Hardy went through the list of street robberies and burglaries, which seem to be targeting Asian women on the street. In the last month, there had been a hundred street robberies in an area that ran from Ilford to Bow, and twenty-five Asian houses had been broken into in the Ilford/Barking area alone. DI Hardy didn't know why certain Asian homes were targeted, but the robbers always seemed to get away with a vast amount of gold. He wondered if Jazz had any thoughts on this. Jazz nearly detected a smile on DI Hardy's face as he asked Jazz for help, but it was most probably wind.

It was all pretty obvious to Jazz. The house breaking was easy to answer. He asked if the houses broken into were homes of Asians about to have a marriage or a party of some sort. DI Hardy wasn't visibly impressed by this. He said cautiously that they might have been. Jazz was getting annoyed; a straight answer was all he wanted. He kept his patience as best he could and added soothingly, 'So, what you need to do, if I may say so…' Then, close up now, he shouted, '… is tell them to take down the fucking fairy lights!' He certainly had DI Hardy's full attention now. Calming himself, Jazz took a deep breath. 'Of course you wouldn't be aware that at every special event in an Asian family calendar such as weddings, special birthdays, etc, fairy lights are put up outside the house. All special events have gold jewellery given or worn. If I was going to burgle a house, I would burgle an Asian house for the gold jewellery. The fairy lights are an invitation to every burglar – *that there is gold in them there houses.*' He added this with a flourish of a bad American accent. Getting back to normality, he stated, 'You know the house burglars are most probably Asian. The only way you can enlighten Asians is through their temples or their publications. A lot of women still don't speak English so it would be better to talk to them in their own language. I can visit the Gudwara locally for you, if that helps.'

DI Hardy visibly relaxed. Jazz was an odd one to work with but he was grateful for his easy offer of help. He knew if Jazz said he would do something, it would get done – which was more than he could say for other officers, he thought darkly.

On his way home, Jazz went to the Gudwara (a Sikh Temple) in Seven Kings. He found one of the elders on the committee who look after everything that happens in the Gudwara. The Seven Kings Gudwara was somewhere Jazz had started to gravitate towards. He didn't know why, but his Sikhism seemed to be more important to him of late. He would go into the Temple and kneel and join in prayers for a while. Then he would go into the community room where the food was prepared and served free to all of those who wished to avail themselves of it. All the food was provided free by Sikhs, while the cooking, cleaning and serving were done by Sikhs voluntarily. There would be the usual clique of gossiping aunties who came every day and prepared and cooked food. They were wonderful women who knew everything that was going on in the community. Without them the Gudwara would not function. They were usually older women who didn't have so much responsibility at home for bringing up children. Some were very old and Jazz realised their work made them feel welcome, and part of the community. He was beginning to understand how great Sikhism was. It was that they practised what they preached. He did his bit; he would take a cloth and go to the racks where people left their shoes and polish them for half an hour, just to feel part of everything. When visiting a Gudwara it was required that everyone covered their head and removed their shoes. At any one time there could be up to a hundred pairs of shoes in the racks provided.

Deepak was always at the Gudwara. A retired businessman who was recently widowed, he found solace in the Gudwara and enjoyed the companionship there. He now worked as a committee member for the Gudwara. He was a wise man and seemed to recognise something in Jazz that needed nurturing. They would talk for many hours over a vegetable curry and tea that had fermented in a heated container for many hours with milk and water added regularly. The tea was thick, strong and vile-tasting, but Jazz was getting used to it.

He talked with Deepak about the burglaries and the robberies of Asian gold. Deepak would ensure everyone was made aware. He would advise women when going out to hide their jewellery with a scarf or not wear jewellery when going out shopping. He'd heard of a few women from the Gudwara who had been robbed in the street and the fear this had caused all the women he spoke to. As for not putting up fairy lights, well, he thought that would be difficult. It was traditional, and no one wanted to lose face by not doing things properly. He said he would ask if there was something else they could do. Jazz said he would speak to his team and get someone to be available to visit homes to talk about burglary prevention. He didn't want to tell Deepak that his 'team' consisted of only one man. He left the Gudwara with a hug from Deepak and kind words to take care and keep safe.

On the way home he rang Ash and asked him to make himself available to help with burglary prevention for Asian families. Ash wasn't happy. Again, these stupid jobs! He'd become a DC to do real detective work, not this sort of stuff. He promised himself again he would talk to Jazz about letting him work more closely with him on the next case. He was fed up working alone and realised other teams were taking the mickey out of him for the baby roles given to him. He was not a happy bunny and Jazz didn't realise that if he wasn't careful Ash would put himself in danger just to get an exciting job.

CHAPTER SEVEN
The best laid plans

On the way home Jazz was buzzing. He would meet with Tom Black tomorrow, as he wasn't available today. He had spoken to Ash who was now busy visiting Asian homes. He wanted to go and see Mad Pete for some business he wanted to get done. But for now he would go home, sit down and watch some TV. He really wanted a drink. He'd fought the need for a drink for a while but now it didn't seem so important. Perhaps just one drink this evening, he told himself. He didn't think he would go back to how he was before. He'd worked hard, he deserved some relaxation, and a tipple always helped him relax. He tried to find a reason not to buy a drink but his heart wasn't in it. He gave in far too quickly and stopped at Sainsbury's, where he bought a bottle of vodka: a full bottle, because the half bottles were a waste of money, he told himself. He wrapped it in two carrier bags so it wasn't visible and bought some crisps to fill out the bag. The walk to De Vere Gardens would do him good. He quickened his pace, wanting that drink. By the time he arrived home, he was salivating at the thought. It had been so long since he had his last drink and he remembered that wonderful taste as it slid down his throat, and how every tight muscle in his body relaxed and let him feel wonderful and powerful. He smiled at the thought.

He had just put his foot on the first step and his hand on the rail when Mrs Chodda opened her kitchen door. Those words of, 'Oh, Jazz, have you a minute please?' filled him with dread. He wanted to say no, and to tell her to leave him alone, but good manners didn't allow him to talk to her in that way. With a sigh he smiled and followed Mrs Chodda into her kitchen.

Since he first began boarding with Mrs Chodda she had seen him as an excellent husband for one of her relatives; some had been very distant relatives indeed. She'd seen how successful he was in the police force and what good prospects he had. Over time, she'd become quite fond of him and wanted to see him happily settled with a good Sikh virgin who would cater for his every need. She'd tried to ignore his drinking, but then again, Sikh men enjoy a good drink and it never did them any harm. So, regularly and without notice, she would arrange for suitable female relatives who were available for marriage to be in her kitchen when Jazz arrived home. It was good traditional manners to never offend and Jazz could never be rude to Mrs Chodda; she was like an auntie to him, and he had taken to using this Sikh endearment when addressing her. He had got very comfortable with Mrs Chodda but the string of young women and their mothers was getting on his nerves. He had laughed, in private of course, at the beginning as he understood her motives, and his manners always contained his irritation as time went on. Now he was getting fed up with the interference. He presumed, unkindly, that he had already seen all the girls worth seeing and now they were scraping the bottom of the barrel.

As he expected, there was an older woman staring disconcertingly at him as he entered the kitchen, with a rather gorgeous girl beside her. This vision of loveliness smiled shyly and looked at the floor as is becoming of a virgin bride in the making. He really didn't want this tonight. The thought of not being able to sit quietly relishing a drink depressed him intensely. 'Good evening, Auntie,' he said warmly and respectfully to Mrs Chodda. Mrs Chodda introduced her cousin's husband's sister-in-law Pali, who had brought her beautiful, single and intelligent daughter Amrit to visit. Jazz nodded courteously to Pali, and smiled and nodded to Amrit. Apparently Amrit was a budding lawyer. She was studying hard at university for her degree. Jazz's interest was sparked a fraction as they talked about her studies. Amrit continued to look down at the floor in a demure fashion. They were all encouraged by Mrs Chodda to sit at her big heavy table which dominated the kitchen, and take a cup of tea with a selection of her home-cooked samosas and pakoras.

Jazz tried to start a conversation with Amrit and she looked up at him and smiled. Her smile was gruesome; she had tombstone teeth that she had hidden very well. Still, he thought, he shouldn't be so shallow and go for looks. With great interest he asked what part of her course she enjoyed the most. Her voice seemed to boom at him with a thick Brummie accent that locals in Birmingham would have difficulty understanding. When demure and still she looked like a goddess; when speaking and animated, she was scary. Once unleashed, she didn't stop talking. She went on and on about something he had no idea about. Her accent was strong and her voice, he thought rather unkindly, sounded like a foghorn. Even Mrs Chodda looked like she was developing a headache. Amrit would never make a lawyer with that voice. This torture went on for an hour. Jazz marvelled at the fact she hadn't stopped talking. Thank God there were no questions! He wouldn't have known what she was asking. He just nodded and smiled and tried to look interested. He sipped the tea and ate the samosas, which were at least hot and tasty. When there was a suitable gap, he explained he had to be up early in the morning for a meeting. With good grace he thanked the ladies for their hospitality and wished Amrit well.

As soon as he escaped to his room, he poured a triple vodka. Well, he deserved it after that. Jeez, what was Mrs Chodda trying to do to him? After a couple of glasses of vodka he giggled about the fact that even Mrs Chodda was surprised at the girl. That will teach her to set me up, he thought. The vodka felt so good. He didn't want to go to bed. He just wanted to sip and enjoy the warmth of the liquid slipping down his throat and the bonus of a hot surprise as he swallowed. Relaxed and at peace he sat smiling; he had missed the after-feeling of peace, joy and contentment vodka gave him when he was chilling out. At this moment all was well with the world and there was cricket on the TV. It couldn't get better than that.

Again, he promised himself he would have a word with Mrs Chodda and tell her he didn't want a new wife.

Every time this happened his manners never let him say anything. But every time he promised that next time he would make Mrs Chodda stop doing this. A part of him was flattered that she was so committed to marrying him off, but he really didn't have time for all of this socialising and having to be nice and polite with these dragged-in Sikh virgins with their straight-faced mothers. Nothing ever seemed to happen afterwards so he presumed the mothers didn't approve of him. This hurt his ego a little but hey, he wasn't interested and was in no mood to court any woman at the moment. Again, this was all in his head and the conversation with Mrs Chodda was never going to happen. He didn't want to hurt her feelings.

CHAPTER EIGHT
Hi ho and off to work we go

He woke the next morning with a thick tongue and a head that wasn't quite right. You never get a hangover from vodka but you can feel a bit muzzy. He thought it might have something to do with the fact he had only three hours sleep. He looked at the vodka bottle and was a little dismayed to see it had only enough left in the bottle for a single shot. He had drunk the lot in one evening after being off drink for a long time. He promised himself that he wouldn't do that again. Next time, he would have only a small amount and would make a bottle last him a week. He nearly laughed at such an absurd thought; he knew he would never be that focussed.

The shower made him feel better and more in control. He was on his way to see Tom Black to tell him about Musty Mary's lead. He liked Tom Black very much and he was the only person he almost trusted in the police service. Bob had done a lot of damage, but in thinking about him Jazz had to smile. The bastard was damaged goods himself. His legs would never be the same again after the beating he took in prison. It had cost Jazz a lot of money but it was money well spent. That bastard would never have an easy life after what he did to get DC Tony Sepple murdered. Villains are bad enough but one of your own being a turncoat and helping cause the death of an officer should be a death sentence as far as Jazz was concerned. The beating had been so bad that apparently it was touch and go if Bob would recover. Jazz still rued the day that he did recover but at least he would never be the same again with broken legs, arms that would never be right and a smashed face that would scare his mother; it was a small consolation.

Tom Black was in residence in Ilford Police Station. As Jazz climbed the stairs to the CID office he heard his voice booming his usual profanities. 'I'm gonna kill the fucking bastard who touched my sodding in-tray.' The words rang through the air as Jazz went into the murder squad area. 'Great threats for a murder squad,' he thought ironically. Clearly Tom Black was not in a good mood and he glanced at Jazz with a cautionary look that said *Think carefully before you speak.* Jazz was about to turn tail and get the hell out of the area but Tom remembered their conversation yesterday about the canal murder, as it was known. It was a thorn in his side. He knew this murder had been arranged and was some sort of signal. This wasn't just a drunken murder; this was a gangland killing. What he couldn't understand was why gangs in London were using the Columbian code of murder. A Columbian necktie had never been seen before in England and it just didn't compute. Killing someone was one thing but to go to the trouble of cutting his throat and pulling his tongue through the opening in his neck was just too surreal and too fucking pernickety for all the gangs he knew. Yes, there had been tortured bodies found, mutilated bodies, but never something this creative. It was a sign for someone; he knew this, but the frustrating and bollocking thing was who was it aimed at?

The canal murder was one of ten murders he had on the go at the moment. His team were busy sorting through all of them. Most were what he called kiddy gangland killings. Teenage miscreants who thought they were tough and used a knife and some used guns. Kiddy turf wars, drugs and just plain egos were the main cause of the murders. It was becoming a problem but they knew who had done the murders, or which gangs were responsible, but it was more which member had done the deed. The public didn't know just how bad things were out on the street. Most murders were inter-gang related so they just murdered each other. The general public was reasonably safe. The canal murder was different.

He beckoned Jazz over and almost smiled but it didn't quite make it to his face. Jazz could see Tom had calmed down and was safe to approach. Tom Black was a law unto himself. Jazz knew DI Tom Black was the finest and sharpest detective in the Metropolitan Police. He didn't fit into the candy-assed Pretty Politically Correct set that was being drummed into every officer. What it meant was his record for solving murders was better than most and at the same time his reputation was barely above sackable level. It was no wonder Jazz and Tom got on so well. They were the two detectives that the Met Police couldn't do without but sorely wished they could. Neither got any national recognition for their work. They were let out to solve crimes and then pushed under the carpet when the press came sniffing around. Jazz and Tom were the guilty secret of the Metropolitan Police hierarchy. Neither Jazz nor Tom understood their role but neither cared. Getting results was what it was all about and they were both given a wide berth by those wishing to climb the corporate ladder and those wishing to stay out of trouble.

The two men went outside for a cigarette. Jazz told Tom about his visit to Musty Mary and about Mr Barry Jessop. Tom dragged hard on his cigarette and chewed on the information. Jazz knew bits about the case but he wasn't working on it so he listened with interest. A good murder enquiry was always something to relish and solve. After a few minutes of thinking Tom murmured to no one in particular, 'So, he was taken from bloody London and brought to fucking Dagenham. That makes some sort of pissing sense.' Before Jazz could ask why, Tom turned to Jazz and told him determinedly that he had to be right all along! All the potential killers had rock-solid alibis; the killing was something you watched on a fucking, bollocking Godfather film on the telly. This didn't happen in East London.

Jazz knew all the potential people who had a huge grudge against Barry Jessop had rock-solid, gold-plated alibis, but Jessop had been brought to Dagenham of all places, murdered, mutilated and dumped in Barking Creek. *A Columbian necktie* was what the mutilation was called. It happened in America when gangs wanted it known that there had been a gangland killing. Musty

Mary had given them the time and date, although forensics had already told them everything they needed to know about when Jessop was killed, but she had confirmed it. Until now they didn't know where he was killed; now they had to find out why.

Tom thanked Jazz for the info and gave him a heavy-handed pat on the back that sent him flying. Tom left saying he would talk to Musty Mary's bloke and recheck the alibis for the Gascoigne Residents Association members who had been duped out of hard-earned money and Lottery donations to make their estate better. It was interesting that it looked like the men who had taken Barry Jessop mentioned his victims. Tom was tempted in his excitement to say, 'The game is afoot,' but he resisted the Sherlock saying and just said, 'This is the best fucking lead for a sodding long time – I owe you one, my fine fucking friend.'

For now, Jazz was going to check up on Ash to see what he had been up to since yesterday and to talk about the Asian burglaries. He had to make out a report on his teamwork. For the past year or so he hadn't had a lot to do with Ash. Still giving him baby jobs, he just checked up on what he was doing. If nothing else, he knew he had kept him safe. He wasn't going to lose another officer on his watch. The bonus to this way of working was that Ash cleared up all his jobs and their team record was high. With so many small jobs cleared up the numbers were good. The other CID teams were jealous of his clear-up results and, with Jazz doing well with his jobs, on paper they sat pretty high in the statistics. It wasn't fair and it didn't represent the types of cases other teams had, which took time and legwork to clear up, but as far as the Chief Supers were concerned Ash and Jazz were riding high.

Jazz was unaware of what Ash was about to say and he arrived at the meeting in a state of bored optimism. It wouldn't last; Ash was about to make him sit up and take notice.

CHAPTER NINE
The worm turned

DC Ashiv Kumar had enough of the situation and he was going to change it. Jazz might have thought he was in control, but no more! Ash had done everything asked of him but he wanted to be a Detective Constable working in the CID. He didn't want to be this namby-pamby joke of a detective working continuously on cases that even the rawest, newest of police officers would be overqualified to deal with.

He was sick of the mickey-taking. He found a Pampers disposable nappy on his desk one morning. Thank god it was clean! But he understood the inference and wondered what he had done to deserve being given such embarrassingly little crimes to solve. He solved them all; he should have felt proud but they were so easy it didn't take much brainwork. Even the youngsters in the area were taking the mickey out of him. They could see he worked alone and only on bike and shed robberies. Kids in the area were streetwise and knew everything to do with law and police. They knew a normal CID officer didn't spend that much time on kiddy crimes. He was known as Dumb and Dumber Kumar. Although no one had ever said it to his face, nevertheless, he had heard what his nickname was and now CID officers were using it. He'd had enough of it.

Jazz and Ash met in the canteen as arranged to discuss the Asian burglaries and follow up on yesterday's meeting. Milly, the legendary canteen lady, was waiting for Jazz. 'Hello darlin', what can I get you?'

As usual, Jazz replied, 'How about excited?'

Milly giggled, blushed, and went to get him a special cup of tea, newly brewed especially for him. She had been working in the canteen for more years than anyone remembered. She was past retiring age – it was thought she must be going on for seventy – but she loved the work in the canteen. She got to chat and joke with such lovely young officers and she ruled the roost there. She had her rules of tidiness and courtesy and she made the officers adhere to it. All, that is, except Jazz. She had a very soft spot for him. She hovered for a while just making sure he had everything he wanted. 'I have some lovely fresh buns, darlin', if you fancy,' she ventured. When he had said no to all the cakes and biscuits on offer, she left them, but only on the promise that if Jazz needed anything at all he was to call for her. Ash tried to hide a smile at this very unusual and inappropriate flirting.

Jazz outlined what had been happening with Asian burglaries and street robberies of Asian gold jewellery. He wanted Ash to be available to visit Asian families to discuss what they could do to make their homes safer and what to do with the gold jewellery they all possessed. Ash grimaced. This was a job for a community police officer, not a Detective Constable, and he said as much. Jazz was shocked and affronted. Ash had never complained before. It occurred to him that perhaps most of their conversations were one way: his way. Having been so busy with the murder of Laura, and any other interesting job that came up, he hadn't given Ash much quality time.

Now Ash had started, he was determined to continue. He saw he had Jazz's full attention, and he was determined and desperate to show him how much he had learned. The information he was about to give him should clinch his position as a good sidekick. With an excitement Jazz hadn't seen before, Ash showed him the list of burglaries of Asian homes within the last three months. The jewellery was worth at least £1,000,000 but if melted down and used as gold the worth would be less, but still a good haul with the gold market running so high. Furthermore, someone had to fence the stuff and to be capable of shifting the huge amount. Gold was worth a small fortune these days and along with lead and iron it was the preferred metal to steal and sell.

Jazz listened, wondering what was coming next. He got a little worried; Ash was working off the radar. He wasn't supposed to do this. Ash took the silence to mean he could go on. He saved the best bit until last. 'I've looked through intelligence and deduced who is fencing this stuff and it's Barry Bentall.' He waited for the praise. After all he'd worked all day and night on this, and it was a pretty good deduction.

Trying to keep calm, Jazz asked, 'So have you made an enquiries out on the streets to find this information out?'

Ash nodded. 'I've spoken to a few groups out there and I've built up some contacts through my work, and they confirmed Barry Bentall is fencing a huge amount of gold. He'll know who is robbing these houses.' Again, he waited for praise and got silence.

After what seemed like ages, Jazz spoke quietly. Tight lipped and steely-eyed, he told Ash he was the biggest fucking idiot in the Met Police. 'Your kiddy gangs have set you up.'

Ash looked around and up at the ceiling, trying to put into place the words buzzing through his head – the only word that came out was 'But, but…'

Jazz saw his face and felt sorry for the poor sod. It came in a blinding flash and he wished he never learned things in this way but he saw he had let Ash down. 'Look, Ash, it's my fault. I suddenly realised I have left you alone for far too long. I thought I was keeping you safe but I bloody well let you get into more potential trouble than any newbie would get into. You've now set yourself up for a slapping or something worse so we've got to make it right. Mr Barry Bentall is the Bird Man of Barking and someone you just don't mess with. He knows everything that's happening in his town and you can bet your bottom dollar the fucking kids have set you up and told him what you are doing. Yes, he is a dangerous man and yes, he could be fencing the gold but we don't have any clear evidence of that. Until you have clear and chargeable evidence you don't mess with the Bird Man of Barking. He's a nasty piece of work and there has been talk that he was responsible for various other miscreants of the first order being knee-capped, beaten to a pulp or given concrete slippers for paddling in Barking Creek. There are teams of officers watching him but he's squeaky clean and covers his arse very well. He doesn't care who he hurts – police, villains, Joe public – he isn't fussy if they get in his way.'

Ash went from bright red to funeral-parlour-slab white. Before he could answer Jazz added vehemently, 'Jeez, you're not going to be Number Three on my list.' He got up from his seat so violently, scraping and pushing the chair so hard, that everyone turned around. Milly came rushing over, thinking Jazz had hurt himself. He smiled, raised his hands in a placatory way and said his goodbyes to all who were still seated there staring. He gave Milly a peck on the cheek and told her nothing was wrong. She watched him with concern as he grabbed Ash's arm and briskly walked him out of the canteen and the station. Once outside he told Ash to stay put while he made an urgent phone call.

Mad Pete heard his mobile ring but couldn't find where the fuck it was. His council flat, given to him in a pristine condition by his social workers, was now a cesspit of stink and filth. He moved papers, clothes, a shoe, and a mouldy plate and finally found the phone. It was Mr Singh, announcing he was coming round and telling him to make sure he was in. That was a bummer; he knew a visit from Mr Singh meant he had to do something or get something, and he couldn't be arsed at the moment.

Mad Pete and Jazz had a longtime uneasy relationship. Mad Pete was a smalltime fence who seemed to know what was happening in the East End. Of service to various gangs, he was used for running errands, fencing mobile phones, and small jobs like that. When pushed, he gave pieces of information to Jazz and in return Jazz protected him from getting arrested. The kiddy gangs loved him and treated him like a hero. He gave them the odd bit of cannabis and bought stolen mobiles off them. He was an ex-heroin addict but was now addicted to the legal alternative, methadone, given to him by doctors. When excited, nervous or worried he could plunge into a druggy fit which made him uncontrollable. Jazz knew how to handle him.

Mad Pete was the only person Jazz truly trusted. Why? Because he knew Mad Pete and what he was capable of, so there were no surprises. Mad Pete would, if pushed, sell Jazz down the river for two pence; his help was certainly anything other than altruistic, more based on fear of what could happen to him. Yes, their relationship was uneasy but true, and it had an honesty about it that most of polite society would never recognize.

Jazz and Ash arrived quite quickly. Mad Pete had just enough time to clear away the odd spliff and various pills for recreational use. Mr Singh knew he had these habits but there was no point in drawing his attention to them; you never knew how Mr Singh was going to react. With a wide sweep he pushed all the papers and dubious bits off his settee and offered them a seat.

'Bloody hell, Pete, when did you last do any spring-cleaning?' were Jazz's first words of disgust. Pete shrugged and pushed a greasy strand of hair behind his ear. He didn't go in for much preening. He seemed to shave with a blunt razor and his T-shirt was always the same one, just with more stains on it. He walked with a stoop, giving the impression he couldn't be bothered to stand straight. His social workers were hoping that, through rehab and social security, he might learn to be a model citizen and even an asset to society. But Mad Pete had the life he wanted. He got by quite happily in filth.

No introductions were needed; Mad Pete knew who Ash was, of course – he knew most things going on in the streets of East London. This was Dumb and Dumber Kumar, whom the lads out there laughed about. He looked quite contemptuously at Kumar. Okay, he had made quite a few arrests but he only got the Referral Order youngsters and that didn't mean anything. They just got a slap on the wrist and a community order: nothing much in anyone's books. The gangs had run rings around him and taken the piss when he wanted information. Now, Mr Singh was a different kettle of fish and he wouldn't mess with him.

Jazz didn't want to stay here any longer than he had to so he got on with it. 'Okay, Pete, what's out there about DC Kumar. Is the Bird Man of Barking involved?'

Mad Pete sucked in his nicotine-stained teeth, shook his head and, in a smug voice, began, 'Now, Mr Singh, where do I start and what do you want to know?' In a flash movement that made Ash jump, Jazz grabbed Pete by his stained T-shirt and pulled him forward until he could smell his foul breath. He pushed him back in disgust. 'What on earth have you been eating to get breath that foul?' he asked. Not waiting for a reply, he carried on with gritted teeth, 'Now don't test my patience, you lump of shit, tell me what I need to know and stop pussyfooting around.'

Pete put his hands up in a placatory way and apologized quickly. You didn't mess with Mr Singh when he was in one of his moods.

'Look, Mr Singh,' he started in a diplomatic way. 'It ain't good. Him...' he pointed a nicotine-stained finger at Ash, '...is in big trouble. The Bird Man is spitting nails. His good name has been disparaged by a little erk and you know how he protects his reputation?' Ash was about to step forward and take umbrage at being called a *little erk* when Jazz put a cautionary arm across his chest. Not wanting to spook Mad Pete, Jazz asked gently, 'So what is The Bird Man planning to do?'

Mad Pete almost laughed, but thought better of it. 'He's gonna stick him like a stuffed pig is what I heard.'

Bloody hell, thought Jazz, the man was capable of it too.

'He has to show everyone that he ain't taking no flack from no one,' added Mad Pete.

'Okay.' Jazz was thinking on his feet. 'Can you contact him and ask for a meeting? For me and DC Kumar,' he added, in case Mad Pete didn't understand. It was important to cap this before there was more trouble.

Mad Pete thought about asking what was in it for him but he saw Mr Singh's face and his eyes told him not to get cocky. 'Okay, Mr Singh, I'll see what I can do.' As an irresistible parting shot , he turned with a smirk to Ash. 'You gonna be Number Three in Mr Singh's hit list of dead DCs? No one lives very long when they work with him, you know. Even me – I nearly got killed, didn't I, Mr Singh?' Unable to help himself he burst out laughing, but the warning look on Jazz's face made him contain himself. He looked at his feet and mumbled something about how he would contact him soon.

Jazz nodded to Ash and said he would meet him in the car, adding that he'd better go check it. Left too long and someone would have nicked the tyres. He wanted a word with Mad Pete alone. When the door had closed and Ash was out of hearing, Jazz turned to Mad Pete and said, 'I need a favour from you.' Mad Pete thought he was going to get a bollocking but instead the tone was very sweet. He nodded and waited. 'I need a contact in the Triad. Someone who will talk to me. Can you help?'

Mad Pete was being asked for his help, not told. This was unusual for Mr Singh. He could have got cocky and played hard to get but there was no point. 'They ain't happy with me, Mr Singh, after the last lot with Bam Bam. I've steered clear of them since then, just in case.' He wasn't too happy to be close to any of them at the moment but if that was what Mr Singh wanted he would do his best to set up a meeting.

Jazz left with the start of a plan that would ultimately end in a revenge killing. That would do nicely, he thought. He smiled at the thought.

The meeting with The Bird Man of Barking was arranged quite quickly and Jazz received a summons to attend his residence in Barking the next afternoon. Jazz knew where it was and he set about instructing Ash to leave all the talking to him and just to look suitably remorseful. Ash wanted to argue that this upstart was a villain; why were they doing all this and pandering to him? Jazz said there were reasons and he'd tell Ash later. For the moment he should shut up and act stupid – which, Jazz muttered, he shouldn't find too difficult.

CHAPTER TEN
The Bird Man of Barking

The Bird Man of Barking was a law unto himself. He was about sixty-five, 6'3" tall and built like a brick shithouse. He was a one punch and knock out man. No one got up when he hit them. He prided himself that no one could take him on in a one-to-one fight even though he was getting on a bit. Over the years he had learned the techniques of boxing in the East End, in Spinks Boxing Club, but it was the dirty tricks of fighting on the streets of London that had made him fearsome. When he looked at you with his intelligent, steely blue eyes you were on your guard. He was no one's fool. With one glance he had you sized up, and the warning glint in his eyes made you want to take two steps back.

Jazz and Ash arrived on time and were shown into the lounge. Jazz, usually cocky and smart, felt small and vulnerable. Quietly, he waited for The Bird Man to talk first.

The Bird Man seemed unusually affable. He lived in a very nice house in Barking near the park. It was fairly nondescript on the outside but once inside it was palatial. Crime does pay, thought Jazz as he looked at carpet that was so thick he nearly lost sight of his shoes, and the sort of furniture you only see on the TV. There was flock wallpaper of a different era but it wasn't Indian Restaurant cheap, it was very fancy and expensive. He asked if he should take his shoes off, this place was far too opulent for his trainers, but the Bird Man said no. He told them to follow him out into the backyard.

The garden was big and immaculately laid out. At the side was a huge brick shed, covered in ivy, but towards the end of the garden Jazz could see an aviary, full of budgerigars of different colours. This was why Barry Bentall was called The Bird Man of Barking. Barry loved his birds and was known to spend most of his time looking after them. For the past two decades he had unsuccessfully bred budgies to find that elusive champion budgerigar.

Inside the shed there was a small but comfortable sitting room with TV, kettle, cups and biscuits. It looked as if he received visitors here, because there were three comfortable chairs set out around a coffee table. The door off this room led to the budgies' nesting boxes, and the aviary. Jazz, uncharacteristically, was lost for words. This was a strange place to hold a meeting. Ash stood surveying the area. Everyone had heard of The Bird Man of Barking, they'd all seen his picture on the video links sent to all detectives with intelligence information, but this was the first time both he and Jazz had the misfortune to be in his company. It didn't feel comfortable.

Up to now The Bird Man had said nothing much. Again he gestured for them to sit down and he went through the door for a few moments, but came back holding something small. The look on his face and the way he held this precious item make them think it was made of pure gold. He pushed the yellow budgie towards them and waited for a response. Perplexed and unsure of what was required, Jazz stammered and said what a lovely yellow it was. Ash nodded in agreement, also not understanding what was wanted of them. Jazz cleared his throat and smiled. Both almost held their breath wondering what the fuck were they doing here. He opened his huge hands a little and showed them a yellow budgie. The Bird Man almost smiled at their ignorance.

In a loud and commanding voice, The Birdman pointed at the bird. 'This one will win the *best in show* and is heading towards being a champion bird. Look at its blow, how beautifully it stands up.' Seeing their ignorance, he pointed towards the head of the bird and showed how the feathers stood up and how they surrounded the beak and covered the eyes. 'There is a good depth of mask and good spots as well. You'll never make it to the bench (show) if you don't have good spots.' Jazz and Ash nodded, not knowing what the fuck he was talking about. 'We have a chance of being *best in show* at the world show next year,' said The Bird Man.

Jazz nodded and said, 'Oh right.' He shifted his position on the chair a little and tried to look interested.

'Oh yes,' The Bird Man continued, savouring the moment. 'That means it's like my bird winning the bird version of Crufts. I will be the dog's bollocks!' He looked at them, turned and left the room. Jazz and Ash looked at each other, not knowing what on earth was going on.

In a moment, The Birdman returned with another bird, but it was different. 'Now this little bird ain't gonna do nothing. It's small, with a short mask, no spots and fine, not fluffy, feathers. It's a runt. So what do we do with runts?' Before they could answer, in one swift move and a jerk of the neck he had killed the budgie. He tossed it into the bin in the corner. 'It ain't no good to anyone so best got rid of.' He sat down and looked straight at Jazz and Ash. Although it had been quick it was unexpected and quite shocking. Both were momentarily taken aback and unable to speak. They read volumes into this small act of violence and wondered if it had been done to show them just what he was capable of.

The Bird Man leaned forward and in a quiet voice that was just as frightening as his words said, 'So, I think you have some explaining to do. I ain't a happy man.' His steely blue eyes never wavered as they locked on Jazz.

Jazz cleared his throat and shifted uncomfortably in his seat. He wanted to fill the ominous and oppressive silence that weighed heavily on his shoulders. It was important he got this right. No smart comments or jokes, just a straight apology for Ash's enthusiastic stupidity. He spent a long time explaining how Ash was new and was being wound up by the kiddy gangs, that it hadn't been done out of disrespect, more out of stupidity. Ash sat and squirmed at his name being trashed and ridiculed. He had to listen to Jazz taking the mickey and telling The Bird Man on the quiet what an utter pain in the neck Ash was. The Bird Man was nearly sympathetic to Jazz's plight of having to work with him.

It was left that Jazz promised to take Ash under his wing and not let him get out of hand again. The kiddy gangs would know that the police had backed off and The Bird Man and his name and standing were intact. The apology was embarrassingly full and this seemed to placate The Bird Man. Finally Ash gave his full and cringing apology, which confirmed what an arsehole he was, as Jazz had put it.

In a frightenly calm tone The Bird Man stated 'I know everyone in London worth knowing, remember that,' Jazz and Ash nodded and The Bird Man continued 'I have taken on nearly every scumbag in London and they don't mess with me. Do you know Big Pete from Plaistow? You wouldn't upset him. Twenty stone of rippling muscles fuelled by steroids and suffering from 'roid rage that hits boiling point before you can say *bugger this I'm getting out of here.*' With much pride he said, 'He got out of line with me, he forgot to give me respect and I needed to teach him a lesson. Tough? You think he was tough? You don't mess with me; we fought one on one and I nearly done for him. Big Pete now sucks his food through a straw.'

Ash looked at The Bird Man and out of a silence you could cut with a knife he said, 'I nearly killed him too.'

The Bird Man snarled at this little pipsqueak. 'You? How?'

Looking straight into his eyes Ash said, 'I got stuck in his throat and he nearly choked.'

The Bird Man looked puzzled for a second and then the laugh came from his belly. By the time it had reached his throat he had patted Ash on the back and shaken

Jazz's hand. 'Okay, I accept your apology, now go and behave and show some respect in future.'

Once outside, Jazz looked at Ash with new eyes. Perhaps they would get on. He would see. Ash was growing on him.

They left Barking in the undercover police car with Ash boiling with rage and mortification at such a trashing. He was ready to resign and punch the lights out of Jazz for the insults he'd had to endure. It was going to take many hours of talking to calm him down and get him to see what was really going on. Tomorrow, said Jazz, they would sit down and he would explain everything. He tried to ignore the dark brooding look Ash gave him. He figured a bit of embarrassment was better than a few nights in hospital and tomorrow Ash would thank him.

Jazz thought better of going to the police station at this hour. He told Ash to go home; a detour to Sainsbury's for some light refreshment and home to a quiet night in front of the telly was on the cards. It wouldn't be long before a quiet night at home would seem like a pleasant distant memory.

He got to De Vere Gardens and put the key in the door. As soon as he opened it Mrs Chodda's kitchen door opened and he groaned and prayed to all the deities in the celestial heavens that she hadn't set him up again. He just wanted a quiet night –in, just this fucking once! As he entered, trying not to clink the bottles in his Sainsbury's bag, he was surprised to see a not so young strange woman smiling at him through the open kitchen door. She was beautiful in an assured way and he could see she was intelligent and interesting; he smiled back. She looked down for a second in embarrassment and apologized for startling him; she had thought it was her uncle, Mr Chodda, coming home. She said goodbye with a beautiful smile and returned to the kitchen. Jazz was quite stunned. No call from Mrs Chodda, no introduction. For a second he was disappointed, and then he almost laughed at himself. *'What are you like Jaswinder Singh?'* He took himself upstairs for that drink he'd promised himself.

CHAPTER ELEVEN
Teamwork

He woke the next morning to the all-familiar feeling of thick tongue and thick head. He glanced at the bottle, not wanting to believe he'd drunk so much. He swore at the nearly empty bottle but vowed he wouldn't drink during the day. He wasn't going down that road again. His hip flasks, all three of them, sat in a cupboard calling him. He could almost hear them saying *it doesn't matter, just fill me and keep me for emergencies in your pocket.* No, he wouldn't do that, not today anyway.

He was going to work with Ash today. Talk to him, do a bit of fence-mending and team-building. If you could call two a team, he thought with disgust. He still smarted that he'd only been given one newbie to work with.

Ilford Police Station was as busy as ever. He picked up a case of street robbery. It was Asian gold again. He found Ash and they went to take a statement. The robbery had taken place on Green Lanes, Ilford, and there was plenty of CCTV. The victim was an elderly Asian woman called Mrs Vijay who was badly shaken and now too scared to go out. Her manners, even in her shaken state, didn't stop her making tea and offering samosas and pakoras to Jazz and Ash. They had to stop her going off to cook some rice and meat for them. Her English wasn't good, but Jazz understood her and spoke to her. She couldn't remember who had mugged her and as much as she tried she just couldn't tell Jazz anything. In the end she started to get upset and covered her head with her shawl. Jazz reassured her that the CCTV would tell him everything he needed to know. Ash just watched, understanding nothing.

When they left Jazz told Ash that they were off to Green Lane to see where the robbery had happened and which CCTV copies would be best looked at. Some shops had CCTV that showed the outside of their shops, and then there were the CCTV cameras in the street. Ash organized copies of CCTV from a sari shop that had cameras pointing outside and Jazz organized the street CCTV film. They went off to Ilford Police Station to sit and look through them. For the first time Ash felt part of a team and, although still waiting for some explanation about The Bird Man of Barking, he liked the decisive feel of doing something right.

They found the film that showed Mrs Vijay being mugged and a good picture showed the mugger. Ash sat up when he saw the close-up of the mugger's face. 'Hold up, hold up, I know him!' he shouted, more loudly than necessary. It felt good to get something right. 'It's that little shit who's been causing me problems with The Bird Man of Barking. And I know where the fucking bastard lives.'

It took only one hour to get Kevin Winston Bobby Moore Chibwesi into the interview room at Ilford

Police Station. Kevin was only fifteen but he knew his rights; in fact he knew more about the law than most police officers. He, Jazz, and Ash sat together in the interview room, waiting for Kevin's mother to arrive as his appropriate adult. Jazz suggested to Kevin that perhaps they could while away the time and talk about the mugging. 'It ain't me and nuffink to do with me. I don't know wot you are saying, man,' was the reply from Kevin. They questioned him, taking turns to fire questions at him, and he just sat there, arms folded, saying, 'No comment and I want my lawyer.'

Jazz said a solicitor was on the way and in the meantime perhaps Kevin would like to look at some film. They showed him the CCTV and he smirked. 'That ain't me, that could be anyone. You ain't pinning that on me, man, I want a lawyer.' Jazz knew he couldn't do anything more without an appropriate adult present and he knew Kevin knew this. It was frustrating but standard stuff.

Eventually Kevin's mother arrived. She was a kindly woman who smiled and introduced herself as Christine. As a single mother, she had her hands full. Kevin was her eldest but she had four younger children all by different fathers, none of whom had stayed with her very long. She was tired and worn down by all the problems Kevin caused. Christine was shown into the interview room and sat down next to Kevin. She tried to fuss a little over him and he roughly pushed away her hands. He was a tough guy and didn't want no mother making him look a *wuzz*.

Feeling a bit daunted but up for trying one more

time, Jazz showed the CCTV again to Kevin and once again started the interview process, now that an appropriate adult was sitting in. The tape was rewound and replayed. Kevin sat with a distasteful bored look. His mother Christine stared intently at the screen before her. She watched the Asian woman walking and the mugging, and then the film was stopped as the mugger looked up. It showed a not too clear picture of a boy in a hoody, which slightly covered his face. Christine sat up and pointed excitedly. 'Hey, look, Kevin that's you.' Kevin paled at this and told his mother to shut up and that it wasn't him. 'Oh yes it is, Kevin, I would recognize you anywhere,' came the joyous response. 'Ooh, can I have a copy please, officer, it's a nice picture of my Kevin and I haven't got an up-to-date picture of him.' This was the final nail in Kevin's coffin. Jazz just stopped himself from laughing and giving Ash a high five. They had got him. He was charged there and then.

A mobile phone was found on him. This was taken away and the IMEI number on it checked against the National Mobile Phone Database to ensure it was his, which was standard practice. The custody officer would be informed of the result. Kevin was bailed and given a date to return to the police station; then he went home with his mother. Now finished in the custody area Jazz and Ash could both go and get on with getting a charge from the CPS and organizing a Nary date, which was the first hearing at court.

Jazz asked Ash to write the MG3 for CPS. There was always some work to do to prepare a charging file. It started with an MG5, which was a full report of the incident, followed by an MG3 which was sent to the CPS for charging advice. These days you had to fax it through to the CPS Charging Centre that had been centralized in London. What this meant was you sat on the phone for as long as it took to get it read and a decision made on charging. This was a done deal, the evidence was good enough and Kevin couldn't deny it. It was a boring and time-consuming job, and Jazz had better things to do. But first a tea break was on the cards. The MG5 and MG3 could be done afterwards.

Jazz took Ash to the canteen for a well-earned cup of tea and a cake served by the lovely Milly. She always served them at their table. No one else got this five star service. You collected your tea from Milly at the canteen counter, otherwise you got nothing. But Jazz always got special treatment and with a big smile too. Milly always flashed her aged and unaligned front teeth in Jazz's direction. He thought it amazing she still had her own teeth at her age.

This was his opportunity to put things right with Ash. In covert terms he tried to give a hint of what was going on. The Bird Man of Barking was a very clever gang leader. Nothing ever stuck to him. Intelligence knew he had fingers in many pies. He made sure he didn't interfere with any of the other gangs dealing with drugs. He dealt with robberies, bouncers for clubs, a bit of protection rackets and prostitutes, and then there was his transport business.

His main business was his transport company. He had a haulage firm called B4 Transport. He built up a big business, fighting off other haulage firms to become one of the countries biggest haulage companies. Everyone knew B4 Transport and the public were encouraged to sound their horns in their car when a B4 articulated lorry passed them. The general public took to this and a B4 articulated lorry completed its journey to a constant fanfare of car horns. The Birdman even advertised on the TV and there was talk of a TV show about his lorries travelling the country. Although The Birdman enjoyed the fame, he put his foot down regarding a TV show. He couldn't afford to have those nosey little bastards checking out what he did and where he went. Even the police didn't have such access to him and there was no way he was going to allow the bleeding media to bugger up his business interests. As it happened another haulage company that ran a lot like The Birdmans was suggested as a better bet for the TV crew and they all trundled off to organize TV footage. That particular haulage company was *legit* (legitimate) which was just as well, with the TV crew looking into every crevice and loophole in their business.

The Birdman had over two hundred lorries and dressed his drivers in B4 T Shirts and trousers so they were recognized. This was his legitimate business and with a business acumen most gangsters don't have, The Birdman had built a multi million business that could go through the books.

He seemed to fill a niche that gangs like the Triads didn't go near. He didn't have many enemies alive and the police had a team of officers watching him but to date they had found nothing. At the moment, there was a *hands off* policy on The Bird Man. The special team watching him had carte blanche over him. He didn't know he was being watched closely and that there was an undercover operation going on that other police officers knew nothing about. So my naïve friend, Jazz told Ash, you could have put the cat amongst the pigeons with your accusations. The Birdman's a clever bastard and he would have hurt you badly if we hadn't stopped it by apologizing and it might have jeopardized the undercover operation going on. Enough said and keep all this under your hat. You deserve to know something.

Ash took all this on board and said he would watch out next time. Jazz said there wouldn't be a next time because they were going to work more closely from now on. Ash asked if that meant he was involved in all the jobs Jazz took on, and Jazz agreed that they were now joined at the hip.

Neither had any idea at that moment just where it would take them and the danger it was about to put them in.

CHAPTER TWELVE
Shake rattle and roll

Ash had gone off to type up the MG3 with all the details for the CPS on Chibwesi, and to wait for a decision. Jazz went off to ring Mad Pete. He wanted that contact name and number. He passed by his fair-weather friend and colleague DI Hardy to tell him about catching Chibwesi and arresting him. DI Hardy nodded. Jazz was getting cocky again and it was getting on his tits. 'So how is Dumb and Dumber doing these days?' was the parting shot from DI Hardy. 'Actually he was the one that identified Chibwesi on the CCTV. He's doing great,' said Jazz, leaving with a smirk that DI Hardy would have been happy to wipe off his fucking face. 'Let's hope he lives long enough to enjoy his success,' he shouted after the swaggering Jazz. They would never know how much that hurt – the bastards! Jazz raised a finger, shouting, 'Swivel on that!' and left the CID office. He was pushing his luck. You didn't talk to DIs in that manner but he didn't care.

After calling in and checking how Ash was doing he thought he would go home for a quiet evening. Ash was bored, holding the phone and waiting for charging advise on Chibwesi from the CPS Charging Centre. Jazz told him to go home as soon as that was done and they would get together first thing in the morning to check out what cases had come in overnight. He promised no stolen bikes.

He went straight home. There was some leftover rice and Chinese in the fridge and a full bottle of vodka ready for consumption. As he put the key in the door of De Vere Gardens he wondered if that girl was still here. He thought he might just knock on the kitchen door and say good evening to Mrs Chodda, just to be friendly of course. She didn't answer his knock. This was the first time Mrs Chodda hadn't been in her kitchen when he came home. Slowly, he opened the door but the kitchen was in darkness. If he felt disappointed he wasn't going to admit to it. He had a quiet night and found some cricket on the TV to watch while he ate his Chinese and drank a vodka or two. This was his type of night so he wondered why he felt a bit restless.

He received a call from IBO as soon as he got into Ilford Police Station. There was a GBH and rape at an address off Green Lane, Ilford. This was what it was all about. He loved it when there were real jobs to work on; there was a buzz in the air. He called Ash and made his way to get a police car from the garage. The BMW had been booked out to another team but when he said it was urgent the garage staff didn't argue and handed over the key. He threw it to Ash and said he would get the address en route from IBO over the radio.

They arrived outside the house but had to park quite a distance away. It was one of those roads chocked with parked cars and where there had been a space three police cars had taken up residence. Jazz and Ash made their way into the house and heard the dulcet tones of Jenny telling officers to stop pissing about and get out of her fucking way. Jazz shouted out, 'Ah, those dulcet tones, I'd know them anywhere. Hello, Jenny.' He heard her response, advising him to do something that sounded anatomically impossible but he appreciated her optimism that he had the size to do it. He laughed and walked off to find someone who could tell him what the hell had happened here.

He got the information from the officer inside the door. 'It's two females, sir,' the officer said. 'The elder woman's in a bad way, it's thought she's suffered a heart attack, and the young girl looks like she was raped and then bludgeoned around the head.'

Jazz went to find out what Jenny was doing. She was in no mood to talk. There was blood and broken glass around and she told him to come back later.

Ash was instructed to go next door and find out what was happening, and to talk to the person who'd made the call to the ambulance service and police. This was an Asian household in an Asian area; someone would know who they were and what they were doing.

It transpired the mother and father of the household and their two sons had gone to Pakistan for a wedding. The grandmother had been taken ill and their daughter was left at home to care for her. The daughter was a beauty by all accounts and just seventeen. She was to be married in the next year and a suitable husband was being looked for. This would now ruin her chances of a good marriage. No man of standing would marry a woman who was not a virgin. This would devastate the family. Never mind she had been attacked and hit around the head with a blunt instrument causing injuries not yet confirmed.

Jazz took himself off to the hospital to see if he could talk to the grandmother and the girl. He asked Ash to get every bit of information he could about the family, what they did, who they knew, etc. A cursory inspection suggested nothing had been stolen. Everything looked in its place and no drawers had been opened, no stuff thrown around – so why had the person broken into the house and attacked the girl?

The victims had been taken to King George's Hospital in Barley Lane. Jazz flashed his badge many times and finally found out where they both were. The grandmother was in a poorly state and Jazz couldn't talk to her. He looked at her through the glass and saw she was hooked up to every machine in the room. She looked so old, with all those machines clamped to her mouth, chest, and arms, and pipes coming from under the blanket. *Poor soul auntie*, he said under his breath. The girl was another matter. She was lightly sedated but semi-conscious. The doctor said she wouldn't remember anything at the moment. Jazz called her name softly. 'Mina, how are you feeling?' She stirred and looked at him with vacant eyes. 'Do you remember anything, Mina?' She didn't answer; she just stared. He could tell she was traumatised and not quite in the same world as him. 'Don't worry, I'll come back tomorrow,' he whispered. Feeling quite emotional from seeing two innocent women destroyed in this way, he could feel the temper rising from his stomach up into his throat. He was going to get the bastard who'd done this.

Back at the house Jenny had found fingerprints on the door: not those of either the grandmother or the daughter. Jenny said she would let Jazz know when she'd put the prints through the machine back at the lab. Jazz was so glad it was Jenny here. Okay, she was bad-tempered with a foul mouth but she was the best SOCO in the Met, and tenacious too. He loved her!

Ash was working hard and had some information for Jazz. They took themselves off to the BMW to talk it through. The radio in the car was red-hot. The team due to have the BMW had been calling up on the radio, and at first had been polite, but after the third hour of calling, the language was getting pretty strong. Jazz turned the radio off so they had no distractions.

The neighbours hadn't seen anyone suspicious. Most members of the Chakravarti family were in Pakistan for a wedding. The neighbours were shocked at what had happened and said they had heard nothing. Mr Chakravarti ran an Indian restaurant and most of the staff were relatives from India. The restaurant had been closed for the wedding and would reopen when he returned to England in two weeks time. The neighbours did say that they had seen the young cousin come to the house a few times whilst the family was away. They presumed he was checking up on the women to see if they needed any help. He was about twenty and had come from the Punjab to work in his uncle's restaurant.

Ash confirmed it was the neighbours who had phoned the police because they saw the back door to the garden was smashed, and they couldn't get a reply when they knocked on the front door.

Jazz and Ash were disturbed by an urgent knocking on the car window. 'Open the fucking door!' It was Jenny, who was getting cross at being held up. She wanted to tell them what she had found by the back door, although it hadn't yet been forensicated: half a pear with teeth marks in it. Anyone else and Jazz would have poured scorn and sarcasm on such a statement but this was Jenny. 'So what makes it special?' he asked.

'Pears go brown very quickly and this one must have been recently bitten into because it was only just starting to go brown. It's within the timeline and I can take a cast of the teeth marks. There could be a match further down the line.'

'God, Jenny, I so love you,' came the joyous response from Jazz.

'Fuck off, you daft prick,' was the blustery response from an embarrassed but flattered Jenny. She had a *thing* for the cheeky bastard, and quite liked the banter with him – but of course he would never know what she hoped.

Ash had got all the names of the family, and the name of the young cousin. The neighbours were a mine of information and knew where the lad was staying. Apparently they'd promised to keep an eye on the women and had said the lad could come to them if he got into any difficulties. His English wasn't too good, he was twenty, and he had only been in England for six months and was not used to the ways of England.

Jazz thought this very interesting and asked to speak

to the neighbours. Ash took him to their door and introduced Jazz as his Detective Sergeant. They were very pleased to talk to a fellow Sikh and invited them both in. Mr and Mrs Manku were very pleased to talk to Jazz about their neighbours. The gossip started with the question of who was Parminder. They whispered that the family wanted the women to be safe and they had specifically asked that Parminder, as a young man, would not call on the grandmother or Mina during the family's absence. It wasn't appropriate for a young woman at home, almost alone, to be in the company of a young man; it wouldn't look good for Mina. They leaned forward and said that Parminder had visited a few times. Mr Manku said the boy had never stayed late but they had made sure to visit the grandmother and Mina the last time he was there, to ensure they were supervised. Mrs Manku added that they had both thought he was very attentive to Mina and as dutiful neighbours they suggested he didn't visit again during the family's absence. He had agreed to this.

Jazz asked Ash to find Parminder and bring him to the police station for questioning. There were a few things he needed to clear up. In the meantime, a cup of something and a sandwich was on the cards. He wished he had filled his flasks that morning. He could do with just a taster of vodka, nothing much, just a little. He went outside, lit a cigarette and dragged on it long and hard. It felt good and relaxed him. He had an idea of what had happened in the Chakravarti household but interviews would tell him later.

He went back to the Ilford Police Station and

decided to maybe just get a half bottle of vodka on the way, just as a back up. He only wanted a sip, nothing much, it would go nicely with a cigarette. It was getting on for late afternoon and he hoped to have Parminder interviewed before the day was out. As he walked back to the station he took a call from Mad Pete and confirmed a meeting that evening.

Milly made him a fresh bacon sandwich. It was a bit late for cooking bacon but she got a nice couple of rashers out of the fridge for him and he sat and thought about what he was going to do as he drank a fresh cup of tea lovingly presented to him. The bacon sandwich was worth waiting for. She was a love and he told her so, much to her delighted embarrassment. He enjoyed the quiet moment to sit and plan and think. Things were going to happen.

It was about 6 p.m. before Ash returned with a scared and quaking Parminder. He was taken to an interview room and left for a twenty-minute pause for thought. By the time Jazz and Ash returned he was shaking and pleading to go home. His English was very poor and a Punjabi interpreter was called for. At this stage a solicitor was not necessary because, as Parminder was told, this was just the police asking for help with their enquiries.

He was made comfortable and brought a cup of tea, offered a toilet break which were both accepted. In another fifteen minutes they were all seated along with a female Punjabi interpreter. The interview was pretty slow going, with Jazz having to speak in English and then wait for the interpreter to interpret and answer back. It was actually very interesting for Jazz, who spoke Punjabi, to watch and listen. Parminder kept asking the interpreter to tell them he had nothing to do with the crime, that he'd been in the flat his uncle had found for him all evening and had never left it. After a time he became quite comfortable knowing all questions were filtered. No pointed questions that he couldn't answer or didn't have time to answer. He looked relaxed and less tense. Jazz saw this and he was having none of it. He wanted a tense and scared person: much easier to get them to tell the truth. When Parminder started to laugh and flirt with the interpreter Jazz knew it was time.

In Punjabi Jazz asked, 'Why did you do it?'

The smile was instantly wiped off Parminder's face and he stuttered and muttered, 'No, no, not me, I didn't do anything.'

The shock of Jazz speaking in Punjabi and the question itself stunned him and almost made him sick. Ash sat up, not knowing what had been said but seeing the reaction. Parminder may not have known much of England but he knew enough to say, 'I want a lawyer, I won't say anything else until I have a lawyer.'

Jazz nodded, and beckoned for Ash and the interpreter to leave the room with him. They left Parminder alone, scared, and not knowing what to do. He had plenty of time to think.

It would be an hour before the solicitor for Parminder arrived. Mr Mason was harassed and tired after a long day and fed up because now he had this interview, which would make him miss his dinner.

The room was pretty crowded, what with Jazz, Ash, Parminder, the interpreter and Mr Mason. The tape was put on, as this was now an official interview. Jazz introduced himself and everyone present and said he was interviewing Parminder Chakravarti about the GBH and rape of Mina Chakravarti and the GBH of the grandmother. Parminder fidgeted and looked petrified. Jazz smiled and said for the benefit of the tape that Parminder was here helping them with their enquiries but he requested a solicitor be present. He confirmed the solicitor was present. He didn't take his eyes off Parminder. Parminder squirmed even more.

The questioning started simply and comfortably: when did you last go to the Chakravarti house, when did you last see Mina and her grandmother. Parminder's answers were noted. It went along nicely for ten minutes with the interpreter working between Punjabi and English. Jazz thanked Parminder for his help and then picked up all the papers on the desk, shuffling them together and looking ready to finish the interview. Parminder visibly relaxed. Suddenly Jazz stopped and said in Punjabi, 'Oh by the way, I know why you raped Mina and I can tell you exactly what happened.' Parminder sat frozen on his seat. He wasn't the brightest spark in the world and didn't know what to do or how to get out of this. The solicitor requested that Jazz ask his questions in English.

In English Jazz said to all present that Parminder was the person they were interviewing regarding the GBH and rape of Mina and the GBH of the grandmother. He said that under PACE he could keep Parminder for twenty-four hours without charging, and that he needed a bit of time to collate the information he was waiting for that would prove Parminder was in the vicinity of the house at the time of the offence. Parminder was put in a cell and the solicitor and interpreter said they would be back tomorrow at 2 p.m. as agreed.

With everything done Jazz told Ash he had an appointment in an hour and would see him back at Ilford Police Station at 9 a.m. tomorrow, when he would explain everything. Ash was getting frustrated by all this cloak and dagger stuff. He went home mumbling that Jazz was an arsehole to work for.

Jazz got home very late. He put the key in the door of De Vere Gardens at midnight. He crept in, knowing the house would be asleep. His eyes automatically went to the kitchen door but of course no one was up, so no visitors. Unconsciously he sighed and decided he was pretty tired. A quick drink and the McDonald's he'd bought down the road would do him fine for the night. He slept the sleep of the contented. His plan was on track.

He was up bright and early the next morning. He walked to Ilford Police Station; he liked that, it gave him time to think. He phoned Jenny as he walked and asked if the teeth indent in the pear had any DNA on it and if a mould of the teeth was ready. Had she written a report that stated the pear had been bitten within a timescale that could be recorded as similar to the crime that had taken place? Jenny asked him if he thought she was fucking superwoman to get all this done in such a short time. He answered yes, she was superwoman. She liked that and told him he was fucking right for an arsehole and yes, she had it ready for him because she knew what an anal dick he was for getting the villains. He said he would get a car and come and pick up the mould, and get her a DNA sample from their suspect in custody. She was pretty impressed and secretly thought that between them they made a good team. Of course she didn't tell him that. She just called him Clever Fucking Clogs and hung up.

It was a good day. Granted it was raining, and granted it was dark and grey – but it was a fabulous day, a day when things were going to happen. When Jazz got into Ilford Police Station he went straight to custody and asked the custody sergeant to organize a DNA sample from Parminder Chakravarti, and an impression of his teeth.

Jazz asked how Parminder had been that night. The Custody Sergeant looked through the log written up by the night Custody Sergeant and said apparently Parminder hadn't slept very much, and had paced up and down for most of the night. He'd fallen asleep about 5 a.m. Jazz was pleased to hear that. He had got Parminder worried.

He met Ash in the CID office at the desks they had taken as their own. The other officers weren't happy about this, as they had to hot desk, but Jazz and his other half kept a desk to themselves in the corner. Just another thing that put Jazz on everyone's hit list. He sat down with Ash and told him his strategy. Ash could see he was right but proving it would be difficult. Then Ash thought and said unless, of course, the forensics came up trumps... For a start there would be semen from the suspect and if that matched Parminder he would be banged to rights. Also the pear. Ash said it was a done deal if these samples proved to be Parminder. He would also tell Parminder why he did it. It was obvious to Jazz but Parminder would never guess anyone else would know.

Ash was beginning to realize that Jazz was a natural old-fashioned detective and had something others didn't. He hadn't figured it all out yet and he hoped he would live long enough to figure it out. Everyone he came into contact with told him his time was limited if he was working with Jazz. 'You will be dead by the end of the year, mark my words.' It wasn't the best of introductions to Jazz.

The DNA sample had been taken and the impression of the teeth, and a Met Police motorbike rider took it over to Jenny's lab straight away. By the time they left to go there Jenny would have examined the DNA and would hopefully have a result for them to look at. 'Fingers crossed,' said Jazz. 'We could be putting this one to bed today.' They didn't know at that moment that they would need all their time to investigate the three tortures and murders that were about to be brought to their notice. They would need all their energy, time, intelligence and nerve to work through them.

They got a quick cup of tea and Jazz got a biscuit for free from Milly. Ash looked at him and said he was 'a jammy bugger'. Jazz smiled and said, 'It's actually a jammy dodger, but if you got it, flaunt it.' They wiled away about thirty minutes talking about the interview of Parminder. 'It's 11 a.m. and time to go get the DNA and see if the slipper fits Cinderella's foot,' said Jazz. Ash thought him a little mad, but he was beginning to like Jazz more. They left the police station laughing.

The interview arranged for 2 p.m. had Jazz and Ash ready in the interview room with all the paperwork they needed. The solicitor was on time and the interpreter was waiting. All were shown into the interview room and Parminder joined them within a minute of everyone settling down. The solicitor had spent a short while with Parminder and, using the interpreter, had a prepared statement for the police stating he was innocent and hadn't been in the house or area that day. It was listened to with due respect and noted on the interview tape. All well and good, and Jazz graciously thanked Parminder for his effort in this. Parminder felt it was going well. The solicitor who had some experience of Jazz in the past wasn't so sure. He could feel the cockiness just behind the smile. Something was up.

Jazz politely asked Ash if he would be so kind as to hand him the piece of paper near him from the lab. Ash, in the same mode, said he would be delighted to pass the paper to him. The interpreter was translating this little conversation to Parminder who suddenly felt this wasn't right.

Jazz quoted from the lab paper on the DNA discovered in the semen and on the pear and compared it to the DNA swab from Parminder. To a point of several million it was correct. The teeth marks in the pear were also a match of Parminder's pearly whites. Jazz looked up, not smiling now, and said that

Parminder was charged with the rape and GBH of Mina Chakravarti and the GBH of the grandmother. He was read his rights and Jazz waited for a response. Parminder, knowing he was beaten, asked how Jazz knew it was him in the first place.

Smugly Jazz settled back. Ready to amaze everyone, he started at the beginning. You are a young man in a strange country. You don't know the language and quite honestly you are not the best looking fellow I have ever seen. You can't chat up the girls without language skills and you are feeling a bit frisky. Mina is gorgeous, she is the nearest you have been to a woman you want. She rejects your advances and you have visited a few times and now the neighbours are telling you to stay away. You are fixated and so horny you want her no matter what. While the family are away you make your move and you break in the back way so the neighbours won't see you. I don't think you meant to attack her or the grandmother but you had to keep the grandmother quiet because she could still shout so you whacked her with the metal bar you broke the window with. After you had raped Mina, she said she would tell everyone and panic set in, so you beat her with the metal bar in fear of being found out. You are a nasty piece of work and there are no excuses for what I am saying. You deserve everything you get.

With that, in disgust, Jazz told the police officer present to take Parminder away. They would contest bail.

Again, Ash was given the job of typing out the MG3 and sitting on the phone to the CPS to get a charge. It felt good to get this one but his feel-good factor ended with a phone call to say the grandmother had died and that Mina was in intensive care. It was thought a bleed in the brain had been discovered and there didn't seem much hope for her. The Chakravarti family had been contacted in Pakistan. Jazz sat with Ash whilst he was hanging on the phone to the CPS and told him he would have to change the charge. It was now a manslaughter charge as well. The adulation and joy of a charge left both Ash and Jazz. They felt pretty depressed and promised themselves a drink in the pub when the charge was set by CPS. The rest of the case papers could be worked on tomorrow.

Jazz got home later than he thought again and a little wobbly. The drink in the pub turned into quite a session. Ash drank the odd half pint of beer and Jazz had double shorts. Ash didn't stay too long; he said he had to get home to the wife and check the children were in bed and if he had time to say goodnight to them. Jazz tried to show interest. Ash had a boy, Ashok, who was seven, and a girl Tara, who was five. Apparently they were the brightest children in the infant school they went to and the most beautiful children ever born. Jazz suspected Ash was maybe exaggerating a little but liked his pride in them. When Ash left the pub to go home, Jazz took the opportunity to have a few more doubles before setting off home. The Lion in Ilford was used to seeing Jazz on and off over the past few years.

When Jazz entered De Vere Gardens he saw the kitchen door open and felt a little let down when Mrs Chodda came out. She just wanted to wish him a good evening and offer him some leftover curry and rice for him to take upstairs if he wanted to. She added it was a mild curry. He thanked her and went into the kitchen to collect the bowls of food she had set out. Over in the corner was the woman he'd seen the other night. He felt good seeing her and nodded hello. Mrs Chodda, unlike her usual ways, just said that it was her sister's cousin-in-law, Amrit Singh, who was visiting. She didn't ask Jazz to join them in the kitchen. He left with his bowls of curry and rice feeling a tad miffed, although he didn't know why he was bothered at all.

The next day Jazz was told that Mina had died. Parminder didn't get bail and was sent to Chelmsford Prison where he would be kept at Her Majesty's pleasure until his trial. This case would go to Snaresbrook Crown Court – maybe even the Old Bailey. It didn't leave a very good feeling but at least they got him. DCI Radley called Jazz into his office, wanting to know what was happening with the case. It had got into the press, DCI Radley was giving a press conference that afternoon, and he wanted to know how he was found, etc. After an hour's debrief DCI Radley thanked Jazz and said he could go. As an afterthought he asked how he was getting on with Ash and was glad to hear it was going well. 'Just keep him safe,' was the parting shot from DCI Radley. Jazz didn't need to hear that.

Jazz kept Ash close and when a call came in that a man was on the ground after being attacked they took the call and went to London Road. The victim was pissed and said he had been hit. CCTV was found and looked at and it showed the victim sitting on the ground holding his head. He said the restaurant owner of the Little Rabbit, two doors away from where he was attacked, actually was his attacker. Jazz went and saw the restaurant owner who said he only attacked him in self defence, that the man had threatened him and he was frightened. He had thrown him out of his restaurant for being argumentative and violent. Jazz asked to see the restaurant's CCTV and the owner got it for him. Jazz and Ash looked through it and they saw the victim sitting on the floor holding his head when all of a sudden the biggest bottle of beer flew into the picture and hit the victim on the head. They could see the bottle was thrown from the restaurant by the angle. They arrested the restaurant owner and took him in to charge. He continued to say he threw the bottle in self defence because he was being attacked and he was scared.

The courts found him guilty but Jazz and Ash were due back at court because the restaurant owner has gone for a Newton Hearing. A Newton Hearing was where you agreed with the guilty verdict but disagreed with how it happened. It would discuss whether it was a self defence action, as said, or an ABH as the police had charged him with. It was all a bit of a nuisance to have to go back to court. Jazz went and saw the restaurant owner and told him that the CCTV would prove he was an attacker and that the stance of the victim was passive. He also said if he didn't think again about what he was doing then Jaswinder Singh would make sure that everyone, especially the police who used his restaurant on a regular basis, would not want to avail themselves of his hospitality again. The Newton Hearing was dropped and the restaurant owner did his community service as his sentence specified.

There weren't many nights off for a while. Ash was working hard next to Jazz and learning a lot. They were called to a robbery. Two men had followed a guy from the Barking nightclub 'Blings' to a cash point. Suddenly the victim felt a knife at his neck and heard someone saying, 'Take the maximum out of the machine otherwise you get shanked.' The man stuttered he could only get out £170 and then he purposely put in the wrong pin number. The two men were caught off guard and the victim turned and punched the one with a knife and the other ran away. Security guards close by heard the noise and came running over to the victim; they grabbed the remaining defendant and proceeded to give him a good pasting. By the time Jazz and Ash and the police arrived the defendant, whose name was Richie Waters, was not feeling too good.

Richie was taken back to Barking Police Station to be interviewed. Jazz asked Ash to interview the victim; he would take the defendant. He went into the charging room where Richie sat with his head in his hands. Jazz asked if he was okay and Richie looked up saying he had voices in his head saying *hurt yourself, hurt yourself.* Jazz sat down and quietly said he would give him some water to drink to clear his head a bit. Richie thanked him and put his hands around his head again. He said, 'I did nothing, it wasn't me, I was just there.' Jazz nodded understandingly. He could see Richie was high on something. When the water came and the door was closed, Jazz added a little vodka from his flask into the plastic cup of water and encouraged Richie to sip it, just to freshen him up.

Suddenly Jazz spoke. 'Did you hear that?' he asked incredulously. Richie looked up. 'Did you hear the voices? I can,' added Jazz. Richie frowned and listened, and said he could hear the voices.

'They are saying *you must tell me who you were with*. Can you hear that?' Jazz asked. Richie said yes, he could hear that; he was quite excited. 'So who were you with, Richie?' asked Jazz.

'I was with Andy French,' replied Richie.

Jazz went outside and told the sergeant to get a warrant for Andy French. He went back into the room with Richie just as his phone was ringing. Richie answered it and said, 'Hello Andy, I'm in custody at the moment so I can't talk.' The phone went dead. Jazz did a 1471 and got the number and had it checked.

When Andy French was brought in, both Richie Waters and Andy French were charged. Jazz told Ash to put in the report that they had found Andy French through a telephone call made to Richie Waters whilst he was in custody, and Richie confirmed it was Andy French who held the knife and threatened the victim. He didn't want in writing his version of Richie hearing voices, and that was how he got Andy French. The gods were with him, Jazz knew that. The case could have been thrown out if they knew of Jazz's druggy encouragement to get Richie to talk. Ash was a bit rattled by Jazz's methods; he was not used to such ways of working. But it was good to be on the winning side.

Over the next few weeks Jazz and Ash had

developed a reputation that they were unbeatable. Their clear up record was pretty awesome. For some it just made them mutter under their breath that he took chances and okay, he had got lucky so far but look at his history – they saw trouble ahead. Jazz was riding on the crest of a wave that was about to drown him.

Jazz found himself quite often drawn to the Gudwara in Seven Kings. He would idle for an hour there. He went in, kneeled and offered prayers, and then did his bit for the Gudwara by cleaning shoes or helped dish out food. He wouldn't admit to himself but he was becoming closer to his religion: something that hadn't happened before. Deepak seemed to always be there and they would take tea and sit and chat. Jazz got much from these talks.

CHAPTER THIRTEEN
If you go down to the woods today you're sure of a big surprise

It was about 11.30 a.m. when the call came in. A dog walker had uncovered a body deep in the woods and, although not in a good state, it appeared to be someone known to the police as John Carpenter. The note around his neck said so. The paper had been carefully protected in a plastic cover so the police knew they were meant to find it. The question was being asked: *why would anyone do that?* You don't usually want murder victims to be found because of clues on the person that would find the killer.

Jazz was contacted because he'd dealt with the case of John Carpenter and the family of the victim Laura Kent. With Ash they headed to Epping Forest and were shown the area John Carpenter had been found. They couldn't get very close because an intensive search was being conducted of the area. Colleagues of Jenny were there in their white suits. Jenny was back at the lab looking at the body. Apparently it was pretty gruesome but Jazz was to find out all the details when he spoke to Jenny.

A forensic team had gone to John Carpenter's flat

and on first sight it seemed that the acid had been administered in the flat, with traces being found on the carpet; there were also signs of blood and bone splinters, minute but there, and from that Jazz assumed at this time that John Carpenter, although alive, would have had to have been carried from the car to the site where he was found. The forensic evidence from the flat had to be confirmed but Jenny gave it to Jazz on the quiet; she would give him the confirmed evidence as soon as possible.

He looked at where the body was found and the distance it would have taken someone to carry the body or frog-march him to this area of the forest. They knew he wasn't dead when dumped in the wooded area because they found evidence of a live body having been dumped there. His bowels had opened on many occasions and this had seeped into the ground under him. Samples of everything were being taken by the team. Tyre tracks were found and it was suggested the walk to where the body was found would have taken about ten minutes. It was off the beaten track for most walkers. It was in quite a dense area of scrub and not somewhere anyone would normally go.

Apparently the dog walker was at the police station. Jazz needed to talk to him. He and Ash went back to the station. As Ash drove Jazz took a deep breath and wondered how he felt. John Carpenter was a scumbag of the first order and some would say he deserved what he got. Jazz needed to know what had happened. The family came to mind straight away. He was fearful they had done this. The mother, Amanda, was mad enough and vengeful enough to do the deed but she was too off the wall to do it covertly. The rest of them he didn't think would do it, but who knew; he hoped they had nothing to do with it.

The dog walker was Alex Hardy, a fit sixty-five-year-old man who'd been taking his dog for a walk. He was having a cup of tea when Jazz saw him. He was still in shock at what he had found and no one could get a clear sentence from him. He was asked again to tell what he found and what took him to that area. Alex hadn't been able to talk clearly since he found the body. He kept crying, and then he talked in gibberish. He just couldn't focus properly. Jazz saw this and went and got some biscuits off the typist. He suggested that a dunking biscuit would go well with the tea. Alex looked up and took a digestive biscuit out of the tin. Jazz said that they were his favourites, and he took one too. After a few sips of tea and a couple of dunks of the biscuit Alex looked a bit more settled. 'What type of dog have you got?' Jazz asked. Alex said that he had a cocker spaniel. In answer to another question from Jazz he said that the dog's name was Freddie and he was three years old. He went on to say he was a bundle of energy and the walks wore out Alex more than Freddie. Jazz laughed at that and then asked, 'Why do you go to Epping Forest to walk Freddie? Do you live close by?' Alex said he always went there but today he went to a different car park in Epping Forest. He'd wanted a change of scenery and it made a change for Freddie. Jazz coaxed him along, talking about Freddie and how long he went out for walks, what was Freddie's favourite treat, etc. Alex was feeling a lot more relaxed and Jazz asked what was wrong today with Freddie. Alex said he got spooked by something or had spotted something; he'd just run off barking and wouldn't come when Alex called. Alex wondered if he'd seen a rabbit and was chasing it. The conversation was getting closer to what Jazz wanted to know.

'So, what did you do when he didn't come back?' asked Jazz. Alex said he'd got a bit mad and scared. He didn't want to lose Freddie in the undergrowth. He could hear Freddie ahead barking his head off and he seemed to be stationary by this time. By the time Alex had reached Freddie he was as cross as hell but then he saw what he thought was a dummy – like one of those shop window dummies. When he got closer he saw it was a man's body, in a terrible state.

Alex couldn't go on any further. He started to cry. The sight of a human being in that state was something he would never forget or get over. He managed to say it was about 10 a.m. when he found the body. Jazz thanked him and patted him on the back. A doctor had been called to check him out for shock and give him some medication and then he would be taken home.

Ash had watched Jazz talking to Alex and was impressed with the way he handled the man so sensitively and cleverly. Jazz was a much better detective than officers at Ilford Police Station had given him credit for. To be quite honest Ash had thought Jazz was a waste of space and someone to steer clear of. His reputation had been shredded and scattered. Not many had a good word to say about him. But now Ash thought he was actually quite a pukka guy, and this was to be the turning point in their working relationship.

This was Tom Black's case as DI in the Murder Squad so Jazz went off to find him, dragging Ash with him. Now they worked together and although Ash had wanted this for a long time, he would wonder as the days went by if it was such a good idea. DI Boomer Tom Black was in full throttle. 'Where the fuck is my team?' he boomed at some poor officer walking past his office. Jazz approached head on. When Boomer was in full throttle it didn't do to surprise him. He had been known to floor anyone coming up to him on his blind side. He was a big man with long arms and big fists. No, he didn't fit the Metropolitan Politically Correct Police either but he got results and in the monthly statistics he was king.

Just for the moment Jazz wanted to speak to Boomer by himself. Together they concocted things that were not recognized as good working practice and he didn't want Ash to hear his conversation. 'Ash, do me a favour?' he called. 'Go see Laptop over there and find out if there's any news from the lab yet.'

Ash looked puzzled. 'Laptop?'

Jazz explained. 'Laptop is that small P.C. over there: PC Graham; it's his nickname.' Against his better judgement Ash smiled and went off to find Laptop.

When he had gone Jazz asked if he could be involved in the case. Boomer knew why; it had been a very difficult and emotional case. With none of his team around he was glad of the help. They discussed the family and whether it was possible that one of them could have done this. There were no doubts that within the Pringle family John Carpenter was the most hated man ever, but it didn't seem possible that any one of them would have the strength or the ability to kill him and take him to Epping Forest. Boomer asked Jazz to go and visit the family to see what he could find out. They would wait to see the family until after they saw Jenny's report. At this stage no one was aware of the tortuous death and extensive injuries John Carpenter had endured. Tomorrow would be the start of the investigation after Jenny's results had come in. It would be the start of an unbelievable string of coincidences and facts that would lead Jazz and Ash into mortal danger.

Ash wasn't stupid; he knew he had been pushed to one side whilst Jazz and DI Tom Black discussed something he wasn't supposed to be privy to. Laptop wouldn't know anything. It was obviously too early for a report to come out of the lab yet but Ash did as he was asked, although he was still not sure about working with Jazz. Trust was something the man didn't have, not with him anyway, and that was quite depressing.

It was 4 p.m. and there was still time today to make things a bit right for Ash. Jazz had taken a quick look at his emails and seen the email launching yet another MPS-wide initiative but this one took his interest. It was the launch of an *Ending Gang & Youth Violence* in the East End of London. Officers had been assigned each day of the three days of action. This was day one and Jazz contacted DI Cunningham who was organizing teams. With full approval from the DI, he found Ash sifting through paperwork and told him they were off to get some retribution. The atmosphere around Jazz was expectant and the ripple of interest and smugness was infectious.

A puzzled but mildly interested and nearly excited Ash followed Jazz to a police car that just happened to be available. Jazz tossed the keys to Ash and told him this was to be his investigation; Jazz would just watch and enjoy. Of course Ash had read the email regarding the initiative regarding gang and youth violence called *Operation Victorious*. He wondered who sat and made up the names for the many and different operations that went on. There had been Operation Witham, Operation Skywalker, and other such names. This one had taken his interest and now he saw how he was going to be involved. 'What was the name of the scrot who landed you in trouble with The Bird Man of Barking?' asked Jazz. 'It was that bastard Billy Tower from the Dag Boy Gang,' muttered Ash, still angry and frustrated he had fallen for the information given to him by a smug and far too clever for his own good Billy. It was known he was the top member of The Dag Boys and he'd become far too cocky around the police.

'Today my friend, you are going to search Billy's home under the new initiative. I bet we find quite a bit to put this little scrot away for. We know he pushes drugs; his gang regularly robs other little scrots for their mobile phones and money.'

The search warrants were ready and because Billy Tower was high on the list of gang members to target there was one ready for him. Jazz had asked if he could take this one. No one minded. There were enough to go round and any help was welcomed.

They arrived in Bentry Avenue. Billy Tower lived in the far left house in the banjo that was Dagenham's version of cul de sacs. The trouble was you could be seen from the house and, in the time it took to walk along the Banjo, drugs could be flushed away. Jazz suggested they go to the house next door first to allay any fears they were after Billy. Mrs Dale, an old lady who had lived in Dagenham most of her life and remembered when the place was full of Dagenham car workers, lived there. She loved to reminisce but not many gave her the time these days. Jazz asked if they could go over the fence at the back into the next-door garden. Mrs Dale was intrigued; she was always happy to help the police. Both Jazz and Ash saw how she had kept her home looking as it must have in the 1950s: austere but clean, smelling of lavender polish. There was old-fashioned brown lino on the floor, with a carpet runner leading to the kitchen. She still had utility furniture built after the war but it was in good condition and looked as if it was in a time warp. It was pretty impressive.

Swiftly Jazz and Ash nipped over the fence and knocked on the back door. A surprised Tracy Singer, mother to Billy Tower, opened the door. Billy was her eldest son by a boyfriend who had left before he was born. Since then she'd had three more children by different fathers. Life was difficult for Tracy and Billy was the cause of many of her problems. The search warrant was waved in front of her and Ash rushed into the house and up to Billy's room at the back. Billy was lying on his bed playing with his X Box and he looked up in surprise as Ash walked in. After the initial split-second shock, Billy adopted his sneering, dismissive tone. He thought Ash was a nonce and not worth much. "Oi! Get out of my house, pig!' shouted Billy. Ash was enjoying this and responded smugly, 'No way, sunshine, I have a warrant and I am searching your room for contraband.'

'Contraband? What the fuck is that?' was the incredulous response.

'Behave yourself, Snot Nose, I've had enough of you for now. I'm searching your room and I would ask that you remain where you are whilst I do this.' Just as Billy was going to argue the point, Jazz entered the room and stood quietly with arms folded while Ash searched the cupboards and shelves. Billy could see he was outnumbered and he knew you didn't mess with Jazz.

It took only a short while for Ash to find a box with small plastic bags of white powder. There were about five packets, more than enough to make Billy a dealer. Ash peered under the bed and pulled out a shoebox hiding amongst the fluff and bits of tissues and papers. When he opened it he exclaimed, 'Well, well, well, what have I found here, Billy, it looks like a starting pistol to me.' Jazz looked down the barrel of the pistol to see if it had been decommissioned but there was no Y-piece metal down the barrel to make it safe and legal. It was now a re-commissioned lethal weapon. It was known in the trade as a *gang bangers' special*.

Another small box under the bed contained four live shells individually wrapped in tissue. Ash held them up to show Jazz. Jazz took one look and shouted, 'Hold up, hold up. Put them down really carefully.' His tone was urgent but almost soothing, which suggested danger. Ash obeyed unquestioningly and put them down, almost sweating with the effort of making sure he did so without any sudden movement. Both he and Jazz took a deep breath once the bullets were back in the box. Startled and scared, Jazz looked at Ash. 'Didn't you learn any fucking thing at Hendon? You don't mess with bullets when you don't know who loaded them. One wrong move and they could have exploded and you might have filled me full of fucking holes, never mind bollock-head here.' He pointed at a sullen and silent Billy who had just been looking on, knowing he had been nabbed. CO19 were called to come and deal with disarming the gun. With great pleasure Ash read Billy his rights and took him in handcuffs to Ilford Police Station.

Billy was locked up in cells whilst they sorted out the paperwork and talked to CPS for charging. Ash looked at Jazz and thanked him for letting him arrest Billy. It gave him back some street cred as a detective. The gang members would know it was DC Ashiv Kumar who had arrested Billy. Jazz nodded and shrugged. 'It was your call, Ash.' He was actually trying to make amends for the neglect of his team member over the year.

Jazz beat himself up with the thought that he didn't seem to have learnt anything. How fucking stupid was he to think if he ignored Ash and gave him baby jobs to deal with he would be safe? All he'd done was make Ash a laughing stock with police and criminals alike. He didn't like himself very much at the moment.

There would be a lot of work to do in finding out what the Dag Gang was doing with a gun. Knives were the norm but now guns seemed to have entered Barking and Dagenham, and that was a worry. Ash was thanked for his police work by Trident who dealt with gun crimes and gangs and seemed to have a particular interest in the Dag Gang. The case was handed over to the newly formed Trident Gang Crime Command. They would now deal with Billy. It was a good day for Ash.

At the end of the three-day operation the Commander for the new Trident Gang Crime Command had sent out an email to say how absolutely delighted he was that the carefully planned operation had yielded such excellent results which included:

A large number of weapons seized including fourteen guns, thirty-seven knives and other bladed articles, and twenty-five other weapons including CS canisters, a cross bow, a Samurai sword, seventeen coshes/metal bars and one dangerous dog. Firearms included a sawn-off shotgun, eight hand guns (two semi-automatic), three imitation firearms, a taser and a gas-powered gun. Officers also seized a huge haul of drugs including half a kilo of crack/cocaine in Stratford, and sixty-seven grams of heroin in Barking (with a street value of approximately £3,500), and they also uncovered four cannabis factories around Romford and Dagenham.

At the end of the three days there were celebrations in the local Barking Dog and Bone pub with officers toasting their success. Jazz was there with stories and anecdotes and lots of vodka to toast their success. There were many toasts that evening and Ash was toasted for his find at Billy Tower's. By the end of the evening Jazz had toasted just about everyone in vodka and was ready to go home.

Meanwhile another group of officers were working quietly and confidently trying to help young people leave gangs or help them to turn their backs on gangs. They didn't have as much to celebrate.

But for now Jazz said goodnight to Ash and arranged to meet him in the office at 11 a.m. after he'd met with Jenny and got the results of the autopsy on John Carpenter. At least he'd done something good for Ash and now he could concentrate on the murder of Carpenter.

For now he would go home, heat up a pizza and possibly have a couple of drinks. He made his way home to De Vere Gardens. Mrs Chodda was at her kitchen door when he arrived. For once he was glad to see her. He wondered if she was going to introduce him to that girl he had seen in her kitchen. Mrs Chodda invited him into her kitchen but his face dropped just for a second when he saw yet another girl from some part of Mrs Chodda's family who was in need of a husband. He changed his look into one of suitable politeness but his thoughts were dark and mean. He wondered if Mrs Chodda was related to most of Great Britain's young women of marriageable age. He stayed for a cup of tea and a samosa or three, listening to inane conversations, and seeing a girl nearly young enough to be his daughter giggle and blush and say very little. He explained he was working on a very important case and needed to get his sleep for an early start the next day. He noted Mrs

Chodda nodding in appreciation to the mother of the young girl. He could almost read her mind. She would be saying, *see, I told you he was important*. He smiled to himself as he walked up the stairs. Perhaps he was a little disappointed it wasn't the young woman he had seen in her kitchen, but hey, he was tired and okay, not so hungry, but he was looking forward to a drink of the liquid nectar that he called vodka. He sat down and with the help of two or three large vodkas thought about John Carpenter and the Kent family. Tomorrow was going to be a difficult day.

CHAPTER FOURTEEN
Kindness, karmas, and killers

Jenny had worked very late last night and this morning she wasn't at her sprightly best. 'What the fuck do you want, DS Singh?' was her welcome.

'My darling,' said Jazz, 'I just couldn't stay away from you. Having seen you yesterday in the light of early afternoon and the twinkle in your eye, I have looked forward to this morning all night.' He thought he might have waxed a tad too lyrical even for Jenny but hey, he enjoyed the banter. Again she retorted with a request that he did something disgusting with his inner digit. He couldn't help it; he had to laugh.

Jenny was an amazing SOCO and her repartee may have needed a little work but he loved her for it. She had a very warm spot for him but she would never let him know that. In her sixties and not mindful that long grey hair swept carelessly into a ponytail was not a sexy sight, dressed in an ill-fitting tracksuit, Jenny lived her life for her work alone. Her mannerisms acquired over the years did not endear her to anyone and if it wasn't for her work she might have felt lonely. Jazz was the only person that ever tried to engage her in conversation or flirt with her, and she enjoyed it immensely. At home she had her cat but it wasn't the same. Jenny had never married and never had a boyfriend that anyone ever knew about.

Jazz knew where she kept her coffee and biscuits and asked if he could make her a cup of something and they could talk. She tried not to care but said if he wanted to help himself, she would have a coffee with milk and two sugars. He went over to the corner of her room and boiled the kettle. Her office was a mess. She had bits and pieces everywhere. Plastic see-through bags containing the odd piece of cloth, or a coat or a piece of wood all neatly labelled. She seemed to have half of Barking stashed on one side of the room. He spotted a particularly vicious knife in a rigid see-through knife container and wondered which miscreant had that tucked down his trousers. He looked in the fridge for the milk and rummaged amongst test-tubes of blood to find the milk. He tried not to feel too squeamish.

Jenny watched as he walked carefully across the room, balancing the biscuit tin on top of the steaming mugs, his tongue just out as if it helped him balance. She nearly said Boo!! But she didn't think that would be funny especially as he might spill her coffee onto the piles of papers that lined the route to her chair. It was 9 a.m., which for most was the start of the day, but she had been in her office since 7 a.m. and now she had a lot to talk to Jazz about.

She threw him a freshly typed report to read. He looked at its thickness and admiringly exclaimed, 'Gosh, Jenny, you must have worked through the night to produce this.' She smiled, and replied that she had not quite worked that long but near enough. She knew this was important. Jazz sat and read quickly through it, frowning and cursing under his breath when he got to parts that shocked him. He looked up and asked Jenny to confirm what he had read; it was unbelievable. Yes, she told him, John Carpenter had been blinded with acid and acid had also been put down his throat. The pain must have been excruciating, she added unnecessarily, as Jazz had a good idea what that might have been like. Carpenter's shoulders had been smashed with a large and heavy blunt instrument, and his knees and thigh bones had been shattered with a heavy blunt instrument too. Jenny added that a lot of strength would have been needed to shatter the bones in this way. With disgusted amazement Jazz asked if it was right that Carpenter was alive when he was left in the forest. Grimly, Jenny answered yes. Faeces had been found under him: his own. It looked as if he'd lived for about three days after the acid and broken bones attack. Jazz asked what killed him. A combination of shock, dehydration and hypothermia, said Jenny. She didn't think the various bites and tearing of his flesh actually killed Carpenter but it must have contributed to the general state of shock. When he was found he had nearly been eaten and there wasn't that much flesh left. Both she and Jazz shuddered at the thought.

'This is the second weirdest and most insane murder I have ever had to deal with since I became a SOCO many years ago,' stated Jenny as she sipped her coffee. She added that both had happened within months of each other. Jazz asked if she was referring to the

Columbian Necktie murder in Barking Creek and she nodded. She had dealt with many, many murders in her working life and some were particularly gruesome with a tortuous and painful ending but nothing so – and she thought carefully about the word – so theatrical in its way. She added disparagingly that she didn't think anyone in Barking and Dagenham had the sort of imagination and flair to commit such an act.

Jazz, deep in thought, added that John Carpenter was a particularly nasty piece of work; some would say he deserved everything he got and this looked like a revenge killing. So was the Columbian Necktie killing of Barry Jessop, a scrot who preyed on the naivety of good people and stole their money. He'd also got away with his crime. But all of the victims had good alibis for the murder of Barry Jessop. He couldn't believe any of the Kent family would be capable of committing such an act but he would have to visit them. At present the murder of John Carpenter was under wraps and the press hadn't been informed yet. He wanted to talk to the Kent family, Amanda in particular, and also James, the father, who always hid himself away. He asked how long Carpenter had been dead and Jenny said about one week. Animals had carried on eating him and there wasn't much left, but no animal ate anything near his eyes and throat because of the acid.

Jazz made his way to Ilford Police Station a little late; it was now about noon. He had spent a lot of time with Jenny. You just couldn't read such a report and not ask questions and confirm the facts. It felt strange. John Carpenter deserved all he got but this was something else.

It was the work of a madman or madwoman. No normal person would do this. He would take the report to Tom Black and discuss it with him. Ash would be waiting for him as well and he needed to get him on board. No more leaving him out. He had promised Ash he would be involved in everything – well, nearly everything. There was still something Jazz was organizing that no one else needed to know about.

Ash was waiting for him. Ash was always punctual and not used to someone being late; it made him edgy and cross. He had information for Jazz and had tried to ring Jazz on his mobile but it had gone to answer phone. Last night Jazz had asked him to find out when John Carpenter had missing. They needed to correlate when he had been taken and when he died. On his way to work Ash had gone to Carpenter's residence. A caretaker had told him the last time he had seen Mr. Carpenter and that his newspapers hadn't been taken in. They were able to establish when he was taken within a few hours.

Jazz looked at his watch and beckoned Ash impatiently to follow him saying loudly *The game is afoot Watson!* Ash thought darkly that Jazz sure wasn't Sherlock Holmes and he wasn't Dr Watson! He moved quickly though and caught some of the infectious excitement emanating from Jazz. They both strode towards Tom Black's office. All the way along the corridor Jazz gave a potted version of what was in the report on Carpenter. Some of it was so graphic Ash almost stopped in his tracks not believing what he was hearing. This was beginning to feel good; he, DC Ashiv Kumar, felt part of a real investigation and he wanted to stop and savour the moment. Jazz was having none of it. He grabbed Ash's sleeve and pulled him along, saying there was a lot to get done before the press got wind of this.

Tom Black was in his office and took a quick look at Jenny's report. His face was a picture of disbelief. He and Jazz talked for a while about the case and what was happening next, while Ash sat and listened. Jazz wanted to go and speak to the Kent family before the press got wind of the story. He wanted to see their reactions.

Having rung the Kents to say he was on his way and that he had some information for them, he arrived to find the front room just as he had left it last time he visited. The dining chairs were arranged against the wall as if there was going to be a party of people arriving. This time, the grandmother, Grace, was the only other relative with Amanda and again James was missing from the room. Jazz presumed the rest of the family felt they had done their duty and disappeared; he didn't blame them. He introduced Ash and all nodded at each other. Amanda looked very skittish and Jazz wasn't sure if she was going mad or had already reached that state. Grace looked older than he remembered. The lines in her face were deeper and she looked as if she carried the worries of the world on her stooped shoulders. Jazz felt so sorry for her. She was patting Amanda on the back in a motherly way but Amanda's back was taut and she looked like a piece of string about to snap under the tension; it made Jazz almost stand back from her, not sure what she might do.

Knowing where James would be, he beckoned to Ash to follow him, promising Amanda and Grace that they would be back in a moment. Jazz knocked on the door of the shed and entered a different world of order and quietness. A shed full of woodwork and gardening tools neatly hung on the wall or behind cupboards that James had built himself. There were a few pots of well-tended plants near the window, just about to flower. James had placed a chair in the corner, with a tired but comfortable cushion, and had put in a small TV to go with his little radio. A kettle in the corner and a paraffin heater showed he spent more time out here than indoors.

James looked up, seeming unsurprised by their appearance. He never said much and his hello and a nod of his head were about the best Jazz and Ash would get. Jazz asked him to come into the house, to sit with Amanda and Grace, because he had something to tell them. Again, James didn't look excited or enquiring; he just nodded and followed them into the house. By now Amanda had started to pace. She had become an ace pacer since Laura had been murdered. The worrying thing was that, when she paced, she ranted and the more she paced the more worked up she became; if not controlled she would start to hurt herself. Last time she had banged her head on the wall and caused a nasty gash. The tablets helped but there was nothing other than a full comatose medication that would keep Amanda controlled. Many tired relatives had muttered she would be better fully comatose. Jazz reckoned she was half a centimetre away from being sectioned and perhaps that would be better for everyone. This was Ash's first sight of the Kent family and he was glad Jazz was organizing the meeting. He stayed in the background away from what looked like a dangerous situation. Amanda looked capable of doing serious damage to someone if the wrong word was said to her.

In the edgy, electrically charged atmosphere, Jazz asked everyone to sit down. Maybe a cup of tea would help, he suggested. Hearing this, Grace got up and disappeared to the kitchen. Ash went with her to help. He was glad to get out of the front room; the atmosphere was giving him a headache. Grace was past tears. She told Ash she had cried herself dry and now she was left with a severe indigestion that didn't allow her to eat much. He thought she looked thin. During the time it took to make a cup of tea Ash and Grace connected, and he left the kitchen worried and emotional about her. This was a new experience for him and he didn't like it.

The pleasantries were unspecific and Amanda was getting seriously rattled. She asked in a controlled yet agitated manner why had Jazz come to visit? The weather wasn't important to her: never had been, and certainly wasn't now. James' plants in the garden were bloody useless and she couldn't give a tinker's cuss if they bloody flowered or bloody turned into bloody vegetables. Her voice rising to a crescendo, she finished loudly saying that it all didn't matter, nothing mattered to her any more. She had built herself up again into a worrying rant. Grace tried to calm her and patted her on the back but Amanda aggressively flicked her hand away. James just stared at the carpet as usual. Everyone sat in their own padded cell of silence without any human warmth between them. It was a daunting sight.

Jazz wasn't sure what the right way would be to start, but he had to do it. Ash, as asked to earlier, would watch carefully for reactions from Amanda, James and Grace, although an aging grandmother would be laughable as a murderer; she didn't have the strength or inclination to do such a thing. Jazz told the family that John Carpenter was dead, that he had been viciously and tortuously murdered and had been found in Epping Forest.

Amanda, now quiet, suddenly leaned forward which made Jazz lean back, not sure what she was going to do. Amanda asked urgently how he died. Jazz didn't quite know how much to tell them but what the hell, they'd lived through so much they were entitled to know, so he told them some of it: that John Carpenter had been tortured and left to die alone in the forest in pain. James just continued to look at the carpet but Amanda was a different kettle of fish. She rose joyously and shouted *Praise be to God!* She was laughing and thanking Jazz, as if he had committed the crime. She danced around the room, kissing first Jazz on the head and then Ash; she shook James by the shoulders and repeated the news, as if he hadn't heard that the murderer was dead. He nodded to her and agreed it was good news. Amanda hugged and kissed Grace, repeating *God is good, God is good, oh my, God is good* like a mantra. Then she wanted to know all the intimate details of Carpenter's death but Jazz couldn't tell her; it was all classified. Amanda kept asking if it had been painful and had it taken him a long time to die. She was laughing and as she got more and more ecstatic the spittle dripped off her lips. It was all beginning to look a little distasteful. Carpenter was a bastard and he deserved what he got, but normal people wouldn't put on such an over-the-top show of pleasure. Well, the reaction from Amanda was very clear. Jazz asked James how he felt and James just nodded that he was glad Carpenter was dead. Grace was looking at Amanda and worrying about how she was going to get her to settle down: Amanda was a loose cannon and no one knew how she would act and how she would turn. Grace brought her another tablet and a glass of water, looking as if she could do with a *pick me up* herself.

With one eye on Amanda, Jazz carefully picked his way through what he needed to say, not knowing what Amanda's reaction would be. He asked them to provide alibis for the past week. At this James looked up and Amanda said joyously that if it had been her who had killed the foul and despicable John Carpenter, she would tell the world of what she had done and would be proud of it. Grace frowned and said she did the same thing every day, which involved being with Amanda. Jazz tried to make light of it and said that they would be required to come to the Police Station to make statements. It was routine stuff, and it was necessary because they would be obvious suspects and it was important to clear their names. James nodded and said they would come tomorrow. With courteous goodbyes, Jazz said he would see them at 5 p.m. at Ilford Police Station. He and Ash left and once outside they both took deep breaths to rid themselves of the tension.

They made their way back to Ilford Police Station. It was only a couple of hours before the Kents arrived, and there was information to be shared and discussed. They found Tom Black deep in thought. They decided to get a cup of tea and sit in the canteen and talk through the latest information. An incident board was being set up in the CID office and they would go and look at it in a short while.

The lovely and sultry Milly', as Jazz called her, offered him a fresh cup of tea. She'd never let him have a stewed cup, oh no, her Jazz always got a very fresh cup of tea. This upset many other officers who never got such consideration, more, they were told to behave themselves and come when she called when their food was ready otherwise their meals went cold. She was known as a bit of a tyrant but to Jazz she was a temptress. On many levels Jazz was not spoken well of by many officers. *Jammy bugger, lucky sod, and conceited bastard together with cop killer,* were the normal descriptions he was given. The last one was untrue and proved so, but it had stuck to him like glue.

Most days Jazz sat alone in the canteen. But today he had Tom Black and Ash with him, and they sat in a corner discussing what had happened to John Carpenter.

Between them, Jazz and Ash could say, hands on hearts, that no one in the Kent family could have carried and tortured John Carpenter. To start with, Amanda was so off the wall she would have alerted the whole neighbourhood had she been involved, and she would have been proud of it too. The woman wasn't capable of doing anything at present and even if her mother had helped her, the two of them wouldn't have been strong enough. James was quiet and a bit of an unknown quantity but he wasn't a big man, and to carry a limp body all the way into the forest wasn't on: well, not by himself anyway. They would wait and see what James had to say in his statement but these were ordinary people and not the sort to kill, even though they had extreme provocation.

Tom Black had some interesting news. Whilst Jazz had been talking to Jenny regarding the autopsy, Tom had spoken to forensics who had searched the area around the body. They found sixteen cigarette butts on the ground around where John Carpenter lay. It seemed highly unlikely that anyone else would have spent that amount of time in that particular part of the forest. Forensics said there were four different DNAs on the cigarettes. From this it would seem that at least four people were involved in the murder and they'd hung around long enough to smoke four cigarettes each. The question was why? What was the point? If you'd killed someone or wanted to kill them, why would you leave them alive? Presumably this was part of the torture. Carpenter sure as hell wasn't going anywhere with mashed-up legs and arms, but then why had the attackers waited?

Tom added that it would be a hell of a coincidence but the Barking river guy Barry Jessop, as Jazz had found out from Musty Mary, had been grabbed by more than one guy. They'd spoken to Musty Mary's friend Yen, whose full name escaped Tom at this stage. Yen had thought at first that there was a whole army of men outside his cubicle but then he'd heard about four different voices, maybe more, but he wasn't sure.

What was going on in their town they asked themselves. It was agreed they would speak again after interviewing the Kent family. Tom would help and they would take one each when they came in. Tom, Jazz and Ash finished their tea, shared a few jokes and went off to the custody area to wait for the Kent family.

The interviews went well. Jazz drew the short straw; he got Amanda, which wasn't easy. They had all talked about where they were and so their statements were very similar. James had driven to Chester for a few days taking Amanda and Grace to visit his brother, and they stayed there for three days. That was during the time that John Carpenter was taken to Epping Forest, which made their alibis tight. Even if he was Stirling Moss, James couldn't have got back to London that quickly. It was a relief to Jazz; he didn't want them to be part of the murder of John Carpenter. The family had suffered enough without being accused of his murder.

Back in the CID room, they debriefed. Ash had spoken with Grace and she'd told the same story. She said that they had intended to stay the week in Chester but Amanda was scaring members of the family with her hysterical and perverse ways, so after three days they decided to return. Tom said James didn't say much but he confirmed they were in Chester and therefore couldn't have had anything to do with the abduction and murder of Carpenter. It seemed as if they had no leads; the DNA matched nothing on their database and no one had seen anything. Tom looked at Jazz and Ash. 'Bollocks!' he said. Which seemed to end that conversation.

They took a look at the incident board in the CID

room but there was nothing much on it yet. Jazz did have a thought and he asked Tom and Ash to be open-minded and listen to his theory. He asked them to consider two unusual murders in the same town. Both were defendants who had been found innocent of the charges. So no justice. Both were unusual murders. Both seemed to involve a vigilante group. They all thought and decided that at present it didn't get them anywhere. If there was a vigilante group what the hell had it got to do with each of the murders? They were different types of offences and different parts of town. The police would know about a vigilante group. You couldn't keep it quiet; someone would talk. For the moment they felt they had talked themselves out of a lead. Door to door enquiries were being made by Tom's team and he promised to let Jazz know if anything came up. In the meantime, Jazz would talk to his contacts to see if there was any change in the idea of a vigilante group in Barking and Dagenham. It wouldn't be long before there was a chink of light at the end of the dark tunnel.

It was time to head home and outside the station Jazz patted Ash on the back and thanked him for his work. Ash left hoping this might be the start of some worthwhile casework. Jazz left with the thought that tomorrow they would search out his contacts that might have something to tell them.

He was running out of vodka so he stopped off at Sainsbury's on the way home. He picked up one of those microwave lasagne meals and also bought some Doritos and Nacho cheese sauce dip for later. He hoped Mrs Chodda would give him a rest tonight. He needed to have a word with her. It was getting stupid with the girls he was being introduced to. But when he got home the kitchen door was open and he saw Mrs Chodda at the stove stirring something; she looked miles away. He shouted out, 'Good night, Auntie!' and saw her jump with surprise. He dashed upstairs, giggling. The day had been full on and he needed the little bit of silliness. A drink would help now, and he put his dinner in the microwave and poured himself a generous vodka. There was nothing much on the TV but he watched some mindless game show and was just about to get his meal out of the microwave when he heard a timid knock at the door. 'Oh bugger,' he thought. Why had he brought himself to Mrs Chodda's attention? She was going to make him come downstairs to meet another distant relative or some such. He wondered if he could pretend he was asleep. But at that point there were loud cheers and claps on the game show. No way could he pretend to be asleep now.

Reluctantly he opened the door and there stood the young woman he had seen before. She looked embarrassed and hesitant. 'I am so sorry to disturb you,' she said in a beautifully deep, rich voice that reminded him of a glass of Baileys. 'My aunt, er, Mrs Chodda,' she added, 'wondered if you might like these.' She thrust a Tupperware box containing some rice and curry at him. He thanked her and smiled. She smiled back and turned to go. 'Oh, sorry,' stammered Jazz. 'Erm, I am Jaswinder, Jazz to my friends. Erm, we haven't been introduced, have we?' She turned and smiled. 'No, we haven't.' She went down the stairs before he could think of anything else to say. He smiled; he liked her coolness. He lingered lost in thought for a second, then pulled himself together. Time for another drink.

He met Ash at 9 a.m. sharp at their desks. He'd spend an hour sorting out his emails and then they would be off to meet and greet and see what was going on out there in the world. Ash had been at his desk since 8 a.m. and was finishing copying his MG11 for Grace's statement. He'd completed the MG5, and all the MG6 series that went to make up a full set of case papers. Jazz was impressed; he'd worked hard and well. Ash asked Jazz if he'd copied his MG11 for Amanda so the file could be put together. Jazz gave it to Ash and said that, as he was so good at it, perhaps he would like to photocopy his for the file. Ash didn't mind; it was good working with someone for a change. He was looking forward to today.

Jazz and Ash checked in with Tom Black before they left, to see if there was anything else worth knowing on the John Carpenter case. Up on the board was a forensic picture of Carpenter at the scene before he was carted away. It was the most gruesome picture, beating anything anyone had ever seen before. He had been eaten and was half a man. The maggots had started breeding and anyone with a weak stomach would have retched for weeks. Another picture showed the surrounding area where he'd been found and Jazz muttered that, judging by the state of the undergrowth, the way it was flattened, a herd of something or other had been there. The cigarette butts had been found in the area, confirming that several people had paced around and waited there for a while. Again, the DNAs on the cigarette butts were not known. So far the house to house enquiries had given them nothing to work with, except nailing when Carpenter was last seen, which was over a week ago.

All the girls on the campus who were taught by John Carpenter would be interviewed and it was hoped this would bring something to light. In the meantime Jazz and Ash were off to check out the vigilante theory.

First they went to the Gascoigne Estate in Barking. Jazz wanted to see Charlie Griffiths, a fifty-year-old man who had lived, worked and drunk on the estate. He was now medically retired with his back which didn't allow him to walk far. Luckily he could see his local pub from his first-floor flat. He spent his days gossiping with the women in his block and his nights gossiping with the men in the pub. He was a mine of information. Jazz knocked on his door and waited. It took a while for Charlie to reach the door, but they could hear him cheerfully shouting that he wouldn't be long. When the door opened they saw a very dapper man with his white fairly short hair greased down slickly, wearing a white shirt and dark blue trousers; he looked like an office worker on a break. His home was immaculate, everything polished, in its place and hoovered. Charlie made them a cup of tea, using a teapot and real tea leaves. It was all rather quaint and Jazz and Ash sat patiently waiting for the tea to brew. Charlie was quite excited to see Jazz. He hoped he was bringing a nice piece of gossip he could share with his lady friends when they came for tea.

Over tea and some bourbons he had in the cupboard,

Charlie asked expectantly what he could do for Jazz. They talked for a bit about the local gossip with the drugs changing hands and how the kiddy gangs were grafitti-ing everywhere, and about who was sleeping with who, and who had just gone into or come out of prison. After Charlie had shared his gossip, he was ready for Jazz to reciprocate. Jazz knew that every word he said would be repeated, exaggerated and whispered around the estate. He picked his words carefully. Of course Charlie knew about Barry Jessop being found in Barking Creek. What no one officially knew was about the Columbian Necktie, and Charlie wanted that confirmed. He leaned forward and asked Jazz outright if it was true that Barry Jessop had been found dead with his tongue pulled through a slit in his throat.

Jazz knew he wasn't going to get much help if he didn't confirm what Charlie and his friends already knew. He looked hard at Charlie and asked him not to repeat a word. Charlie whispered that every morsel of information was safe with him, of course. Jazz sat up straight and sipped his tea. Charlie, hardly daring to breathe, licked his lips as he waited for the tasty morsel of information. With great deliberation Jazz put down his cup and whispered that Barry Jessop had been tortured and murdered, and that yes, a Columbian Necktie was what he'd been given. Charlie sat back and sighed deeply. His mouth shaped the word *oh* as he exhaled. He was thrilled with such a gorgeously tasty bit of information. 'Now!' said Jazz. 'I need your help.' Charlie was all ears; if he had been a cat he would have been purring. 'What can I do for you, Mr Singh?' He hadn't heard of a vigilante group in Barking at all. If there was one he would surely know about it. He'd ask his lady friends to ask about. He also said the speculation on who had committed the murder of Barry Jessop was still a huge talking point with his ladies and his drinking pals. No one had come up with any concrete ideas. 'So,' said a ponderous Charlie, shifting in his seat, 'Was Barry Jessop dead when they cut his throat and pulled his tongue through?'

Jazz didn't know but said he was probably alive because that was common in Columbian Necktie murders. 'And,' added Charlie delicately, 'did they shoot him in the head afterwards?'

Jazz didn't want to get into this. He finished the conversation with, 'In the back of the neck, Charlie, and that's all I can say.' This was enough to please Charlie but there was one more question.

Charlie, as a good gossipmonger, had thought carefully about what Jazz had asked him. 'So, Mr Singh, when you ask if there's a vigilante group, it beggars the belief that there has been other cases. When you say vigilante groups, it usually means they're sorting out other misdemeanors. Am I right, Mr Singh?' He enquired soothingly. Jazz smiled and said that at present there was nothing to add. He said he would see Charlie tomorrow and he hoped there would be some information by then. They left a very happy Charlie Griffiths. His talk with Mr Singh would be the topic of discussion at this afternoon's tea session and tonight in the pub.

As they walked down the stairs from the flat Ash asked why Jazz had told such a gossipmonger classified information about Barry Jessop. Jazz explained that Charlie and his cohorts already knew what had happened to Barry Jessop; he was just confirming it. He needed information from Charlie and his lady friends and they would talk of nothing else for a while and then make all sorts of enquiries for him because the gossip would be good. They would be told far more than Jazz could find out. John Carpenter would stay under wraps for the time being. Ash nodded; he was beginning to get a feel for what Jazz was all about and how he worked. He felt uncomfortable in a way because it certainly wasn't textbook stuff but part of him was enjoying the excitement.

Their next stop was Mad Pete, who lived on the Gascoigne Estate. But he was out and wasn't answering his mobile. They wandered the estate for a while but there was no sight of him. Jazz said that they would go back to the station for a few hours and see if anything had developed.

Something wasn't right. Murder had its own way of working. It happened for all sorts of reasons and the idea was to kill. These two murders were something else that didn't fit the usual modus operandi. Murder used to be a rare occurrence. Now there were gang murders; knives and guns were being used to kill and maim, and there were the domestic violence murders. There were more murders on the street than could be reported in newspapers. Only the unusual murders got into newspapers these days. The John Carpenter murder was about to be reported not only in the local but also the national newspapers, and on TV. DCI Radley was going to be busy again, thought Jazz.

They would drag up the case of Laura again and he thought he ought to visit the Kents and warn them. Amanda needed watching in case she went on the pill munching phase again. He asked Ash if he wanted to go back to the station and work on the case papers for John Carpenter whilst he went and visited the Kents.

He found all the Kents in their home. Amanda didn't seem to stray very far these days and Grace was always there to look after her. Again, James was in his shed. Jazz could see their lives had been ruined and perhaps they would never return to normal again. Grace said she would keep a firm eye on Amanda and reassured Jazz not to worry. He thought she was a wonderful woman. Every time he saw her she looked ten years older and he wouldn't be surprised if she didn't last much longer. It was a depressing thought. He sought out James who still had very little to say and refused to come out of his shed. Jazz had done his job and warned them all of the impending press stampede. He left the Kent home in need of a stiff drink.

On his way home he popped by the Gudwara and said hello to Deepak. All was going well with his talks with the Indian ladies and their jewellery. He did say the fairy lights were another matter and he was having no luck with that. What was a worry was Sikhs were asking male members of the family to stand guard during festivals and special occasions when the fairy lights were out and gold jewellery was in abundance. Deepak said he hoped it didn't turn into a problem. Jazz stayed at the Gudwara for a little while. It was beginning to feel comfortable and the gossiping aunties made sure he ate something before he left. Deepak always had time for him and they chatted about this and that and business in the area. He went home feeling better.

The key in the door of De Vere Gardens attracted Mrs Chodda. Again, before he had got halfway up the stairs, she came out of the kitchen. She reminded him that on Sunday he was going to a family wedding with her as he had promised. He had forgotten all about it. In truth, he had only agreed to attend with Mrs Chodda just to get away from her. He didn't want to go but perhaps it wasn't a bad idea. There would be a bit of good food, conversation and a dance or two which sounded actually quite good. He lied that he hadn't forgotten and that he'd see her Sunday morning all suited and booted. It was going to be held in the City Limits banqueting suite. He had been there before and if he got bored he could go downstairs and play tenpin bowling. Sounded good to him! The food at weddings would be the best of the best and there would be chips for the children which would suit him well. The drinks always flowed liberally. Yes, he would go just to keep Mrs Chodda company.

CHAPTER FIFTEEN
Retribution

He had kept himself to himself. No need to go out much, he told himself. Since those women had found him in the supermarket and surrounded him and frightened him, he had to be moved again. The police, Social Services and the Council were liable for his security and they moved him to Barking. He was now on the Gascoigne Estate.

This huge sprawling estate full of high-rise flats and a selection of lower blocks of flats were crammed into the area designed in the infinite wisdom of the architects. All in all, when empty, Gascoigne Estate looked boringly and coldly functional. Now, full of various families and single people with infinite problems, it was a heaving mess of misery, criminality, and resentment. It would be wrong to say that everyone on the Gascoigne Estate had problems. There were many families struggling to bring up children in an area with so many temptations. Gangs, drugs, drink, and criminality was rife. The Council in their wisdom saw the Gascoigne Estate as a dumping ground for all the problems in the area. No one would move there by choice. Johnny Peters was a huge problem and he had been ceremoniously dumped in a one-bedroom flat on the top floor of a high-rise block on Gascoigne Estate after he was recognized and chased by women shoppers in Asda in Romford.

They called him a paedophile: a horrible name. He was just someone who loved children. Johnny related better to children. His favourite age was seven. He liked boys as well as girls. Children were sexual beings, he knew that. All the clever people in the world and they didn't know this? He knew they were lying. His home was child-friendly. He had lots of sweets, an X Box with all the latest games, and a selection of Sylvania Family for the girls to play with. His home was a fun place to be. He liked to film his play time and had cameras slightly hidden, so the children didn't feel self-conscious in the lounge, bedroom and bathroom. He had a camera in the bathroom to watch them pee. He liked that.

He had been utterly miserable. He dare not make any new friends for a while. The police had warned him that he was being watched and he didn't want to be chased again by those awful women. He didn't deserve it. He had been in Gascoigne now for about six months and he had found a new friend.

The time in court was really terrible. The child wouldn't go to court and the parents wouldn't go to court which was a relief. The things said by the prosecuting counsel and the police made it sound so basic and terrifying. They said nothing about the love of a child and the reciprocation that love gives. He had loved that child and he missed her dreadfully. He used to call her seven-year-old Sally, known as SS. He had laughed at that. Yes, of course she was a little scared.

Real love is scary but he was kind and gentle when he made love to her. How it was thrown out of court he never understood. All he remembered was the rush to get him out of court and hidden away before the baying crowd got hold of him. They had found his homemade DVDs and they took them away from him. He couldn't even have some comfort in watching them. But it was a relief he didn't have to go to prison.

He had walked by the local school but he had to be careful. The police might have been watching him but they could do nothing at the moment because he'd been found not guilty. During his first three months on the Gascoigne Estate he had watched and seen Little Tommy, who was a latch key child. Tommy lived across the road in another block of flats. He was a quiet boy and didn't seem to play with other children. Johnny felt sorry for him. His mother didn't get home until 7 p.m. and he had to play by himself from 3.30 p.m. until 7 p.m. Johnny said if he wanted he could come and play on his X Box. He had the Star Wars game. He told Tommy that it was for twelve years and upwards, but he thought that Tommy, at eight years old, would smash it.

Now Tommy came to him straight from school. Johnny waited in anticipation every school day. He had taken it slowly. He had romanced and flirted with Tommy. It was a month before he made any real advance. It had been awful with Tommy, scared, crying, and shouting, trying to run out of the flat. Johnny didn't understand what had gone wrong. He knew Tommy wanted him too. He was frustrated and angry now. All this time in courting Tommy and he acted in this way?

He had given him everything he wanted. He didn't have a lot of money but he'd spent it on Tommy, who had taken everything. He found his hands around Tommy's neck, squeezing. It wasn't long before Tommy was still and Johnny kept him there for hours just looking at him and touching him. He was a slip of a lad and it didn't take much to put him in a shopping trolley that was hanging about the hall by the lifts; he had a bin liner to put him in, and he put boxes over him and wheeled him down the road to Barking Creek. It was dark and quiet by Freshwharf and he pushed the shopping trolley into the black waters of Barking Creek.

It took only a day for the police to find Tommy. They knew it was him but they couldn't prove it. They tried their best and said they would get him eventually and that he was being watched. So now he sat in his flat and didn't dare go out. Someone had let it be known who he was and he had to have all his food delivered by Tesco because he couldn't go out. The Council were looking to move him again but nothing had happened yet. He was considered to be reasonably safe in his top-floor flat. His door had six locks on it and every now and then someone would bang angrily on his door and he would hear vile things said. He didn't have a letterbox in the door and he covered the bottom of the door so nothing could be posted through to him. It was scary and he hoped he would be moved soon. He felt bad about Tommy. He didn't want to kill him; he'd just wanted to love him.

He was getting stir-crazy. He had been in his flat for two months since Tommy died. He still couldn't go out and the Council hadn't done anything for him. He rang them every day but they said he was reasonably safe where he was and they were looking for safe accommodation for him. He flicked the TV on but there was nothing he wanted to watch. It was dark outside and he used to quite like looking at the lights spread out across London but nothing excited him any more.

The phone call was late but it was a Council worker saying they had found him a new place to live that would be very safe. The only thing was they had to move him now. People in the area were watching out for him so a night move was imperative. He protested that he needed to pack, he wasn't ready, and why hadn't they told him earlier. The answer was crisp and clear. He had to go now for his own safety. They implied there was going to be trouble from the residents. With that he agreed and they said a knock on the door in five minutes would be his cue to open the door. He agreed, scared now at the thought there might be a lynch mob around the corner.

He got his coat, wallet and cigarettes and waited nervously for the knock on the door. When it came he opened the door to four big burly men waiting for him. The front man smiled but the smile didn't reach his eyes. The two men behind looked around nervously and the other man stared hard and straight at Tommy. It didn't feel right and he was about to argue he wasn't ready. He wanted to close the door on them. The front man said soothingly that they had heard about fifty residents were amassing around the corner to come and beat his door down, so they had to get him away urgently. The blanket over his head as they frog marched him to the lift was for his own safety. He understood that and went with them willingly and fearfully, his feet barely touching the ground as two of them took an arm each and rushed him to the lift. They told him to be quiet because his voice would be known. He stayed quiet, almost scared to breathe. He was bundled into a car and as he tried to take the blanket off his head he was tasered. The shock was enormous; he found it hard to breathe and then thankfully he went unconscious.

The journey took just over an hour and they made their way along the A127 towards Southend, Essex. When they got to the Tesco roundabout they took the Rochford turning and arrived at Paglesham Village at midnight. The boatyard just past the village was secluded and dark. They were on a tight timescale because the full tide was expected in at 2 a.m. They tied him up and put gaffer tape across his mouth. His feet were tied and a large concrete slab was tied to his feet. They had a lot of work to do and they tried to keep as quiet as they could. There was no one around the boatyard but just in case one of them kept a watch. They all had tracksuits on and now they donned boots. The quayside was all mud but it filled full of water when the tide turned and came in. The water from the estuary, lit by the moon, was still a long way out. Johnny was coming round and they wanted to get him in the mud quickly. It was soft mud and when they lowered him down the weight of his body and the concrete slab sunk him up to the tops of his legs. His eyes widened in fear and they could hear the muffled shouts of fear and pleading. As he struggled he got a little deeper into the mud so he stopped still; the only part of him moving was his eyes, darting in terror towards them and his situation. One of the men had an infrared camera and was filming him.

Five cigarettes later the tide was lapping around Johnny who was by now so scared and cold his body trembled. He felt the water rise slowly but relentlessly. The men watched and wondered how high it would get. They had been told that tides vary in height. After about an hour of utter fear and terror the water had reached Johnny's lips and he could only breathe through his nose. He kept his head as high as he could and his neck was aching like mad. After what seemed a lifetime, he realized the water was very slightly receding. *Praise be to God!* he thought euphorically. The tide had turned. His chest was pounding, his breathing was laboured, and his head was giddy with fear and now with relief. He swooned slightly but was held fast in the mud and water. The elation was short-lived. He looked up at the sound. A huge Deutz engine had been gunned and was now throbbing heavily in anticipation. A Dutch barge can move in three feet of water. The size and width of the barge began to blot out the moon. It was at this point that one of the men, on all fours on the quayside, leaned out to Johnny and ripped off the gaffer tape across his mouth. The screams and pleas, and the shaking to release himself were all filmed. The look in Johnny's eyes of unspeakable and unstinting terror was captured on film.

The high-pitched scream of terror rang through the air as the barge glided towards Johnny and hit his face full force, pushing his unyielding body under the water. The majestic barge continued its journey over his head and stopped a few feet after Johnny disappeared into the black abyss that would now be his place to rot in hell. As the tide went out the barge settled on the mud and the huge weight of two hundred tons of a thirty-metre metal barge sank heavily into the mud. Johnny would be buried forever. It had been a strange few hours and the four men thankfully left the boatyard that had now resumed its peaceful tranquillity that ramblers loved to visit.

In the morning, when the curlews resumed their search for food in the mud and the local fisherman came to check their nets in the estuary, there was no sign of the trauma of the night before and the Dutch barge sat quietly hiding the murder of a paedophile that would cause the rejoicing of many in the East End of London.

CHAPTER SIXTEEN
Confusion and clarity

The rest of the week was shit. Jazz had told everyone within sight and sound that nothing made sense. He and Ash had visited Charlie the next day for updates on the gossip and Charlie had nothing to add except his ladies and himself were tirelessly investigating every avenue. Jazz could almost hear him purring again. This had made Charlie's year and he would milk it for as long as he could. This was good news for Jazz. As soon as Charlie had any information he would contact Jazz.

Again, Mad Pete was out and Jazz was seriously pissed off with him. He wasn't answering his phone either. They needed to get back to the police station for a meeting with Boomer on the latest updates on the John Carpenter case and anything new on Barry Jessop. Jazz would sort out Mad Pete later. He and Ash had been officially seconded to Tom Black's team. The two murders were causing problems for DCI Radley. The press were having a field day and something needed to be settled soon, otherwise the big boys would descend on Ilford Police Station from Scotland Yard and take over. No one wanted that.

As usual, any meeting with Tom Boomer Black and his team was sprinkled heavily with Boomerisms. He started his motivating talk to his team with Jazz and Ash in attendance. 'Someone is fucking about and taking the piss out of us.' Everyone looked up at that statement. He was referring not to the usual stabbings or blunt instrument murders of which they had enough to deal with, but the two murders that bore no resemblance to any others so far in the East End. He reminded them all that they had had their fair share of strange murders such as bodies being fed to pigs, or found in pillars to hold up flyovers, or minced up, but none compared to the creativity of the Columbian Necktie murder and the Babes in the Wood murder, as the John Carpenter murder was being called. He asked all present to look closely at the facts. What had been done to the two men seemed to be a message but to whom? Who was doing this and why? Were the two murders connected or were they just random creative murders? No one thought that was the case. The whole East End was quiet with no whispers. House to house investigations were going to happen again, he told his team. The forensic details were going to be looked at by someone else in the team. A fresh set of eyes and thoughts were needed.

It was clear to everyone, and all felt the frustration, that it was as if they were being taunted by someone. Each case smacked of vigilante killings but there was no sight at all of a vigilante gang working out there. Each man had done something that would piss off people and cause vengeance, but those involved had clear and watertight alibis. Boomer asked officers to swap their notes and get a new officer to check the alibis. He finished by adding, 'The sodding press are hot on the heels of John Carpenter's murder and we are going to get a fucking bollocking from everyone if we don't stop pratting about and solve these fucking murders. So go off and sodding well come back with something, you bastards.' No motivating quote like *hey, lets be careful out there*, from DI Tom Black. They all left smiling, knowing what he was like; his men were very loyal to him.

Jazz and Ash were given a free hand to look into the cases. Boomer sincerely hoped that as comparative outsiders to the two murders they might come up with something useful. Jazz felt a bit depressed at Boomer's optimism. He hadn't a clue where to look. Up to now all roads had come to a dead end.

They set off to find Mad Pete. In times of need Mad Pete could often provide information that was helpful. He never told freely but Jazz had a way with him. Their relationship was based on fear and favour. It would amaze both of them to say they needed each other and that they were quite symbiotic. Jazz sorted out any problems with the police for Mad Pete. He still fenced mobile phones and there were plenty of them being offered to him by his kiddy gangs who had robbed another scrot for their mobile phone. The same mobile phones were recycled in the district by Mad Pete. Then there was his drugs which he needed and Jazz protected him from the police.

Mad Pete furnished Jazz with lots of information about what was going on in the area. He seemed to have his finger in every pie and knew what was going on with whom and where. It amazed Jazz just what Mad Pete was into and how he never seemed to get into the real trouble. He ran errands and did little bits and pieces for some very hefty gang members. They were known to mete out some serious slaps to anyone who crossed them. Jazz presumed that, although Mad Pete was a hero to the kiddy gangs, to the big gangs in the East End he was just a snivelling scrot who ran errands for them. They should have taken note that he listened to everything and wasn't as stupid as they thought. A consummate coward, Mad Pete always looked frightened and was scared of his own shadow. He scuttled around the East End like a rat, gathering a bit of money here and there. Jazz was going to find him and sort him out. He had left so many messages on his mobile, and Mad Pete always had his mobile with him, but there was no reply as yet.

It was going to be another day of no Mad Pete. He was nowhere to be found on the Gascoigne Estate. Ash went back to the station to look through CRIS reports to see if he could find anything of interest. It all sounded incredibly boring to Jazz who wanted to do something more interesting. It was Friday night and he decided to go home. Monday was another start and he had a fucking wedding to get ready for. His suit, hardly ever used, was in good condition but he needed another white shirt. He took himself to Marks and Spencer down the road and bought himself a stunning white evening shirt. He had a bowtie somewhere and he was going to look fabulous. A bottle of vodka was also bought in Sainsbury's, as well as a Sainsbury's Finest shepherds pie that he could whack in the microwave. He was going to sleep in on Saturday and think. There was something he was missing and it felt close but not close enough to touch yet. There was something similar to the murders; there had to be a link somewhere. It had to be something like a vigilante group. He was to hear from Charlie on Monday and that would be the catalyst to send Jazz on his way to hell.

Sunday came and at 4 p.m. Jazz went downstairs suited and booted, and suitable enough for Mrs Chodda to be proud of him. He was fond of her and her funny ways and he liked the fact she wanted to show him off to her family and friends. A wedding is an opportunity to wear your best and show off your riches, family and potentially marriageable children. Everyone was in some way related to the other. It was a good time to be seen and to seek out others.

When you married into an Asian family you took the family on as your own and they would all be invited to occasions and weddings and birthdays. An Asian event was always a huge event with anything from two hundred people or more to cater for. Jazz knew of one family who had a thousand guests at their daughter's wedding. Of course they were a rich family and guests came from as far away as the Punjab, Africa and Canada. That had been a wedding and a half. Most weddings last days with the bride's family wedding reception; the groom's parents will also have a wedding reception, and then there's the pre-wedding party. This family had parties that went on for weeks with other important members of the family hosting wedding parties for guests. Jazz's mother had been alive then and he remembered escorting her, and just how tiring it was but also great. Those were the days, he reminisced.

Mrs Chodda gave him the once-over in a glance. He looked good and she smiled. He would do nicely. She'd told all her friends how Jazz lodged with her and what a wonderful man he was and how important in the police force. She was quite the envy of her friends to have such an important and handsome young man lodging with her.

City Limits was originally just a bowling alley but the upstairs had been transformed into many rooms that constituted banqueting suites. It was owned by a Sikh family, and the food was exquisitely Indian, of course. The chandeliers were stunning and changed colour during the evening. The bar was well stocked and buried under Sikh men who frequented the bar and stayed there. The food was wonderful and the bride sat in a special place looking demurely at the floor. She was fed sweetmeats by various members of the family. She looked stunning in her red gown, with plenty of bling around her neck, on her ears and from her nose, not to mention long arms full of gold bangles that nearly made Jazz reach for his sunglasses. She had sat all day in this position and now she was released into the family custody and to her new husband. By 10 p.m. the men were quite drunk and Jazz was merry too. The Bangra music started and most of the men, especially the younger ones, took to the floor to show off their Bangra moves. Jazz watched in awe. Sikhs really knew how to rock. He was pulled onto the dance floor by a young man, and he danced competitively. As each man danced fast and more intricately, others would mimic him and better him. By the end of the evening the dance floor was quite frenzied with young Sikhs dancing for their honour. The older Sikhs had long given up and returned to the bar. The young women danced around the men with their eyes on those they quite fancied. Parents looked on and watched the young people enjoying themselves. Jazz knew some would be making notes of suitable prospective wives or husbands for their children. Of course, the family itself would need investigating first. It had to be suitable. You married the family as well. Both sides of the family become as one. Sikh marriages were far more complicated than western marriages and he was glad not to be part of it.

He had had quite a few drinks and was merrier than he should have been. He spotted that girl sitting in a corner talking to someone old. It was the one he had seen in Mrs Chodda's kitchen, the one who didn't give her name when she brought him some food. He shouldn't have gone over to her, he was far too tipsy to be sensible, but what the heck, he wanted to say hello. She watched as he sashayed over to her. She wasn't going to bother talking to him in his state. Before he got close enough she had got up and walked off to the ladies. He was confused when she got up and walked away but he was getting tired now and just wanted to go home to sleep. Mrs Chodda got him a taxi so he could go before her. She was busy talking to one of the bride's relatives from India. Jazz got home and fell up the stairs into his room. His bed was the only thing he wanted. He had a lot to do Monday morning and needed his sleep.

Charlie had Jazz's mobile telephone number just in case. Jazz should never give out his private mobile number but he trusted Charlie and wanted any information he might have. The sound of a phone ringing woke Jazz. He must have slept with his mouth open because his tongue felt huge and his mouth very dry. He felt around for his mobile with his eyes shut. Having no luck he tried to open his eyes slowly but there was a stabbing pain in his head. He found his mobile under his pillow and before he could ask himself why it was there he pressed the answer button and heard Charlie's voice. Charlie asked with concern if Jazz was all right. It was, after all, 9 a.m. and Jazz sounded as if Charlie had called in the middle of the night. Jazz pulled himself together and said it had been a long night and he was catching up with sleep.

Charlie commiserated that Jazz's work was very time-consuming and he deserved time off. These cooing words of consideration gave Jazz time enough to grab some Fanta from the fridge and take a swig. Now he felt a bit better. Charlie was still talking about police working hard and that crime rates were high etc. Jazz asked how he could help him and Charlie understood he had to talk straight. Charlie had heard about Johnny Peters, the paedophile who had been given a place on the Gascoigne Estate. He told Jazz that everyone was up in arms with him being there. He whispered that he had heard of many men who were looking to cut him into little pieces. 'Well,' he added breathlessly, 'I have just heard that he hasn't been in his flat for a few days now. His door was left open and his lights were on.' He didn't know who had found this out but it was true. He asked if Mr Singh knew what had happened to him. Jazz didn't but said he would make enquiries. 'Why are you so worried about him, Charlie?'

'Oh, I'm not, Mr Singh. We would just like to know where he is. We don't want him on our streets talking to our children.'

Jazz realized this was what Charlie's women friends had been saying to him and they were concerned. He said again that he would make enquiries and he reminded Charlie about the vigilante groups and to call him with any information he might get. Charlie said he would and asked if Jazz could ring him with an update by lunchtime. Jazz smiled at this. He knew Charlie would be seeing his lady friends for tea in the afternoon and he wanted any information he could get to pass on to them.

He moved as quickly as he could. How the fuck had he managed to sleep until 9 a.m.? He needed to get to the police station. He had a quick shower to wake himself up; another drink of Fanta helped. The sweetness of the drink seemed to calm him down and in a short while he was walking to work, thinking about Johnny Peters. What a fucking lucky paedophile he was. He should have been put away but he got off on a technicality. There were times when Jazz wished he could take all the judges and make them live on the streets to see how life really was. They lived in fancy ivory towers and didn't speak to, see or live anywhere near the types of miscreants the police dealt with. He had heard that Johnny was being watched and there was talk of him befriending a little boy but nothing much had happened about that so far. He would ask when he got into the station.

The station seemed deserted. Already everyone was out making enquiries. Ash couldn't be found either. Jazz knew he was late, it was 10.30 a.m. by now, but still, where was everyone? He tried Mad Pete again but still no reply. He was seriously pissed off with him now.

For the moment he went and found someone in SCD5, Child Protection, to ask about Johnny Peters. He found Paula working on something. Paula was a no-nonsense tough cookie. Over the years she'd seen and heard more than anyone in their early thirties should. She had convicted men you wouldn't want within a mile of you and she had to sit in a small room and interview them and talk about sexual acts performed on children and look at pictures of children being compromised that would send a normal person mad, hysterical, deeply sad and depressed. Jazz could see it all in her eyes; she looked haunted.

He asked about Johnny Peters and she looked up and sighed. She was busy and he was not her case. Having said that, she said he was under investigation and added that the bastard wasn't going to be so lucky next time. They would get him. Jazz told her about his door being open and the lights on, and that he wasn't there. She looked mildly surprised, thought for a second, and rang her boss, DI Richard Cunningham. He didn't know what had happened but said he would go to the flat and see what had happened. He thanked Jazz for the tip-off. Jazz then rang Charlie and told him the police were not aware of Johnny Peters moving anywhere and they were sending officers round to his flat to take a look. Charlie was very grateful to Jazz and thanked him profusely.

As a second thought, Jazz asked Charlie if by chance he knew Mad Pete? Of course Charlie knew of him. Jazz wondered if he had seen him around lately. Charlie had and said he seemed to be hanging around the youth club in the Gascoigne Estate. It was pretty posh to call it a youth club; it had turned into a graffiti-ridden shack where youngsters hung out for drugs and anything else that was going down. Nice people didn't frequent the area. Jazz thanked him and said he would go and look for Mad Pete. Charlie said he was always happy to help the police and he would be most grateful for any updates that he could pass on to his Neighbourhood Watch team. Jazz smiled and said he would do what he could.

CHAPTER SEVENTEEN
Come into the parlour said the spider to the fly

Ash was deep in contemplation of CRIS papers and reports he had found. He knew Jazz was good at what he did but paperwork was not his forte. Ash was going to prove he was an asset to the team. He felt he had run behind Jazz, letting him take all the decisions, making the assumptions and getting things to happen. He felt a bit of a *numpty*. He wanted to find something that would help solve the murders, to make him look like someone worth having around.

He'd been kidding himself when he said that he wasn't worried what others thought of him, and that the name-calling from the other CID teams didn't get at him, and that the laughter at his expense didn't make him so mad he was close to landing punches on the bastards. He felt like a spare part at a wedding and that was about to change. He wanted a win and he wanted the adulation it would bring him.

He had to admit that, although he was going through files with a fine-tooth comb to see if there were any links or ideas to help with the murders, it was a fluke that gave him that rich and elusive clue that might solve the cases. The regular updates from intelligence or departmental emails containing snippets and videos of unsolved cases or unidentified suspects sent in the hope that officers would recognize these elusive bits of information were his lucky break.

The tenuous link would never have been seen by anyone else. Ash was living with the paperwork of the two murders. He had all the names of associates, where they lived, and what they thought. Everything was in their statements and in the police documents, and he felt close to all the people associated with the murders. Yes, all the victims or their relatives had fantastic alibis but – and that was the but – the coincidence was that they were the victims, so who else would be interested in murdering the two men?

Ash always read all his emails. There were the video emails of some young and slightly obscure person robbing a late-night supermarket. The CCTV camera above the counter showed someone entering and pulling out a knife. In some cases the shop owner would fight back, and in others they would try and hide whilst they were being robbed. He never recognized any of the villains. Having seen quite a few of such videos of late-night robberies, he vowed he would never want to own a shop. Too many were seen as easy targets. Another police initiative would help put a stop to that. Police would target areas for such crimes and quite a few villains were caught in this way. He thought the operation was called something like Operation Vincent. Again, he wondered where they got the frigging names from.

Then there were the emails with information. One email caught his attention. There had been trouble at a pub in Longbridge Road. It was frequented by some members of a gang associated with Barking. The name was never mentioned in print but everyone knew it referred to The Bird Man of Barking. This made Ash sit up and take note. His brush with The Bird Man had been worrying and humiliating and, if he was honest, downright frightening. By the same token, he was interested in anything to do with him. No one had got anything on The Bird Man of Barking. It was ridiculous to think that he, Ash, a lowly Detective Constable, could do anything better than the experienced officers who watched and noted everything he did. He'd been warned by The Bird Man to behave himself and he understood that warning, but it did no harm to keep an eye on what was happening. He dreamed of being the superhero who got that bastard.

The Bird Man of Barking was never seen in pubs or talking to any of the various dubious men that worked for him. He was squeaky clean, which infuriated the team of officers watching him. But it was known that The Pig and Poke in Longbridge Road was the local haunt for his men. On this particular day there had been an almighty brawl outside The Pig and Poke: some Northern builders who were working in the area and who spent their evenings drinking and fighting. They were obviously strangers to the area. No one in their right mind would cause trouble at The Pig and Poke and bring the public house to the attention of the police. Because of the affray everyone who was in the pub was interviewed and had to give a statement. Some customers, including those men sitting quietly in the corner who were known as associates of The Bird Man, had slipped out the back door when the police arrived – but those not used to disappearing quickly were interviewed by the police. It made a nice change for Officers to be called to the notorious public house and to just take a look at who was there.

Because it concerned The Bird Man of Barking, Ash downloaded all the case papers and took a good look at who had been there. He may not be as quick on his feet as Jazz appeared to be when talking to victims or witnesses, but he was blindingly brilliant at sifting through paperwork. He actually loved the paperwork side of policing, finding it satisfying and neat. He trawled meticulously through all the MG papers and CRIS reports. Nothing very interesting. But then one of the names of someone in the pub that night leapt out at him: James Kent. He knew that name; he looked up the address and yes, it was Laura Kent's father. For a moment he wondered why Kent would be at such a pub. Although he hadn't been involved in the original case, Ash had made it his business to read everything about the case. Since John Carpenter had been murdered he was now involved and working with Jazz, so the Kent family was very important. He got out all the papers on the case and read them thoroughly.

From what Jazz had told him and from what he had read about him, James Kent seemed a quiet and reclusive man. Why would he go to such a pub? The paperwork told him that the members of the Kent family were good, honest citizens who had lived normal and honest lives. Such a pub wouldn't be a place James Kent would go. Ash sat and pondered on this fact but couldn't come up with any reason. He started to doubt himself. He wanted to find something, he knew that. Perhaps he was thinking too deeply and getting everything out of context, making more of it than he should.

He continued to look at the list of names, some of which he knew and some he didn't. He trawled the list a few times. There was one name he knew but for the life of him he didn't know where from. Working in the area you got to know as many names as you would find in a small local directory. It was the name of Peter Daly that made him stop and think. He put the name in the computer and looked through to see what the search brought up. There were a few Peter Dalys. It was a common name. The one that caught his eye and made him sit bolt upright was Peter Daly from the Gascoigne Estate Housing Association. He checked the address for Peter Daly on the CRIS report for the affray at The Pig and Poke. It was the same Peter Daly.

He grabbed the file for the Columbian Necktie murder and looked at the list of names and, sure enough, there was Peter Daly. Daly was the Chairman of the Gascoigne Estate Housing Association that had been raising money for a community centre to be built. This was a strange pub for both of him and Kent to frequent. It was also about fifteen minutes from Kent's home by car, while Peter Daly, according to the reports, seemed dedicated to his area so it would be more appropriate for him to frequent a pub closer to the Gascoigne Estate. Okay, they might travel to a different pub if it had something they wanted in it. That they were both in the same pub seemed a huge coincidence. There was nothing in their lives to suggest they knew each other. Did they speak to each other? Why were they there? Was it a co-incidence? How exciting was this find? All these questions, and Ash would work to get the answers.

It was strange and actually rather exciting. He could feel the hairs on his arms rise as he wondered if maybe he had found some sort of chink in two murder investigations that were sitting in a dead-end cul de sac of no clues. He knew his forte was investigative paperwork. If he had the time to sit and work at it, he would find out what was going on. He had all night to do this.

His wife and children were at his mother's for the next few days so he had the time he needed. It was half term and his mother liked to spoil the grandchildren every now and then. This had caused a few problems with his wife. He hoped the two women would get on. They had a dutiful relationship but it was full of tension. He would cross the road for a takeaway curry and come back and work on his notes until he came up with an answer worth looking into.

For the moment he was going to keep this information to himself. If he gave it to anyone else to run with, he would be pushed aside and he wanted to make his mark, to be a top dog Detective, and prove to everyone he was better and bigger than they were. He wanted Jazz to be proud of him. He knew Jazz thought he was a bit of a numpty but he would show him too.

He sat in the quiet almost empty office dreaming of fame, adulation, respect and the love of his wife and children as they watched him rise in the Metropolitan

Police Force. With history about to be repeated, Jazz was yet again nowhere to be seen to protect his team member. His secret investigations would lead Ash Kumar on a certain route to hell.

CHAPTER EIGHTEEN
Not so silent night

Next morning started not quite as bright and early as Jazz would have liked. He was getting used to the heavy muzzy head in the morning and the feeling of hopelessness when he saw how much he had drunk the night before. Vodka was such an easy drink to slip down his throat and make him feel good. He hardly noticed how much he was drinking.

He had decided that today was the day he would find Mad Pete and give him a slap. Pete had been missing for days and he wasn't answering his phone or returning any of Jazz's calls. Something was up and Jazz was going to find out what. Mad Pete should have known better than to fuck about with Jazz. Their relationship had rules. Mad Pete did what Jazz asked and Jazz kept an eye out for Mad Pete and protected him where he could. It was an uneasy symbiotic relationship but it worked.

Mad Pete wasn't playing the game. He had a top of the range mobile phone so there was no possibility that he hadn't got the messages. It was an *all singing all dancing* piece of equipment that the lads who hung around Mad Pete badly wanted. Those with the best mobiles were top dogs; there was competition over who had the best and latest mobile phone. Mobiles had taken over from the best trainers and the biggest diamond earring in the hierarchy of being top dog. Mad Pete always went one further; he had three top of the market mobile phones. Jazz was disgusted to sit in McDonald's with this bastard talking on three different mobiles. He just did it to show off to anyone watching.

So, with three mobiles, there was no excuse for Mad Pete to avoid Jazz except, of course, unless he had something to hide. Jazz was going to find out what that was. He drank some Fanta to wake him up; the sugary orange drink seemed to help the fuzziness in his head. He couldn't believe it was nearly 10 a.m. At another time he would have jumped up and rushed around but he just couldn't hack it at the moment. There was a cold piece of pizza in the fridge and he chewed it distastefully, just for a bit of something in his stomach. He hoped that would stop him feeling so sick.

At 10.30 a.m. he left De Vere Gardens for Barking. He should have gone via Ilford Police Station but wasn't up for it. He thought about Ash but he needed to find Mad Pete and sort him out himself. He didn't want Ash hanging around. Besides, he told himself, Ash was busy doing his paperwork thing. Automatically, he checked his pocket for his hip flask. Old habits died hard. He was back into the habit of carrying vodka although he'd promised himself he wouldn't go down that road again. He pushed this to the back of his mind and made his way to Barking.

At nearly noon, the Gascoigne Estate had some of its residents just waking up. Jazz went to Mad Pete's flat.

Normally at this time Mad Pete was just getting himself together for the day. His day lasted until the early hours of each morning. Jazz hoped to catch him before he scampered into some dark hole. He could smell rancid fat and the musty smell of neglect as he knocked at the dirt-stained door of Mad Pete's flat. There was no answer. He continued banging on the door and shouting through the letterbox. This wasn't right. Mad Pete was never out this early.

With bad grace and a few stinging words and threats through the letterbox, Jazz left, deciding to check McDonald's down the road, and the hut on the Gascoigne Estate known as *The Youth Centre*. He picked up a Big Mac and chips but there was no sight of Mad Pete. The youth centre was nearly empty. A few lads had just turned up on their bikes and were milling around outside waiting. They were showing off out of boredom, and doing quite expert wheelies and pirouettes on pretty good-looking bikes. Jazz reckoned their skills had been honed by practicing in Barking Park on the skateboard ramps. He smiled ironically at the thought that they must also be able to pedal fast to get away from the kiddy gang members who hung around looking for opportunities. Barking Park was a favourite place for stealing bikes and mobile phones. Years ago it had been full of youngsters and families having fun but today it was quite deserted. Community police officers patrolled it regularly and it was hoped this would encourage people back into the park, which was a big and beautiful area in the middle of Barking.

Jazz knew a few smalltime drug dealers drove up at

certain times with skunk, crack cocaine and E's. If he saw them he would arrest them. He hated the scumbags who fed youngsters these drugs. He knew the game. Give them a bit free, let them enjoy it and when hooked make them pay the price they couldn't afford. Crack cocaine was one of the worst. Instantly and totally addictive, once it was taken a user would do anything for the next fix. Jazz had arrested enough young people who had stolen from their parents, even their little old grans who adored them, to pay for their fix.

He'd been around long enough to see the effects of hard drugs. Keeley Webster was a lively, cheeky teenager when she first took crack cocaine. Now, at twenty-four, she looked as if she was forty and had had a rough life. She'd turned to prostitution to pay for the drugs but now she was in such a state that a blind man wouldn't pay her. Her life had been ruined and she looked past the point of any return. It made him shudder with knowledge and rage at the scumbags who pedalled the stuff. Keeley always came to mind when he thought of drugs. He expected to hear soon that she had overdosed or taken some bad shit and had been found lying in a gutter somewhere. She didn't want to be helped. He'd arrested her often enough and she had the opportunity to change using the prison and probation services available but she would have none of it.

He shrugged off the thoughts and, seeing that Mad Pete was not in the area, he decided to go back to his flat. The bastard was hiding from him and he'd had enough of the cat and mouse stuff. Enough was enough. Mad Pete would not have left Barking so early. He banged hard on the door, rang the bell, and shouted through the letterbox, but to no avail. This time he stepped back and with full force rushed the door and shouldered it. It didn't give way, leaving Jazz holding his shoulder and cursing loudly. He kept banging on the door and ringing the bell. Mad Pete

After ten minutes, just as Jazz was about to give up, he heard bolts being drawn slowly; he counted at least six of them, and then the lock and the latch were being unbolted. After what seemed like another ten minutes the door opened a crack and Jazz caught sight of a miserable face surrounded by wild hair and stubble. Not waiting, Jazz pushed the door open with such force that Mad Pete stumbled backwards and fell on the floor. He looked a useless wreck lying there in a disgusting pair of boxer shorts, which Jazz presumed had once been somewhere near white. Mad Pete screwed his eyes at the light behind Jazz and floundered on the floor, not having the energy to get up and move around. He seemed shocked and tried to mouth the words *what the fuck* but it seemed he couldn't think of the next bit of the sentence.

Now high on adrenalin and mad as hell, Jazz leaned down, grabbed Mad Pete by his arm and pulled him up. Shakily and groggily Mad Pete went off to get his jeans and T-shirt. Jazz would have made a drink but looking at the kitchen and the sink full of mouldy mugs and plates, he didn't bother. Mad Pete lived on McDonald's and pizzas and chips and Jazz didn't know what he needed plates for. Takeaway boxes were strewn around. Just as he was about to have a go at Mad Pete for all his takeaways, Jazz remembered that perhaps he wasn't much different. He hadn't cooked anything for years. Anyway he wasn't Mad Pete's fucking mother, so it was up to him how he lived. He needed to know what was going on.

Mad Pete, now dressed in the same T-shirt and jeans he always wore, came out of his bedroom moaning. 'There was no need to ring on my door like that. I've had a bad night and I don't deserve to be treated like shit, Mr Singh.'

Jazz told him in no uncertain terms that he was shit and he deserved everything he got. He handed Mad Pete a black coffee with five sugars. It was his wake up and get going drink. Mad Pete looked at the coffee, nodded his thanks and held the mug tightly in both hands. He got the shakes first thing but the coffee would help. He had taken his fix in the bedroom so he would be okay soon. Mr Singh knew he took it but no need for him to see him doing it. He knew he was in trouble and needed a caffeine and sugar fix to get him ready.

Jazz squirmed as he listened to Mad Pete slurped loudly at the coffee. He would give him a few minutes. He didn't want Mad Pete to go into one of his druggy fits or fall asleep on him. Something was up and he wanted to know what it was. After five minutes of listening to the infuriating slurping noise, Jazz told Mad Pete to tell him what was going on. If he didn't tell him, he warned, he would get him arrested and he could sit in a cell for the whole of the 24 hours of PACE without access to any drugs. He told Mad Pete that he would take great pleasure watching him climb the walls when he was going mad for his fix. Mad Pete smiled; he had taken his fix and would be fine for quite a while. Jazz, knowing this, added quietly, 'Don't think I would arrest you now. I'd walk you around for hours on end with no access to drugs and then I would arrest you. Your twenty-four hours in custody would start then and I can also get that extended. Wouldn't be difficult to find something worth investigating to detain you longer.' The smile was wiped off Mad Pete's face and was instantly replaced with panic. Jazz told him soothingly not to worry, that wasn't going to be necessary because Mad Pete was going to talk, wasn't he? Mad Pete nodded, hoping Mr Singh wasn't going to ask him about anything to do with the murders.

What should Jazz ask? He knew something was being hidden and he knew how wily Mad Pete was. It was a game of cat and mouse. One wrong question and Mad Pete would know he knew nothing and would tell him nothing. They looked intently at each other. The tension could almost be tasted. In the silence Mad Pete licked his lips pensively. Jazz leaned forward and said, 'So, where do we start?'

Mad Pete looked at him, cleared his throat and finally said, 'Can I have another coffee, Mr Singh?'

Jazz grabbed the mug and went off to make him another coffee, cursing him with every step. Both men used the few minutes to think what they would do next. Mad Pete had much to keep silent about.

This time Jazz cleaned a mug for himself. He sensed there was a lot going on here and he needed to sit and do this right. They both sat with their black coffees in hand

and waited. 'Why are you avoiding me, Pete?' was Jazz's opening question.

Pete murmured something unrepeatable and mildly disgusting into his mug, which got him a slap from Jazz. 'Where are you hiding it?' was the next question. After Mad Pete told him he didn't know what he was talking about, and that he knew nothing, Jazz slapped him again and said enough was enough. 'I know you have the information I want, and I want it now.' He said he'd spoken to someone who you just wouldn't mess with, and Mad Pete's name had been mentioned. This was a lie and although Mad Pete was wiley, he wasn't the brainiest of men. He sat up at this. The shakes had started again and he wasn't happy. Jazz noted this with interest. He didn't know what big man was scaring Mad Pete but he knew how he did little jobs for various gangs in the East End so it could be one of many.

Jazz smiled and calmly reminded Mad Pete that he always looked after him. He should be more scared of Jazz than anyone else. Mad Pete hesitated, and then, with a rueful smile, quietly said, 'Not necessarily true.' He reminded Jazz that Bam Bam had nearly got both him and Jazz killed last time, and he didn't want to go through that again.

This polite conversation had to stop. Jazz got up and pushed Mad Pete hard enough for his cup to go in one direction and his head in the other. 'Listen here, you little shit! I could land you in so much trouble with everyone in the area that you'd never be able to scuttle out of your hellhole again without someone wanting to kill you. Just remember torture comes before murder in their alphabet. Now, do you want to put it to the test?' He paced back and forth in front of Mad Pete; with every turn he told him what he could do to him and what others, mad enough to kill him, would do to a traitor in the area.

Scared now and knowing what Jazz had said was true, Mad Pete made Jazz promise to protect him and to never tell anyone what he was about to tell him. Jazz nodded seriously but inside he was jumping up and down saying *Yes! Yes!* Now the whining started. 'I didn't want to know this, Mr Singh. He made me run errands and I saw a copy and I sort of borrowed it. By accident I overheard a conversation and no one knows I know.' Jazz nodded understandingly but he knew Mad Pete would have earwigged any conversation, always looking for information he could use, sell, or make something on. He was also nosey as hell and always loved having the inside story. 'So what do you know?' Jazz asked gently. Mad Pete got up, went to his TV and picked up a DVD. 'It's all on here, Mr Singh. It's pretty awful so you will need a strong stomach to look at it.'

Jazz sat back to watch the DVD with interest and anticipation. He knew if Mad Pete had been avoiding him there had to be something worth having on it. The footage was very dark at first and then something was turned on to light it up. It was an amateurish copy with wobbling pictures but the light showed someone standing in mud. He was tied up and he had tape across his mouth. He was struggling at first but stopped as he sank deeper into the mud. Jazz didn't recognize him. The film started and stopped. Every time it started the water had risen a bit. The man was in mud up to his thighs and then the water was getting higher. He was mumbling through the tape, sounding pathetic and imploring. After ten minutes the picture showed the man with water up to his mouth. He had stopped mumbling and was very still. He had stretched his neck and leaned his head back as far as he could to keep the water from his nose. All you could see was his eyes, full of terror. Jazz found himself raising his head high and breathing through his nose in solidarity with the man on the film.

The film had been turned off and when it was turned on again the man's tape had been pulled off his face and he was rejoicing and thanking God. The water was now just below his chin and was obviously ebbing. Jazz sat back, relieved, and the tension that had built in his jaw relaxed. It had been the most horrific thing he had seen.

But the horror of what was about to happen was unbelievable. The camera picked up a loud sound and the man in the water looked up. His rejoicing changed into stark terror. He became manic; looking at the camera, he was begging, screaming, praying and pleading. Jazz couldn't see what he was so terrified of but the engine sounded meaty and loud. Now the man was struggling, not caring if he sank further into the mud; he was struggling with more energy than Jazz thought possible. In seconds Jazz saw the horror of what was about to happen as the dark silhouette of a barge moved slowly and purposely towards the man. Jazz jumped up out of his chair in horror, shouting 'FUUUCK!!! *Oh my God!*' as, in a split second, the barge smashed into the man's head, glided over him and stopped. Now silent the barge sat down onto the mud below the swirling red water. In seconds there had been a murder and a burial. In the silence of the night, everything carried on as if nothing had happened, the owls hooting, the moon shimmering off the now ebbing water. The film stopped and, in the silence of shocking nothingness, Jazz held his breath. He stood there for seconds on end. With his fists clenched so hard his nails bit into his hand he could feel nothing but shock and horror. He looked at Mad Pete and shook his head, asking incredulously, 'What the fuck was that. What sick bastard would do that?' For a few moments he was unable to say anything else.

Mad Pete was scared. He realized Jazz didn't know anything at all. He sure as hell didn't know about the man who had organized this. Now Jazz had seen the film, he was going to make sure he got every detail out of Mad Pete.

Mouth open and head shaking, Jazz stared at Mad Pete and with shaking hand pointed a finger at the screen and asked *was this real?* Mad Pete nodded his head almost afraid to speak, not sure what Jazz would do. Jazz sucked air in through his teeth noisily and said he had to look at the video again. This time he was watching and looking for something that might be familiar. He didn't recognize the man about to be killed. He didn't know where the place was; there was nothing to identify it except it was obviously on the water. It could have been anywhere along the Thames. The man shouting in the mud had an East London accent so presumably it was somewhere around London. He wondered if it could be somewhere on Barking Creek. It seemed to be quite a preferred choice for murders these days, he thought ruefully.

Deciding he could gather nothing more from the DVD, he turned to Mad Pete. 'Okay, you fucking bastard, where did you get this from? And no messing around. I haven't got the time, patience, energy or manners to fanny around.' Mad Pete knew he was in trouble. He said he had to go to the toilet because he was busting and then he would tell Jazz everything from the beginning. He made his exit to the hall. Jazz, deep in thought, didn't hear the door click quietly shut. After about five minutes he went to find Mad Pete, only to discover he had legged it out of the flat. Spitting nails in anger, Jazz kicked over Mad Pete's only decent piece of equipment, his X Box, and trod on it for good measure. He vowed to do the same with Mad Pete's head when he found him.

Time was of the essence and he needed to do something fast. Identification of the victim was Number One. He took the DVD out of the machine and made his way to Ilford Police Station to see Ash and DI Tom Black. He wanted this looked at pronto. He didn't know how old the murder was but from the way Mad Pete was acting, he reckoned it was quite new.

CHAPTER NINETEEN
Déjà vu

Ash read everything about The Pig and Poke Public House. The more he thought about James Kent and Peter Daly, the more bloody obvious it was that they shouldn't and wouldn't have been there under normal circumstances. It was a rough pub by their standards and they just wouldn't go there. The question was *what were the abnormal circumstances that took them both to The Pig and Poke.* The answer was so close he felt it but it eluded him until dawn. He had fallen asleep in his chair and woke with a start. It was like a dream when the truth came to him. Although he should have been tired having had only a couple of uncomfortable hours sleep at his desk, he was energized by new knowledge. Jumping up, he gathered his papers and went to the canteen for a hearty breakfast; he sure as hell deserved it.

He ordered a 999 Mega Police breakfast. All canteens had 999 breakfasts on the menu. It was the largest breakfast on the planet and had everything from chips, eggs, black pudding, bacon, sausages, tomatoes, mushrooms, and much more. Again, Ash thought he should tell Jazz what he had found out and again he decided that first he wanted to get all the evidence necessary for an arrest. This would teach the CID lot to behave themselves in future and treat him with more respect. Then DI Tom Black would want him on his team, Ash mused, and this felt good. He sat back and sipped his tea, unaware of the hole he was digging for himself. The hole was beginning to look more like a grave and he hadn't a clue.

Before he did anything else he called his wife and listened for what felt like an hour to her barbed comments on his mother. It had been his wife's decision to take the children there and she should have known what to expect. Two strong women in the same house bickering over how to do things and how to bring up children. He wished he hadn't rung her, but she was his wife and he loved her. It was best just to listen and after she ran out of breath he told her he loved her and had to go. He would talk to his mother later and expected to hear something similar from her. His mother wasn't an easy woman to please and for some reason Ashiv's wife never pleased his mother. For now he was grateful to be away from all the atmosphere and arguments. He would save his call to his mother for later when, hopefully, he had something to tell her that would make her even more proud of him.

The breakfast went down a treat and he finished it with another cup of tea. Anyone watching him would see the self-satisfied look on his face; he was *cooking with gas!*

He was off to see James Kent first. As usual, James Kent was in his shed in the back garden. Ash knocked politely on the shed door. When the door opened, James looked quizzically at Ash and then behind him and to the side. Where was DS Jazz Singh? He only liked talking to Jazz. None too pleased, James invited Ash into his shed and made his way to the TV. He turned it off, muttering how it helped pass the time. Ashiv acknowledged this gem of information with a nod. The uncomfortable silence was eased with the offer of a cup of tea. Ash, still full from breakfast, said he would love a cup. Whilst it was being made and with James Kent's back to him, Ash asked conversationally why he had been in The Pig and Poke. James stopped stirring the mugs of tea for a second; his back tensed up and his head fell forward towards the cups. Ash watched in interest.

After a few seconds James turned to look at Ash, smiled, and shook his head. He said he believed he'd never been in such a pub: where was it? When Ash told him, James pondered for a moment and shook his head again. He really didn't think he had ever been there.

Now the fun would begin, Ash thought wryly. He told James about the police being called to the pub because of an affray happening outside, and about the statements taken and people's names noted – and surprise, surprise, James Kent had been one of the names. To prevent any question of stolen identity, Ash added that CCTV could confirm if it was James or not. He asked James to reconsider whether he'd been to The Pig and Poke just over a month ago. James, fidgety by now, tapped his chin and thought, his eyes darting between the floor and Ash. Hesitantly, he said he might have stopped there to go to the toilet. He told a story of being in Barking shopping and getting caught short on the way home. He had stopped at the pub, popped in just to use the toilet, and then left. Smiling, he said that was what happened; he had forgotten. Ash felt disappointed. He'd hoped he would catch James out. He thanked James for his time and left.

James waited ten minutes in case Ash did a Detective Columbo on him (Columbo always returned after talking to a witness; just as they were feeling relaxed and confident he would say, *Oh, just one more thing* and would throw the cat amongst the pigeons). He picked up his mobile and dialed the number. All he said was that he needed to talk and he nodded as a time and venue were given to him. Picking up his coat, he locked his shed door and left through the garden gate to his car parked outside.

Ash made his way to meet with Peter Daly. He hoped he would get more out of this visit; his investigation wasn't going as he had hoped. But Peter Daly had been pre-warned, Ash could tell by his responses. Yes, he drank at that pub, he told Ash, and asked what business it was of his. Daly was being a little edgy and facetious and Ash didn't like it at all. He made a point of telling Ash that the police had done diddly squat! The courts should all be abolished because they did nothing except pay fat salaries to out-of-date and out-of-touch judges. He was getting pretty aggressive now and Ash subconsciously stepped backwards; it occurred to him he should leave before he got a slap. But instead of stopping there he pushed his luck that bit further and, not quite realising how hard he was pushing Daly, he asked if he knew any of the men who frequented the pub, like Mickey Span or Freddie Link, two of the local henchmen well known in the area and to the police.

Peter Daly went ballistic at such a question. In a temper that resembled the Incredible Hulk, he told Ash to clear off before he did something he would regret. If Ash had had a bit more experience he might have handled it better, but at an absolute loss as to what to say, he left with recriminations ringing in his ears: *just because I live in Barking doesn't mean I am a fucking gangster! How dare you check up on me to see where I drink! This isn't a fucking communist country, I can do what I fucking like. I am ringing your fucking boss and complaining about you.*

No, he hadn't handled it well and he left with his tail between his legs. It was getting late now and he was in Barking, not a part of town he wanted to be in.

Peter Daly watched out of his window as Ash got into his car, sat for a few minutes in silence and then gunned the car and left the area. Daly made a phone call, confirming that Ash had been and gone. When and where should they meet?

CHAPTER TWENTY
The rats are leaving the ship

Jazz found DS Tom Black. He was never hard to find, you just had to follow the sound of shouting and swearing. Tom Black was tearing a strip off one of his Detectives. Jazz couldn't tell what he had done but whatever it was it included fucking his mother and doing something pretty dodgy with the pet dog. When Boomer saw Jazz, he dismissed the detective in front of him. He got up from his chair hoping that Jazz had something interesting for him to work on.

Jazz showed Boomer the DVD and said it had to be viewed in private. Although in the police station most offices had their own DVD players, until he knew what he was dealing with, Jazz wanted to keep it between himself and Boomer.

The Chief Superintendent was out for the day doing something official up in London. Boomer had seen him leave in his ceremonial uniform, all spruced up, dressed to catch the attention of the press. He was well known on the Police Guard circuit for his enthusiastic but authoritarian assistance to the press and paparazzi. His room was off bounds to everyone, but it had a DVD player and TV. Boomer and Jazz knew they wouldn't be disturbed by anyone, and a key was found that fitted his room. As they watched the DVD, both were mesmerized by the horror of such a murder. Neither knew at that moment who the victim was. Tom Black exhaled, cursing everything religious and astronomical. They watched it twice through just to be sure they hadn't missed a clue. At one point Jazz thought he saw a ring on a finger. They rewound and looked again; whoever was holding the camera had put their fingers in front of it for a few seconds. Tom got out his phone and took a picture of the freeze-framed victim's face. The face looked familiar but neither could put a name to him. Whoever was filming this wanted to see his terror and hear the fear and screams and pleading. It was pretty sick. Boomer set off to put the picture on his computer and send it out to all his cronies to see if the victim would be recognized.

The identity took minutes. 'Modern technology is a fucking wonderful thing,' Boomer shouted to Jazz, who was preoccupied trying to get a bag of crisps out of a vending machine in the hallway. A response email had already come through. The man in the DVD was Johnny Peters, the paedophile. 'Bloody hell!' was all Jazz could say at that moment. He knew of Johnny Peters, and he had seen pictures of him, but no way did he recognize the manically terrified man in the DVD. He thought for a split second about how extreme terror and fear can alter someone, making them unrecognizable. He read the email for himself, just to check, and now he saw the Johnny Peters identity picture, he could see he was the same man.

Charlie would be pleased to hear the information that Johnny Peters was dead. Jazz could see him drooling over it. The afternoon tea with the local ladies was going to be full of details and conjecture, something Charlie would savour. Jazz couldn't tell him at this stage just how Johnny had died. It was going to take time to find out what sick bastard had thought this up and carried it out. For now no one knew where the hell Johnny had been murdered, by whom, or why.

Tom Black took a picture of the finger with a ring on it. It was a bit blurred but the ring was quite striking, with what looked like raised swords on it and a diamond in the middle. He sent it out to all officers in the hope it was recognized. Again, it didn't take long before a reply email came through, which rendered Tom Black almost speechless. Then, with a tirade of profanities, he called Jazz to the computer again, and showed him the picture of a heavyweight man in a black suit with his hands crossed in front of him, as if he was protecting his testicles. There on his right hand was a ring that looked very similar to the slightly blurred DVD picture. The email told them it was Freddie Link, who was a close associate of The Bird Man of Barking. What the hell was going on? They were on dodgy ground here. No one took on The Bird Man without authority from the top people in the Metropolitan Police.

Jazz knew there was an undercover operation going on watching The Bird Man. It was *hands off* to every officer and detective who looked in at the Bird Man. He was *Teflon-coated*: a known villain but nothing stuck. All information was to go to the special unit set up. As far as Jazz knew, this special unit had been in operation for over a year and so far there had been no arrests or charges put to the Bird Man. No way did he want to give this information to a special unit that had done diddly squat! He argued with Tom Black that until something more concrete had been found out they should keep *schtum*. Tom Black was as far off the politically correct scale as Jazz; he agreed far too readily and without caution. Both were setting themselves up again for a car ride to Epping Forest and a shallow grave.

For an East End boy with little education The Bird Man had risen in the ranks of the London gangs through his fighting and his ruthlessness. He would do anything to get what he wanted. In his younger days, before DNA testing, CCTV and mobile phones, he could kill off rivals with ease, undetected. The 1960s had been his time when there was stuff out there for grabbing and there was time to build his reputation. It was also the time of motorway building and many bridges including the Bow Flyover and Charlie Brown's roundabout flyover allegedly contained more bodies in the upright pillars and foundations than could be good for the structure. The Bird Man had made his mark and systematically rid himself of all rivals. There were many gangsters who were as ruthless as the Bird Man but his edge was that he also had a very fine and cunning mind.

Today there were many gangs – Asian, Chinese and Romanian – working the East End. More laidback these days, The Bird Man seemed to have settled, allowing others to work on what he considered his turf. He never got into selling drugs like other gangs; he was a bit old-fashioned for most gang leaders but he did have his area of work.

He had many strings to his bow. His main front business was his transport company, a haulage firm called B4 Transport that had become one of the country's biggest haulage companies. The Bird Man even advertised on the TV and there was talk of a TV show about his lorries travelling the country. Although he enjoyed the fame, he put his foot down regarding a TV show. He couldn't afford to have those nosey little bastards checking out what he did and where he went. Even the police didn't have such access to him and there was no way he was going to allow the bleeding media to bugger up his business interests.

Some would say that The Bird Man didn't do anyone any harm if they were honest and law-abiding but that wasn't true. Jazz had looked at his M.O. and he was a nasty piece of work. It was true that he had calmed down a bit over the years, perhaps because he had his work and his area tied up neatly and he didn't need to fight dirty anymore. But they said the same about the Krays and they were no angels either.

There had been gang-related murders in the East End attributed to The Bird Man. Paddy McDowell had got lippy and, in an East End pub, had declared that he could take on The Bird Man. But he was a drunk and no one listened to a drunk. Paddy McDowell was one of those little pipsqueak villains, always looking for something to sell or buy or steal. He was pretty redundant these days. He spent his time making a nuisance of himself fuelled by too much drink.

Paddy McDowell had a smouldering grudge against The Bird Man. Some years ago he had upset The Bird Man, who had made it known that no one on his turf should use Paddy McDowell. All Paddy's work dried up and he lost out on money, women, and friends. His burning hatred of The Bird Man had been kept under wraps until now, but the drink was making him more and more dangerously verbal. One day he went too far and announced to everyone in the pub that *the Bird Man was a fucking poofter.*

If you saw The Birdman you would see he was 6'3" of rippling muscle with a granite chin and hands the size of a digger bucket and just as hard. He was famous for his one-punch putdown. No one had stayed upright with a punch from The Birdman. One man was out like a light for 30 minutes, most found themselves laid on the floor not knowing what had hit them. Paddy was getting more and more frustrated at no one taking him seriously. He had it in his head he wanted everyone to listen to him and he pushed and pushed his luck by shouting in the faces of known associates of The Birdman that *The Birdman of bleeding Barking was a stark staring raving poofter.*

Paddy McDowell was found days later, shot dead in Barking Park. The killer was definitely The Bird Man but nothing could be proved. Everyone knew and everyone kept quiet. The police had this on record and were biding their time.

The beauty of most villains is they are pretty stupid. There are not that many *Raffles* about so mistakes often happen and it's the stupid mistakes that the police pick up on and catch the villains. The Birdman was not stupid and so far had carried on his business without the police getting anything on him. He was sitting pretty and he worked hard to ensure it stayed that way.

With this new barge murder, the questions were frustrating. What the hell had The Bird Man got to do with it and why? It occurred to Jazz and Boomer that this was the third murder that was unusual and tortuous. Perhaps, suggested Jazz, there was a connection? But what it was neither knew at the moment.

Perhaps there was something going on in The Bird Man's patch that he didn't know about. That thought was stupidly outrageous but perhaps his men were working off piste so to speak. There was a lot of work to do and Tom Black was off to have a root around the area and see what he could dig up.

In the meantime, Jazz was off to find Mad Pete. There was more to find out from that little devious, filthy load of slime. There were a few places he might find him and when he found him there were going to be answers given. Mad Pete knew what Jazz might be capable of and he had hidden in fear in the only place he was sure Jazz would never find him.

CHAPTER TWENTY-ONE
Something's brewing

Ash was thinking far too much. He should have thought about sharing the information he had and getting help but he wanted the glory. He was determined to get the evidence, present it to Jazz and Tom Black, and amaze and astound them. He was feeling good and powerful. Yes, by himself he was going to crack this case. Stupidity is blind.

He made his way to The Pig and Poke. It was getting late in the day but if this worked out then he was ready to reveal all and make an arrest. First, he needed to talk to the pub's landlord.

The landlord had always made a point of being there in the evenings. George Phillips was a seasoned landlord and had worked for many brewery-owned public houses but The Pig and Poke was a free house and he could do what he liked. His record was good, and there had never been any trouble at his pubs. No one knew that the money to buy The Pig and Poke, his first owned pub, was provided by a secret sponsor from the East End. George had worked in many London pubs; he had good bar skills and knew how to keep his mouth shut. His loyalty was recognized and rewarded with the money to buy The Pig and Poke. Rumours were always rife in the East End but no one knew it was The Bird Man who had loaned George Phillips the money. He owed The Bird Man big time.

It was a shame Ash didn't know this, it could have saved him from the terror that was about to happen.

The affray that had happened with the Northern builders was unexpected and uncomfortable for George. His clientele expected a quiet drink with no trouble and no police. His reputation was very important to him and he cursed the builders every day for giving the police the opportunity to come into his pub. Having a lot to prove to The Bird Man, he was anxious to get the pub back to its normally calm state. He was on his way to achieving this but now when he saw DC Kumar entering the pub, he wasn't happy at all.

Oblivious to everything Ash went straight up to George. It was obvious that if a landlord wanted to keep his licence he had to please the police and help in any way he could. It made sense to Ash to take George to one side and have a little chat with him. The place was full and it felt as if everyone was staring at him. But he walked tall and strode firmly; he wasn't going to be shaken by their looks. For a split second he did wonder if he should have told someone where he was but he dismissed that thought. What the hell could happen in a pub full of people, he asked himself.

George had already glanced over to the corner of the pub and the men sitting there idling away time with beers and whisky chasers nodded almost indiscernibly. It was a dark little corner with a high-sided wooden bench that prevented anyone from watching closely what went on. Ash noticed that they were smoking, which was no longer allowed in public houses. But perhaps this wasn't the right time to bring this to the landlord's attention. He sensed the tension in the room and didn't want to cause any problems that might erupt into a fight.

The landlord had picked up a cloth and was busily cleaning a glass when Ash got to the bar; cheerfully George asked if he could get him a drink. Sounding rather pompous, Ash said no, because he was on duty. Suddenly it felt as if he shouldn't be here, that this was the wrong place at the wrong time and he needed to get out, but like a runaway train he couldn't stop.

George was very amenable indeed. When Ash said he needed to talk to him in private, George, all smiles, led him to the back room where it would be quieter and more private. Relieved to be out of the bar and away from the staring eyes, Ash followed George towards the back of the pub. The door there was locked and it took George a few minutes to unlock it, smiling all the time. Ash was looking uncomfortable by now, but George pointed out this was a pretty secure place to keep his stocks of spirits and cigarettes, and money from the till: that was why he kept the door locked. Again Ashiv was offered a drink and he turned it down. He thought George was very affable and he hoped he could get this bit of information sorted so he could go home.

Once inside the storeroom, settled and seated, a still smiling George asked, 'So what can I do for you, DC Kumar?' Ash liked George's politeness. He asked about the night of the fight with the Northern men and the people who were drinking there that night. George thought for a moment and said that it had been a really busy night and he wasn't sure exactly who was in at the time. The Northerners had kept him so busy that night, he'd scarcely noticed anyone else. Ash wanted to push him a bit more; he asked if George had seen Mickey Span and Freddie Link that night. George sucked in his teeth and, after a few seconds, said hesitantly, 'I can't say that I did. I get confused, DC Kumar. That night was really stressful for me. We never have fights at this pub. We're a clean and safe pub and that night was quite a shock for me.'

This put Ash on his guard. Whoever heard of an East End landlord who got fazed by a fight in his pub?

They talked for a further half an hour, with George cheerfully vacant and distracting. What Ash got from the conversation was that George had actually seen nothing and knew no one. This was highly frustrating; as naïve as Ash appeared, even he knew it was all bullshit. Just as he was about to give up and leave, George had one of those golden moments. He laughed to himself and then, with a mournful look of apology, said he remembered now. Of course Mickey Span was there that night, and he also seemed to remember someone called James Kent was around. He asked himself how he remembered Kent's name and, like a light-bulb going on, his eyes lit up. 'Ah yes, DC Kumar, I remember now. James Kent introduced himself to me. I remember saying I hadn't seen him in the pub before. A nice chap, as I remember. Is that of help to you?'

Ash felt he was getting somewhere at last. Just as he was about to ask more, George got up and said excitedly, 'I saw my friend Jimmy in the bar tonight, and he was speaking to James Kent. I'll go and get him, and ask him to talk to you. Would that be helpful?' Ash felt things were really moving at last and he said he'd like to talk with Jimmy.

George said he would only be a few moments. Ash nodded and, as suggested, helped himself to a can of Fanta from the shelf beside him. He sat back comfortably waiting. Perhaps his visit hadn't been a waste of time after all. He was unravelling a ball of string and he was going to get to the bottom of this. As he pulled the ring on the can of Fanta and heard the hiss of the gas he missed the sound of the key being turned in the lock of the storeroom. He would sit there for some time before he ventured towards the door and found he had been locked in.

CHAPTER TWENTY-TWO
Mirror, mirror on the wall

Jazz had spent hours looking for Mad Pete in all the dark and dirty corners he usually inhabited. He was nowhere to be found but there was one place still to look. It was the only place Mad Pete would never go unless things were so bad he had nowhere else to go.

Mrs Mad Pete was a woman and a half. She weighed twenty stone and most of that was mouth! She had the biggest, vilest and nastiest mouth in the country. Mad Pete wasn't fussy but even he was embarrassed by his mother. She lived in Beckton in a high-rise flat. She lived by herself because no sane person would live with her. She didn't care that her neighbours ignored her, that the local shops banned her or that the local Community Police avoided her.

Jazz knew what he had to do but he didn't want to do it. He really didn't want to meet Mrs Mad Pete again. Last time she had thrown him out of her flat, shouting from her sixth-floor balcony that he was a *fucking, bleeding, sodding pig and everyone should shoot him.* The gangs in Beckton didn't need her rally call to want to sort out Jazz. He had a reputation for nicking gang members and he steered clear of the estate as much as possible when on his own.

He knocked on her door. As she opened it the waft of rancid fat and bad eggs caught him in the face and he nearly retched. He could see where Mad Pete got his homeliness from. There before him was a vision of loveliness, three double chins wobbling, a fag in her mouth, with a top lip stained nicotine brown and a bottom lip with black hair appearing cheekily in the dip before the chin. Her hair was scraped up in a ponytail and it needed a good wash. He could have sworn she was still in the same stained shell-suit grey bottoms he remembered from last time; the stains looked familiar along with the 'Frankie Goes to Hollywood' vest that had seen better years.

'What do you want, you fucking bastard?' was her opening line. He marvelled that she could sneer and speak so clearly whilst keeping the roll-up cigarette in her mouth. He was mesmerised by the fag ash on the end of the cigarette; it was threatening to break off and roll into her ample but gruesome bosom.

He didn't bother to charm this one. It would have been a waste of words. 'I want to see Mad Pete now,' was all he said. She looked at him as if he was something she had scraped off her shoe and went to shut the door. Quick as a flash he pushed his way forward and pushed past her, even as she loudly and angrily shouted accusations at him about incest, bestiality and strangely religious defamation. All he said as he passed her was, 'I can see you've been reading my profile on Facebook!' He heard her roar and moved quickly into the lounge, just missing the lunge of her huge hands. He found Mad Pete cowering in the corner. Was he cowering away from Jazz or the murderous harridan behind him?

He grabbed Mad Pete and pushed none too nicely past the foul-mouthed bitch who was looking for something hard to hit him with. She couldn't move that fast. Twenty stone was a hell of a lot of weight to move through all the cardboard boxes, piles of newspapers, and stacks of clothes that were strewn across the lounge floor. As Jazz dragged Mad Pete out he heard a crunch but didn't stop to see what he had trodden on under the rags he'd just walked over.

Thank God the lift was working and before long they were out in the fresh air, away from Mrs Mad Pete. They could hear her on her balcony telling the world how *that fucking DS Jaswinder Singh had stolen and kidnapped her fucking son. What the fuck was anyone going to do about it? Kill the bastard!* Jazz got to the car quickly and threw Mad Pete in. He was snivelling, not knowing what was to become of him. He told Jazz in a pitiful voice, 'I know nuffink. Mr Singh. I ain't a bad guy. They'll kill me if they find me and I don't wanna die.'

Jazz knew a really scared Mad Pete when he saw it. He also knew it didn't take much to scare him but to go to his mother's was something he would never do unless petrified.

They drove back to Mad Pete's flat, picking up two drive-through Big Mac meals on the way. As they reached the flat and got out of the car Jazz gave Mad Pete a slap just for good measure and for making him go and find him at his bloody mother's. For the first time, he realized that perhaps Mad Pete's flat wasn't the worst place on God's earth; his mother had beaten him hands down. Almost affectionately he pushed the filthy cups off the cupboard to put the McDonald's down.

Mad Pete had calmed down now. Going to his mother's flat had done nothing good for him. If he was a nervous wreck before, at his mother's he became psychotic, almost ready to jump off her balcony. He was relieved and even a little tearful that Jazz had come and confronted his mother. It wasn't quite the scenario Jazz intended but actually Mad Pete felt closer to Jazz than most other people he knew and that was going to work in Jazz's favour. It could be that as long as Jazz didn't think too deeply about it, perhaps Mad Pete was one of only a few people that he felt comfortable with. Both would argue that they had nothing but contempt for each, but that was not quite true.

They ate the McDonald's which had gone a bit cold by now. The chips had gone rubbery but were still full of flavour for the discerning, and the coffee was hot. They both lit cigarettes and enjoyed the after-dinner feeling of inhaling deep into the lungs and then blowing smoke out of the nose, giving that satisfied feeling. Mad Pete's smoke was a spliff but Jazz let that pass. Relaxed and quiet now, Jazz asked where the DVD had been filmed. He said he knew who had filmed it, but he didn't know why. He knew Mad Pete was the biggest eavesdropper in the world and if there was anything to hear he was always in the right place at the right time.

Glad to be warm, fed and enjoying a spliff, Mad Pete was almost ready to talk. Jazz gave him assurances he was safe, that no one would know he'd told him anything. Begrudgingly Mad Pete agreed and, with the further incentive that Jazz would stick a taser up his arse if he didn't speak soon, he sat forward and in whispers told him everything he knew.

He had been in The Pig and Poke. Freddie Link was partial to the good shit and Mad Pete knew where to get it for him. He'd been on an errand and was looking for Freddie in the pub. Freddie was in the back room away from prying eyes. The pub was closed so Mad Pete made his way around the pub looking for him. Outside the back room he heard voices. He knew it was The Bird Man; everyone knew the sound of his voice. He got a bit scared but the conversation got interesting.

He heard something about a *fucking bastard who was to be whacked* and then something about taking him to a place called *Piddlesham*. 'I had to get out of the way, Mr Singh, I could hear them moving in the room. I went into the bar and sat in a corner until The Bird Man left. Then I went to find Freddie in the back room to give him his shit but he wasn't there. I did find the DVD just sitting on a table so I took it and left. I could see Freddie another time.'

Jazz knew it was unusual to get a connection between The Bird Man and one of his men, especially Freddie who was a particularly nasty piece of work. 'Where the fuck is Piddlesham?' he asked. 'Are you sure he said Piddlesham?'

Mad Pete looked nonplussed. 'Dunno, it ain't in Barking, Mr Singh, that's for sure.' With what was almost a sense of humour surfacing, he snorted, 'All the pissheads, piss takers and piss artists must come from Piddlesham.' He rocked with laughter for a few moments until he realized Jazz wasn't laughing with him. Jazz told him to stay put, he was off to find out where Piddlesham was. Before Mad Pete went all panic-stricken he added that no one would know he'd told him anything and he was safe here in his flat. Mad Pete was scared but realistic; he nodded and told Jazz to get it sorted and keep him safe. As he left, Jazz heard the multitude of locks on Mad Pete's door being shut and bolted. He knew he would be safe in there for a while.

It was very late now. Jazz rang Tom Black and told him about Piddlesham and how The Bird Man and Freddie Link were involved. Tom Black said he would check on the internet to see if he could find such a place. Jazz was on his way into the police station to do the same. It was 11 p.m. when he got there and Tom was having no luck. They decided to look for coastal and riverways fairly close to Barking, reckoning the men wouldn't have gone too far. After painstaking searching the only place they came up with was Paglesham. It sounded a bit like Piddlesham, and it was on the River Roach in Essex, quite close to Rochford. When they zoomed in on it on Google Earth they could see barges there. It was close enough to London and even though they were tired and wanted to go home, they felt sure this must be the place. They arranged to meet the next morning and travel to this strange place out in the far reaches of Essex.

On the way home Jazz picked up a bottle of vodka from the 24-hour Tesco close by. He needed a drink badly.

CHAPTER TWENTY-THREE
Life on the dark side

Ash sat quietly waiting but it had been thirty minutes now, and he was getting a bit concerned. He didn't really want to go back out into the pub; it had been quite worrying to be watched so intently. Hesitantly he tried the door, intending to peek outside. Nothing happened. He tried again, this time turning the handle quite frantically and pulling at the door; it was definitely locked. For a moment panic set in. He was about to bang on the door and shout for someone to open it, but he contained himself. His breathing sounded shaky as he thought about what he could do.

Of course, his mobile was in his coat! He dialed Jazz's number and waited. Nothing happened. 'Damn it,' he thought; there was no signal in the room. He looked around and realized he must be in a type of Faraday cage. The windows had bars on them; it was, after all, a pub storeroom full of cigarettes, spirits, and petty cash. He noticed that the door was metal and he presumed it was impossible to pick up any signal with lined metal shelves around the room.

He banged again on the metal door and shouted, 'Is there, erm, anyone there?' He got no response and he realized he actually couldn't hear anything. The pub had been full of people, chatting and shouting, but Ash couldn't hear any of it. He presumed the metal door was lined as well, perhaps to stop someone breaking in.

He didn't know why he'd been locked in and the more he thought about it, the angrier he became. How dare they do this to a member of the Metropolitan Police and a Detective Constable to boot? He was making plans to arrest the publican for imprisoning a Met Detective when he heard a key in the door.

The first thing he saw was George Phillips' affable, smiling face. He was full of apologies for leaving Ash for so long. He told him that Jimmy had just left the pub when he'd gone out to look for him. A friend of Jimmy's who was there said he was just down the road, so George had gone looking for him.

Suddenly George developed a very Irish lilt to his affable talk. He looked at Ash and, with a sincerity that had to be seen to believed, said, 'God love yer, DC Kumar, I was just trying to help you and got carried away looking for Jimmy.' Ash, still mad, asked why the hell he had been locked in and left for so long. George's face was a picture of disbelief and then horror. 'Oh jeez and God help and forgive me, DC Kumar, I locked you in?' Before Ash could answer he went on, 'I lock the door as habit always. God, these people are thieving bastards and I never leave the door unlocked. Oh Mother Mary and all that is good, what can I do to make it up to you? I know, I'll buy you that drink in the bar. You can't be on duty any longer, right? It's so late.' Stroking his chin, he added, 'I am gonna find you that

Jimmy if it's the last thing I do. I gotta make it up to you.' Good-naturedly he put his hand on Ash's back and walked him towards the door. 'There's someone in the bar I think you might want to speak with.'

Ash allowed himself to be pushed along, unable to get a word in edgeways. Feeling that he was being helped, he willingly and stupidly allowed himself to be trapped.

CHAPTER TWENTY-FOUR
The only way is Essex

Tom Black arrived early, and immediately got on the phone to Eddie Willoughby at Essex Police Marine Unit based in Burnham. A harassed Eddie listened to the tale about a barge that had run over a man in 'Piddlesham', and could he help find the place. Eddie laughed; Piddlesham was most probably Paglesham, just around the corner from them, near Rochford and Southend. He added that there were also barges moored there. Tom sighed with relief. Just as he was about to ask for help, Eddie told him that, as much as he would like to help, it was impossible at the moment.

Before Tom could add a *but*, Eddie listed his problems. He had not only Essex to cover but Kent as well, not to mention the Olympics in London and the Counter Terrorism team they were working with. Taking a breath he added that he was short-staffed and had only eight men working for him; if you took holidays, sickness, and training days into account he was down to so few he could hardly cope with the work in hand.

Tom asked what he could do to help and Eddie suggested he contact Gary Nunn, the boatman based at Paglesham. Nunn was a font of all knowledge for the area and if anyone could help he could. Eddie added as a cautionary tale that Gary was his best contact but he was a wily old devil and as *slippery as a handful of eels in a bucket of snot* so Tom should beware: Gary could always be found at the Plough and Sail pub at lunchtime.

It was all a bit of a disappointment. Tom had fancied riding in one of the patrol boats, which apparently could reach 70 mphand that sounded pretty good. Before he said goodbye he gave it one more try. He asked if there was a chance that one of their patrol boats, Alert VI, Vigilant or Watchful, were in the area; perhaps they could thumb a lift? 'No chance, matey,' laughed Eddie and he hung up.

Bleary-eyed and feeling a tad on the sick side of healthy, Jazz arrived in Ilford Police canteen at 9 a.m. to meet Tom Black. Both were in need of a strong black coffee. The lovely Milly brought it over to them along with a bacon sandwich for Jazz. Tom had to queue for his sandwich, which made Jazz smirk.

Tom had arranged an undercover car to take them to Paglesham. It took another ten minutes to find it on a map. Paglesham was a village set away from Rochford, near Southend. It was a village in two parts, Paglesham Church End and Paglesham East End, separated by farmland.

After a few sips of coffee to help their brains, it was decided that it would take about an hour or so to get there in the daytime traffic. The A13 was always a bloody nightmare during the day.

On the way, guided by the Satnav, they tried to work out why The Bird Man might have wanted Johnny

Peters murdered in such a way. He wasn't usually that creative and what the hell was the link between the two men?

The traffic on part of the A13 was moving very slowly; fed up and wanting to get there, they put the blue lights on. This always worked and it wasn't long before they reached Sadlers Farm, another nightmare with all the road works. Once past Sadlers Farm it felt as if they were in another world. There were fields and winding roads and blue skies. They speculated that a village so far out of London must be full of six-fingered inbreds. They laughed at the thought of who they might have to talk to and if the interviewees would understand London English. This was way out of their radar and league.

They reached the Plough and Sail in good time for lunch. The pub was what they had expected: quaint, little, and old, with locals sitting outside amongst flowers in pots. It was a pretty place, they'd give it that. Tom Black was more familiar with the countryside than Jazz who, Tom realised, had never ventured far outside of London. Jazz had seen Manchester but that was a lot like London. Motorways let you see countryside but you don't ever get close to it. Paglesham was real and it didn't feel comfortable. Jazz understood towns and city people but this was different.

Both Jazz and Tom, in dark glasses and looking tired and mean, could have been mistaken by the locals watching them for a pair of villains as opposed to Met detectives.

They went inside the pub and Tom asked if Gary

Nunn was about. At the mention of his name, a weathered man looked up from his glass and asked who was wanting Gary. Tom and Jazz sat down beside him. They couldn't quite figure out his age; he looked pretty old but they could see the strength in his hands and back. Perhaps he was about forty, but his weather-beaten skin made him look twenty years older.

After introducing themselves, Jazz asked Gary if he knew anything about a group of men coming to Paglesham Boatyard one night within the last few weeks. He said there would have been lights flashing and muted voices, perhaps screaming and the sound of a barge engine. Obviously Gary wasn't someone who spoke quickly; he considered his comments for a long time before he spoke. After a pregnant pause he moved, making Tom and Jazz sit up expectantly, but Gary was just reaching for his beer.

'Well,' he said, and then there was silence again. Jazz was getting impatient now; he wondered if this man was a cretin or a comedian. It felt a little like he was having them over. 'Have you any comment at all, sir?' asked Tom Black.

Gary looked up slowly and grinned. 'Well, it's like this, sir, we have some funny goings-on down here in Paglesham. What you described could have been the Canewdon Witches Coven meeting by the water's edge. They do this every now and then. It don't do to be out and about when the Canewdon Witches are casting their spells.'

Jazz looked agog. 'Really?'

Gary leaned a little closer and whispered, 'Oh yes, really, sir. Paglesham Boatyard has been cursed many times by the Witches, you know.' At another time Jazz and Tom would have gone into good-cop bad-cop mode to encourage Gary into co-operating, but it didn't seem appropriate here. They weren't sure what to say.

Gary added that on the night of the full moon lights had been seen for about three hours in the boatyard. No one would venture there in case it was the Canewdon Witches; they never took well to being watched. His brow wrinkled as he remembered that a barge engine had been heard that night; the sound had travelled through the night air. The screams had been put down to the call of the foxes. Jazz asked if he could take them to the boatyard so they could see the barges. Gary Nunn nodded. 'First,' he said, 'would you like to sample a Wallasea Wench? You just can't come here and not do that.'

Jazz tried not to laugh. Was this a local custom? In a suitably controlled voice he thanked Gary kindly for the offer but said he preferred to pick his own women. Gary laughed heartily. 'It ain't a woman, it's a beer.' Tom and Jazz declined; they really needed to get on and would like to go now.

But Gary wouldn't be rushed. He added that to get to Paglesham Boatyard they would need to travel there by boat. 'What? Where the fuck is this pissing boatyard then?' Jazz was getting seriously fed up with all this mucking about.

Gary, taking all this in his stride, told them it would take a while to get there but if they came now while the tide was coming in, he would get them there. 'But I ain't going nowhere without payment,' he added. 'It's my boat and it costs.'

Tom Black, also fuming, tried to control his temper and asked how much it would cost.

'It will take a while,' said Gary, 'and my day rate is £240.'

In unison Tom and Jazz said, 'No way are we paying that sort of money.'

Gary looked at them calmly and said he would give them a discount because they were police, so it would cost them £195.

Jazz smiled. 'We don't carry that sort of money on us so we can't pay.'

'Then give me your credit card number and details,' said Gary. 'I can do the payment on my phone. You'll get expenses when you get back.

At last they were all in Gary's old rusty Vauxhall Estate heading to Wallasea, a fifteen-minute ride away. Wallasea had a huge marina with beautiful yachts moored there. They walked along a pontoon that seemed to go on for ages, past many Fairline Luxury yachts, which Gary said were known locally as *gin palaces*. Tom and Jazz looked open-mouthed at row after row of dazzling white and sky-blue modern luxury yachts they'd thought you only saw on the telly in places like Monaco and Cannes. Gary saw how impressed they were and grumbled, 'Half of 'em haven't a clue what to do. They just go up and down the river towards Burnham-on-Crouch and annoy the seals that congregate on the island. And most are drunk.'

At the end of the luxury line-up of yachts, they found the smallest, rustiest and ugliest tug boat they had ever seen. Gary pointed proudly and said, 'Welcome to

Nancy, she knows what she's doing and will give you a good ride.'

Jazz whispered to Tom, 'Is everything sexual with this man?' They both laughed.

Nancy was wet, slimy and chilly. She had no cabin so they sat at the rear, feeling cold. Gary untied her ropes and turned the engine. She caught with a loud roar and they could feel her power. 'Does she go very fast?' Tom enquired expectantly. 'She goes pretty good and her ride will be pretty smooth,' was all they were told.

They set off past Wallasea Island and on to the River Roach. As if they were on a guided tour, Gary told them about what was happening on Wallasea Island. Apparently the RSPB was going to transform the island back into a magical inter-tidal coastal marshland. Jazz hadn't a clue what he was talking about, but Tom was actually quite interested. He had a great love of the countryside but down Dorset way was his haven. The Wallasea Project was to raise the lowland level. It had started in early 2008 when they were approached by Crossrail, the company that was building a major new railway connection under Central London. Crossrail was looking for a beneficiary to reuse the clean soil from their tunneling. It was going to transform 1,500 acres of tidal wildlife habitat. It would take billions of tons of aggregate. The project was long-term and continuous.

At this point Jazz got interested and asked how the soil was transported from Central London to Wallasea; he was hoping to hear it was with B4 Transport, The Bird Man's Company which would be a result. Gary didn't have to think. 'It goes by barge from London down the Thames to Southend, chuck a left when you reach Foulness Sands, round the Maplin Edge to the Whittaker Beacon and bung a left at the Beacon into the Crouch. Watch out for the seals at the *Buxey Buoy*. Piece of cake!'

Jazz wished he hadn't asked, it was more information than he needed to hear. But he did wonder why they used barges and lorries. Gary, now in full swing, said, 'A barge can carry about ten lorry loads in one go, and it takes eight hours using the tides to get here. Simple!'

Jazz was disappointed; he'd really thought The Bird Man would have a finger in this pie.

They sat in silence for a while and then Gary went back into his commentary which Tom found very interesting. The RSPB was something he belonged to. He enjoyed shooting birds for eating but he liked the wildlife of birds. He was fascinated to hear the types of birds that came to Wallasea, he had no idea Essex had such interesting places. He turned to a bored Jazz and said he might come here again on a day off. Jazz looked at him as if he was mad.

Gary said that if he liked birds he could see Avocets, Black-tailed godwits, Redshank, Spoonbill and of course Brent geese, there were lots of them around. He lowered his voice and said that even the Great White Egret had been seen at Wallasea together of course with the little egrets. Tom was quite impressed by that.

They continued on the journey, with Gary talking about various types of birds. Jazz, bored, tried to light a cigarette but had great difficulty owing to the gale that seemed to be blowing up. After a few minutes he got a bit concerned; the boat bobbed up and down ferociously, and he discovered he suffered from seasickness. After a further thirty minutes of torture as they passed round the back of Potton Island and under Potton Bridge, they arrived in Paglesham Reach. He was looking forward to getting onto firm land. They moored on the floating pontoon, which was rocking and rolling with the small boat. The water in the Reach was turbulent and aggressive. The waves weren't big but they were strong and persistent. It took several minutes and a torn pocket before they were able to scrabble off the boat onto the pontoon.

Tom and Jazz made their way down the pontoon looking like a drunken pair of mobsters in their city suits. Gary, following behind, laughed at the sight. 'What a pair of tossers,' he thought.

There were six barges moored at Paglesham Boatyard. Something went *ker-ching* in Jazz's head. Aggregate: who else moves aggregate and who would work with the barges? He tried to ring Ash but the bugger wasn't answering. Pissed off he asked Tom if one of his lads could make some enquiries for him. When he finally got off the phone both he and Tom looked intently at the barge in front of them. They noted the tide was in but it didn't come in very high. Gary confirmed that when the tide was out the barge sat in mud, and the water usually only came up about three or four feet. He also confirmed that barges only needed three feet of water to move, when empty, of course, and not full of aggregate. Jazz asked if the barges were busy working back and forth from the X Rail project to

Wallasea Island. What the heck were six barges doing sitting in Paglesham? Why weren't they busy on the river? According to Gary, the coastguards liked a couple of days a week break from having six barges going up and down the Thames to Wallasea Island. And the barges had a few days overhaul. It all made sense and Jazz began brimming with excitement. If he got the answers he hoped, then he had a link to The Bird Man.

They would need to organise for the barges to be moved and for a camera to check out whether a body was found under the mud. The quayside looked like the only place at Paglesham in which a man could be stood in mud until water came up to his mouth and ebbed out, and a barge came forward. A DVD could be filmed from the quayside, and the angle looked right. They needed to get back to London to process the information and organize a search of the mud. They turned to Gary who was walking back to his boat, and shouted that they were ready to return to Wallasea. Gary said there was no need. He pointed through the boatyard and said if they followed the road, it would take them to their car at the Plough and Sail. It should take about ten minutes to walk. It took a few minutes for this to sink in. The bastard had taken them the long way round and cost them a fortune in an unnecessary boat trip. They were ready to throttle him. But by now Gary had fired up his tug and was out of reach. He waved to them and shouted his thanks for their business. What had they been told by the Marine Police? *He was as slippery as a handful of eels in a bucket of snot!* And they hadn't believed anyone living in the sticks could be cleverer than they were.

They felt like a pair of dickheads and promised each other never to mention it again.

Tom got on the phone to Eddie Willoughby at Essex Police Marine Unit. Now Eddie had to help. Reluctantly Eddie agreed to take a few of his men off a patrol and do the checks Tom asked for. As Tom was about to say goodbye Eddie asked if he had seen Gary. By Tom's tone Eddie knew just what had happened and he laughed. The London Police were always full of themselves and it was good to hear that a local had got one over on the London lot. He would hear about it later when he went down to his local pub. Gary would tell all his story of how he had duped the London Police, and it would keep him in free drinks for quite some time.

Tom and Jazz walked back to the pub, disgruntled that a six-fingered bastard of a carrot-cruncher had stitched them up. They decided to have half a Wallasea Wench and a pub burger and chips before they returned to Ilford. The beer was cold, tasty and hit the spot, and with the food, it all went down a treat.

When Jazz's phone went and Peter confirmed what he'd thought, Jazz let out an excited whoop of *yesss we've got him* which made the locals look up. The journey back to Ilford was full of ideas and thoughts; both men were excited by the thought of getting The Bird Man. No one had done that before and they were going to be the pair that had done the impossible. By the time they arrived at Ilford Police Station they were giggling and saying to each other, *You are the man*. Other officers thought they were drunk but although half a Wallasea Wench was potent stuff, it wasn't enough for a seasoned drinker like Jazz.

He tried to ring Ash again but still got no reply. No one had seen him all day. Someone said he had burned the midnight oil the other night and perhaps he was sleeping. Jazz wasn't happy at all; he'd read Ash the riot act next time they spoke. For now, it was late, and he and Tom wanted to get together the following morning and plan the next stage. They knew they had to be careful when dealing with The Bird Man.

CHAPTER TWENTY-FIVE
Sting in the tail

The time had flown by; it was past closing time and the pub was empty. Ash needed to go to the gents. He'd been banged up in the storeroom for what must have been a couple of hours. No wonder he was tired, hungry and wanted to pee. George took him to the gents which seemed highly unnecessary but Ash reckoned it was George's way of making up for locking him in the storeroom. He thought George was very affable but not very bright.

A meal was produced for Ash and a cup of coffee brought to his table. George was still being very attentive. It was getting on Ash's nerves: too much overseeing of what he was doing and too much niceness. It was beginning to feel claustrophobic and he wanted to go home. He'd been promised that someone wanted to meet him but as yet they hadn't appeared and he didn't want to wait any longer. It had been an evening of false promises. He finished his bangers and mash and got up to go. He was in the middle of thanking George for his hospitality and for his help but at that point George jumped in and said the man he wanted to introduce him to was here, and he pointed to the corner. Surprised and shocked, Ash looked over and there was Freddie Link.

The pub was completely empty. Freddie Link was a monster of a man and not someone he wanted to meet in public, let alone in a deserted pub at this time of night. The graveyard shroud of fear crept from his feet up to his head; as the feeling rose, it sent icy fingers into every part of his body and he felt cold, so cold. He had never felt such fear before. It paralysed him and he couldn't move. There was no smile or acknowledgement from Freddie Link. He rose from his seat and walked to Ash. One punch in the side of the face and he was on the floor out cold. George and Freddie picked him up; although he was quite slim he weighed much more when unconscious. They grunted as they carried him through the back door to a car in the backyard. They pushed him in the boot of the Mercedes and Freddie nodded at George and drove off. All of this happened without a word. Each knew what they had to do.

It was the next day before Ash fully recovered. He found himself on a bed in a dark room. He saw there were blinds, which were closed. He had no idea how he'd got there or why he was there. Again, the fear of what was happening over took him and he shook with terror. He scrabbled in his pockets for his mobile but couldn't find it. 'Oh Jesus, what have I got myself into?' he thought in panic. He didn't know what anyone wanted with him. Now it was coming back to him; as his face throbbed with pain, he remembered the pub and George and Freddie Link. What had he done?

He was not tied up so he got up and tried the door. It was locked. He went to the window to look through the blinds but they turned out to be metal shutters and he couldn't move them. He felt tears of frustration and fear rising up and quickly he wiped his eyes; he didn't need to break down now, he needed to think. He went back to the bed and sat down. There was nothing else in the room except the bed with a pillow and duvet, and a light switch on the wall. At least the light worked. He wanted to bang on the door and demand to be let out but he was too scared. He wasn't sure that he wanted anyone to enter the room. If someone came into the room they might try to kill him. He knew Freddie Link, and if free he could arrest him and George. There was no way they would allow that to happen. They were going to kill him, he knew that. He wanted to tell his wife and his mother how much he loved them. His children – his gorgeous, clever, bright and loving children – he might never see them again. Now he cried loud and hard; it was all too much to bear.

Just as he was trying to sleep, as he had been awake for hours and wanted to escape the torture of not knowing what was going to happen, he heard the door being unlocked. Instantly he was wide-awake; his heart was pounding and his breath was laboured and making him dizzy. Freddie Link entered the room. He had a bottle of water and a McDonald's bag. He threw them on the bed, said, 'Get on with it,' and left.

Ash heard the key turn in the door and a bolt being shut. He sat for a moment wondering why and when and if. He didn't know what to make of it all. He sat and ate the lukewarm Big Mac and chips, and drank some water. He was hungry but his taste buds were on strike and nothing had any flavour. He felt numb.

Whom had he upset? Obviously it was The Bird Man but how could he kill a Detective Constable in the Metropolitan Police Force and expect to get away with it? Alone in the room with no visible means of escape, Ash sat in fear and spent the hours contemplating his death.

CHAPTER TWENTY-SIX
Payback time

Jazz was to meet Tom in the canteen and he found himself an empty table in the corner. Milly was pleased to see him again. There was a queue of police officers waiting to select their breakfast from the hot buffet but she stopped serving them to take a fresh cup of tea over to Jazz at his table.

Tom Black arrived a little later. He'd been held up by one of his detectives. Apparently no one had seen Ash for over a day. He didn't add that the last time this happened Jazz's detective was found shot dead. He'd made enquiries and found out that Ash hadn't gone home; he hadn't rung his wife or his mother for a day and that wasn't like him. He felt as sick as a pig but he had to tell Jazz there was trouble brewing. Okay, it might mean nothing, Ash might have gone on a bender and be holed up somewhere with a massive hangover – but it was highly unlikely. Reluctantly he sat Jazz down and told him that no one had seen or heard from Ash for at least twenty-four hours.

Jazz's first instinct was to jump up and go and look everywhere, but he held back. The sinking feeling in his stomach made him feel sick. What had he done? He'd said this would never happen again. He promised Tom that when he found Ash he would rip his face off for doing this to him. Tom nodded sympathetically but urged Jazz to get into the office and find out what he had been doing and where he might be. Jazz tried his mobile number just in case this was just a storm in a teacup. He hoped and prayed Ash would answer his phone, but it just cut off with no voicemail. Sombre and quiet, he and Tom went to the office in which Ash had been working and searched his desk. Going through the paperwork there Jazz repeated the mantra of 'Fuck, fuck, fuck, fuck.' It didn't make him feel any easier.

In the meantime, a search was made for Ash's mobile phone. No signal had been picked up. It seemed as if it could have been dismantled but the last place it had been picked up was Longbridge Road. It looked as if he was in The Pig and Poke. The feeling of uneasiness overtook Jazz and he tried to control his breathing.

He searched Ash's computer. He knew Ash's log-on code and he checked out what he'd been looking at and working on. He picked up the report on The Pig and Poke affray and read what Ash had read. It was frightening to think he might have taken this information and gone to research it. Jazz showed Tom what he'd read. The look on Tom's face confirmed his fears. 'The stupid, idiotic, fucking prick of a bastard has gone to the pub, hasn't he?' asked Jazz, wanting to hear 'no' but Tom nodded. A detective given the job of checking number plates on the cameras in most areas had picked up Ash's car travelling from Barking to Longbridge Road, and the last camera showed him heading in the direction of The Pig and Poke.

In a second Jazz was off down the corridor with Tom running behind him. 'Where the fuck are we going?' asked Tom. 'To The fucking Pig and Poke, I presume?' Jazz nodded and they headed for the station car park, where they grabbed an undercover vehicle.

It was morning and the pub wouldn't be open yet, but they would find the landlord who lived above the pub. On the way Jazz tried to calm down. He didn't believe anything had happened to Ash; this was all a mistake and he and Tom were jumping to conclusions. My God, why would anyone want to take Ash. He was a medal-winning dipstick of the first order. He couldn't solve anything above bike thefts. Even The Bird Man knew Ash was a numpty and not worth much. But then Jazz stopped trying to convince himself and wondered if Ash was a better detective than anyone had seen. He hoped to God he was wrong and that Ash was the load of rubbish he thought he was. There was only so much he could tell Tom. The Bird Man was dangerous and he didn't want to put Tom in danger by giving him too much information. Tom wasn't stupid, he knew that anyone involved in any way with The Bird Man could be in deep trouble; he also knew that Jazz and Ash had been to see him recently and there was a problem. Tom was a better detective than Jazz gave him credit for.

They parked the car in the empty car park of The Pig and Poke. Jazz felt chilly and shivered slightly. The day was bright and sunny but there was an edge to the air; it felt as if someone had walked over his grave and he didn't like that feeling. They banged on the pub door and shouted, 'Police! Open up.' It took a few moments but in a little while they heard bolts being thrown open and the key turning. The smiley, friendly face of George appeared around the crack in the door.

When they questioned him, George thought hard and long and said he just couldn't remember a DC Ashiv Kumar coming to the pub last night. He said it was busy as usual and he might not have seen Ash. Jazz went through the motions of describing him to George, who shook his head and confirmed that, nope, he just couldn't remember seeing anyone of that description. They asked if they could look around and George opened the door wide for them to enter; he took them around the pub and they checked chairs and tables. They went into the toilets and any door they could find that opened. They came to the storeroom and tried the door, which was locked. George explained that he kept drink and cigarettes and money for the tills in there. They nodded understandingly and asked if he would mind opening the door. George got the key immediately and showed them into the room. They found nothing to do with Ash there. With a thank you to George for his help they left. Jazz drove the car around the corner and stopped. He didn't want to talk to Tom within earshot of George or his cronies.

They discussed what they knew and why they both thought The Bird Man had something to do with this. As yet they were not totally sure Ash was missing. Just because it had happened before to Jazz didn't mean it was going to happen again. But neither of them believed that. There was a link to The Bird Man on the barge murder. It was a pretty good link and by the same token they could link the other two murders to The Bird Man.

The three murders were unusual. There had been nothing like them before. If one was attributed to The Bird Man, could the others? The two men, James Kent and Peter Daly, were at The Pig and Poke according to the statements Ash had been looking at. Jazz looked at Tom and ventured, 'I don't know about you but I wouldn't go near a pub that had anything to do with The Bird Man. He is a serious piece of bad news and can do a lot of damage if he feels like it. Now what are the odds of James Kent and Peter Daly going to a pub like that and being there at the same time?'

Jazz looked at Tom and asked "Is this making sense to you or am I making it up as I go along to fit the pieces? Tom said slowly, 'It all fits but why is Ash a problem? That's the question. What did he make of it all?'

'Perhaps he had also made the connection between the murders,' said Jazz, 'and the stupid fucking idiot came here and asked pointed questions. It would have been like poking a stick in a hornets' nest. Someone could have got upset.'

So the question again was *Where is Ash and was he still alive.* Jazz ached with tension. What the fuck should he do now and where the fuck should he go? He had to find Ash and keep him alive. At present it looked as if he had pissed off The Bird Man or his men, especially Freddie Link who, although not in the pub when the statements were taken, was known to have slipped out the back way. He spent a lot of time in The Pig and Poke.

His girlfriend went there and so did his mates. He wouldn't have been happy to have a Detective Constable walking around his territory asking questions. Freddie was funny like that. The pub was his territory and most people who went there were as frightened of Freddie as they were of The Birdman. Freddie lorded it by taking up residence in the seated booth in the corner where he could watch everyone come and go and he would invite his cronies to join him at his table. Jazz thought that Ashiv would be stupid enough not to realise you don't mess on Freddie's territory.

Again, Jazz hoped he wasn't kidding himself, but surely Ash being there wouldn't have warranted a whack (murder) – more a good slap for disrespect. God, he hoped so. He was as near to tears as he could get. He should have watched Ash like a hawk. How had he gone from giving him no space or interesting jobs to letting him get on with it? Again, he wondered if he deserved to be a Detective Sergeant. Perhaps everyone was right. He was a fucking danger to all police officers.

Tom was off to supervise his team. He was going to find all the haunts of various miscreants that worked closely with The Bird Man and lean on them a little to find out what they knew. At present no one had officially registered the disappearance of Ash and before that happened Jazz wanted to try and find him. If Freddie Link had him, he would have to ask The Bird Man what he could do. Nothing happened on The Bird Man's turf without his permission.

It was agreed that Jazz would drop Tom off at Ilford Police Station and he would collect his men and go and search the dark and dirty corners of the East End of London and route out whatever information they could. Jazz kept quiet, but he knew what he was going to do.

CHAPTER TWENTY-SEVEN
The rat pack

Jazz arrived at Mad Pete's flat with coffee and burgers in hand. He knew Mad Pete was chilling out; he could smell the spliff from the front door. He banged hard on the door and shouted to be let in. It took a few moments. Mad Pete was most probably away with the fairies but the shouting and banging brought him back to reality. It took him a few moments to realize it was DS Singh at his door. He got up unsteadily and, grumbling that he just wanted a bit of peace, slowly he unbolted his door.

Jazz thrust the coffees and burgers at him as a peace offering and told him they were getting cold. He realized he wanted a favour from Mad Pete and he needed to calm him down a bit. He knew he wouldn't want to do it but he needed his help.

After they had finished the burgers and chips, they sat and drank the coffee, which was pretty lukewarm by now. Jazz told Mad Pete he had lost Ash. 'That was pretty careless of you, Mr Singh,' said Mad Pete, snorting with laughter.

But Jazz wasn't laughing. It sounded as if Freddie Link had something to do with Ash's disappearance.

'He ain't a happy man if his recreation time is interfered with, Mr Singh,' Mad Pete uttered sombrely.

'So,' prompted Jazz gently, 'does it mean that if Freddie Link had anything to do with the disappearance of Ash, he'd have to ask The Bird Man for permission or something like that?'

Mad Pete nodded. 'The Bird Man has this area sewn up tighter than a duck's arse and no one with any brains would mess with him.'

Jazz was picking his words, trying to take the conversation in the direction he wanted. 'I need to speak to The Bird Man again, Pete, and I don't want anyone else to know I am speaking with him.'

Mad Pete looked at him and knew what he wanted. 'Oh no, Mr Singh. I can't go near The Bird Man again, not for a long time.'

Jazz tried to look innocent. 'Why not? He doesn't mind you, does he?'

Mad Pete was getting agitated now. 'I can't go near him because I took that DVD and showed it to you. He'll know it's me, he knows everything. You're going to get me killed, Mr Singh, and I don't want to die yet.'

Soothingly Jazz told Mad Pete that The Bird Man would never know Mad Pete had anything to do with the DVD. He added that Pete was very cunning and clever and only he knew that.

By now Mad Pete was almost blushing and he thanked Jazz for saying such nice things. Now that he was more amenable, Jazz said, 'I need you to set up an appointment for me with The Bird Man. I don't trust anyone other than you to do this for me.'

After all this soothing of his ego, Mad Pete agreed to contact The Bird Man on Jazz's behalf. He promised to get on with it as soon as Jazz left. That was good enough for Jazz. In the meantime he had other fish to fry. If he was going to see The Bird Man he needed to be armed with as much information as possible.

He phoned Tom to see where he had got to with his enquiries, only to be told that there was nothing to report and no one had seen Ash anywhere. It looked bad and Jazz was getting to feel quite desperate.

Tom had heard from Eddie Willoughby, Essex Police Marine Unit. His men had moved the barge and were in the process of digging up the mud. They thought it might take some time because the barge had compressed the mud and anyone in there would be *halfway to Australia by now*. Tom asked him to keep going until they found a body.

Jazz's phone went just as he finished talking to Tom. It was DCI Radley. He wanted an immediate update on what the hell was going on. Jazz suddenly realized that he had gone off half-cocked and no one knew anything. It was good to keep stuff under his belt but this had got big and you didn't piss off your boss to this extent. With the Essex Marine Police all around Paglesham digging in the mud questions were going to be asked. The press would be there and where the press was, so was DCI Radley.

Jazz spent the next half hour updating the DCI on what had happened. He omitted the bit about The Bird Man, and he didn't mention Ash at this stage, although he would soon if they didn't find him. His finale, and his *pièce de résistance*, was the DVD. He made an excuse for not showing it to his DCI straight away but said if he cared to look in his desk drawer he would find a copy. He added that for the time being he was undercover and searching for clues. "How Sherlock Holmes did that sound like?" He thought. DCI Radley said he wanted to see him in his office tomorrow at 1 p.m. sharp.

With fingers crossed Jazz hoped he would have everything in place by then. If not, he would have to do a disappearing act. He needed to get on. He had to believe Ash was okay and he needed to find him.

Peter, Tom's detective, was still working on Jazz's questions and said he would come back to him within a couple of hours. All was set in place and now he was off to sort out another part of the puzzle. He wasn't looking forward to this part. James Kent was a sad soul and, Jazz thought, quite harmless. He didn't want to have to grill the man but he had no choice.

CHAPTER TWENTY-EIGHT
Dicing with death

Freddie Link was impatient but was keeping his cool. The Bird Man had told him to wait, and waited he had, but now he was getting jittery. He wanted it over and done with so he could get on. DC Kumar was a pain in the arse and he needed to be whacked and gone.

The Bird Man called a meeting of Freddie and George in a house somewhere in Beckton. He wasn't happy. In a quiet but murderous tone he told Freddie and George that they were idiots; what the fuck were they going to do with DC Kumar now they had him locked up in some house? Sure, he was an annoying pratt but that didn't mean he could be killed or locked up. He reminded them that the police would be all over town like a rash unless DC Kumar turned up soon, and if he was released Freddie and George would be put away for a long time. He added that perhaps that was a bloody good thing because Barry Bentall wasn't happy at having been brought into this.

It was the golden rule that Bentall was never linked to anything that happened in his town. Of course he was instrumental in everything that happened and he always kept his finger on the pulse. Now this had happened.

They knew better than to cause this bit of bother. He suggested that perhaps there could be more than one body to get rid off. They both knew what he was referring to and they gulped.

He told them they hadn't thought what they were doing and what the fucking hell gave Freddie the right to take Barry Bentall's law into his own hands. Freddie paled as he watched The Bird Man work himself up into a rage that could have serious repercussions for him and George. George's face had lost its usual friendly look. Freddie was pleading by now. 'But Barry, I just thought he could be topped and disposed of in the usual way. It's always worked before, hasn't it?'

Barry wasn't impressed. 'He didn't need to be topped. He's a stupid little fucker who knew nothing. Now he's a huge impressive fucker who knows enough about you and George to get you put away and by that token the filth would be on my back. You are the most fucking, idiotic and stupid bastard I've ever worked with.' Getting very angry now, he asked Freddie, 'Tell me what he knew, you clever dick. What exactly could he have known?'

Freddie, his eyes darting everywhere, tried to put into words what he was worried about. He worked more on brawn than brains and he wasn't comfortable being put in this position; he was scared. Freddie wasn't often scared of anything or anyone.

George could see that Freddie was no use and interrupted by saying that the DC knew about James Kent and Peter Daly being in The Pig and Poke. He had intimated that he knew why they were there. 'We were worried about compromising your good self,' George interjected.

'So you thought you were my fucking Superman, did you?' retorted an even angrier Barry Bentall. He was so pissed off with all of this. So much *could be*, *might be*, and no real facts. They should have just sent Kumar on his way.

'What idiot panicked?' The Bird Man asked.

Both men denied they had panicked but Barry knew they both had. He could see the scenario. George locks Kumar in the storeroom and goes to find Freddie. Freddie is pissed that his evening is being interrupted and tells George to fucking leave Kumar there and that he deserved to be whacked for being a fucking nuisance. From there it just got worse. You can't lock a Metropolitan Detective in a store cupboard and not expect repercussions. So they decided it was easier to top him. They had the means of getting rid of the body easily and it would never be found. Simple! But they had to ask Barry (The Bird Man) Bentall first for his permission.

Barry wasn't stupid. He knew the repercussions of killing a Met police detective would reverberate for years and his comfy little businesses would become decidedly uncomfortable. Freddie and George had become a big liability and they had to go.

Now the decision was made Barry could become amenable and pleasant. He smiled at both Freddie and George. 'Never mind. These things happen. We'll get rid of DC Kumar when I say so. For now, let's make the best of a bad job and cover our tracks. I don't want to be associated with you both. I don't want any trail coming in my direction. Where is DC Kumar for future reference? And I'll sort out his future for you.'

Freddie was much appreciative of Barry's understanding and told him that DC Kumar was in the storage unit over Bow way and was securely kept there in the room upstairs. Barry nodded and grimaced. 'Not in that filthy bed up there? I meant to get it thrown out years ago.' Freddie nodded and laughed. It was good to have the boss cracking jokes again.

'As for you, George, said Barry, nodding in his direction, 'you'd better get back to the pub before you're missed. I can see you were put in a difficult position and lessons have to be learned.'

George was relieved to leave and get outside. He thought he'd got off lightly and was glad of it.

Freddie left, thanking The Bird Man for his help and saying he owed him one big time. Barry nodded. When Freddie had left, he got on the phone and just said 'Freddie Link'. That was enough. Freddie was never seen again until he was found several months later facedown in a sewerage treatment plant in Becton. It was thought he had been there for months and had been secured by rope and bricks to the bottom of the main treatment pool. The ropes had been gnawed through by rats and Freddie floated to the top in all his putrefied glory.

George never made it back to The Pig and Poke. The East End is full of CCTV cameras but on his way back a car skidded off the road and ran him down. He was all mashed up and identified only by his teeth. No one was ever charged with dangerous driving or his death. This left The Bird Man with one problem. What to do with DC Ashiv Kumar. He had a few options and he would think about it.

In an indecent amount of time a relative of George appeared and claimed the pub, producing a will to confirm it. His name was Paddy O'Brian, and he was a long-lost relative from Ireland. He was to become a very good landlord and friends and colleagues of The Bird Man still frequented The Pig and Poke. They spoke highly of Paddy's manners and his respect for The Bird Man.

CHAPTER TWENTY-NINE
All is revealed

Here he was again. Standing on the front step of Mr and Mrs Kent's home. He rang the bell and after a few minutes Amanda appeared at the door. She looked terrible and almost mad. Her eyes were large and her body tense and strained. Why had he come to see them again? He was no good to them anymore. He couldn't bring back Laura, could he? She was rambling again; he felt so sorry for her, and even sorrier for her family who had to live with her. He knew she was highly strung but now she was as taut as a violin string. One wrong move and he wasn't sure what she would do. He tried the friendly way. 'Hello, Amanda. I just need to have a brief word with James, if I may. I expect he's in his shed?'

She grunted at him. 'He's always in his shed.'

Jazz smiled and eased his way past her, heading for the back door. He felt tensed up until he got into the garden. With a deep breath he made his way to the garden shed which was looking particularly smart with a new coat of paint.

Knocking on the door, he called James' name, to let him know it wasn't Amanda. Jazz thought that if he was married to Amanda he would lock himself in the shed and stay there. James opened the door with a brief smile and invited Jazz in. The interior was as pristine as ever. James put the kettle on. 'Every home comfort in here,' thought Jazz.

With a cup of tea in hand, Jazz started the conversation with some small talk. He asked what James was doing these days and James just shrugged: not much. Jazz looked at him as he leaned against the potting bench; he was half the man he used to be. He had developed a stoop, his hair was thinning and he had a permanent hangdog expression. Jazz felt sorry for him. He looked like a man who was finished forever.

Jazz needed a lead. It was all assumption but you had to start somewhere. He didn't want to aggravate James and goad him, but he needed to know what Ash had got out of the report. He'd thought about it long and hard, and this was the only thing that made sense.

'Okay, James, how did you find The Bird Man and get the deed done?'

James looked up startled, and then he slumped even further forward with his head almost on his stomach. Jazz knew he had hit the right note and was sorry to be asking these questions. He liked James and thought he deserved better. He wanted to help him along. 'Just make a clean breast of it, you know it makes sense,' he said almost kindly. There was a silence for quite some time and they both sipped their hot tea.

In an almost dreamlike state James said that Laura was the finest thing that had ever happened in his life. He loved her like he never thought possible. He told Jazz about Amanda. He'd met her at work and avoided her most of the time. She'd been highly strung even then but she always made a beeline for him. He didn't know what it was but one day when he was having a bad time at work, Amanda had tried to cheer him up.

She offered to cook him a nice meal. He lived alone and just for once he fancied having someone making a fuss of him. It was nothing sexual, he said – he didn't like her in that way – but he supposed he was a bit lonely at the time and she was very nice to him. They drank wine that evening and Amanda relaxed and he remembered they laughed a lot. It was a warm and friendly evening, and after the second bottle of wine they ended up sleeping together that night. A few months later Amanda told him she was pregnant. James looked at Jazz. 'How bloody unlucky was that! Everyone sodding sleeps together these days but they don't get pregnant on the first and only date, do they? He realized he was almost shouting and he apologized. Jazz told him not to worry, and said that if he'd slept with Amanda and she got pregnant he would have been seriously pissed off. Suddenly he realized what he'd said and immediately apologized for saying that, because James was married to Amanda.

For the first time James laughed. He assured Jazz there was no need to apologise for saying the truth.

James married Amanda because it was the correct thing to do. He looked at Jazz and said, 'Why do you think I have stayed with Amanda? I have never loved her and she is totally unlovable. She's been highly strung for all her life and when she had Laura she got worse. I don't know why that happened but it did.'

He was close to tears. Jazz looked away, embarrassed

for the man. James was silent for a moment whilst he controlled his feelings, and then he continued with his story. 'When Laura was born I fell in love with her. She was the most beautiful of babies with a temperament that was angelic. I would sit and just look at her for hours. When she was asleep she would suck her bottom lip and it was the most beautiful thing to see.' His face became wretched and he was silent again whilst he struggled with his emotions. Jazz watched and marvelled at his control.

'When she grew up,' James continued, 'I watched her blossom. She developed her own mind and personality quite young and I laughed when she tried to tell me what to do. She tried to argue with her mother but that turned into a big fight. Laura would come and sit in here with me and we would laugh about everything.' He looked at Jazz sadly. 'You know, I've forgotten how to laugh. It seems such a waste of time these days.'

Jazz nodded and kept silent as James continued. 'You know I wanted the best for her. We talked a lot about her life and what she wanted to do. We did talk about John Carpenter and I knew eventually she would see him for what he was. Her stupid mother drove her into his arms even more with her hysterical rows about him. Laura needed to learn things her way and I knew as we discussed him she would see him for who he was, but it was too late. I have never forgiven myself. I should have done more.' With this James burst into tears and turned away.

Jazz felt close to tears himself. This was just too much to bear for anyone. Stuck with a mad woman because of the love for a daughter and then she was taken away. How fucking unfair and tragic was that.

He had to ask, he didn't want to and he didn't know what he would do with the answer, but he had to ask. 'Did you arrange for John Carpenter to be murdered?'

James looked up. Now he was in control and sombre. In a voice that had gained strength through hatred, he said, 'If I did arrange for John Carpenter to be murdered I would have loved him to have been murdered in the way he was found. To kill him would be too easy. He needed to know pain and fear. I am glad it happened to him and if I had the energy and the strength, I would dance with joy.'

Jazz asked that, if he had arranged for John Carpenter to be murdered, how would it be done?

James smiled: not a happy smile, more a smile of knowledge. 'I would find a knight in shining armour who had the balls to help me to murder him.'

Jazz reminded him that he and Amanda had already been checked out and had a fantastic alibi that was unbreakable for the approximate time of the kidnap and torture of John Carpenter.

James looked straight into Jazz's eyes. 'Exactly!'

Going very carefully now Jazz asked if DC Kumar had come to see James, and asked him if he had contact with Barry Bentall. Quickly James said no. Changing his question slightly Jazz asked if DC Kumar had visited at all within the last day or so, and James said that he had popped by. Jazz asked what he had talked about and James said nothing much. Jazz gave him a look that said *I'm not silly* and James felt a tinge of embarrassment. He wasn't used to lying. He preferred to hide away so he didn't have to lie.

Jazz said to James that he did understand what he had been going through but things had to be put right. DC Kumar was missing and he thought coming to see James might give him some clues. James was upset to think anything might have happened to DC Kumar; he thought him a nice man, although a bit stupid. He apologized again to Jazz for thinking like that about a police officer. Jazz just smiled and thought he wasn't far wrong.

'He asked me why I was in The Pig and Poke on the night of the affray when those men had a big fight outside the pub,' said James. 'I didn't say anything to him but when he left I rang a number I had been given and told them what he asked.' He looked at Jazz. 'Did I get DC Kumar into trouble doing that? I thought I was just keeping others out of trouble by warning them.'

Jazz wanted names but James didn't know any. No one had given him a name, just a number to ring. When Jazz asked for the number he got it out of his wallet and gave it hesitantly to Jazz.

James, calm now and defiant, stated clearly and firmly that he now had nothing to live for. The only thing that had made any sense to him was his wonderful daughter Laura and now she was gone he didn't care. If Jazz wanted to arrest him he could. He was proud of what he had done.

Jazz interrupted, reminding him that he should be saying he would be proud of what he could have done, *if he had done it*. James wasn't that interested in the fact that Jazz was trying to help him. His words were strong and clear; he'd had enough of it all and yes, he was proud to have done what he did. Jazz was perplexed and didn't know what to do with this information so blatantly given to him.

'So does the name The Bird Man of Barking mean anything to you?' he asked.

James answered honestly that no, it meant nothing to him. Jazz pushed a little more. 'How did you get anyone to assist you? Where did you go for help?'

James, now even stronger, said that the knights in shining armour who were his heroes had no names and he wouldn't tell even if he knew. If any one should be arrested it was him, and they deserved a medal for what they did.

This wasn't helpful to Jazz. 'So why were you in The Pig and Poke? Did you meet someone there who helped you?' James answered that he had. But he would say nothing else. 'How much did it cost you or was it for free?' asked Jazz. James said it cost his savings of £10,000 and it was the best use of money he had ever had. The best bargain in the world. He added he would have paid more if he had it but he didn't.

Jazz, seeing James getting stronger and more confident, didn't want to rouse him into any sort of fury that would take him off this path of revelations. 'Did you get a video of what happened to John Carpenter?' James didn't seem sure he wanted to answer this, but he said he got a very small video. They had filmed the bit where Carpenter was in the woods on the ground and it showed the acid had burned his eyes. He was trying to say something but couldn't make any noise because the acid had burnt his throat and vocal cords. His arms and legs were obviously broken and he couldn't move. James said the video was wonderful and he wished it could have been longer.

Such hatred was a rarity for Jazz. Anger, yes, a bit of hatred – but this deep burning hatred was something he hadn't experienced before. Up until now James had always seemed very controlled and quiet. He could see that the poor man was eaten up with hatred. He patted James on the back and thanked him for his honesty and said he would be back if necessary.

He left by the side gate so as not to go through the house and be confronted by Amanda. He waved to her as she looked out of the front room window as he went out of the front gate.

He looked at the piece of paper given to him by James and dialed the number. He put in a 141 first: no point in alerting anyone that he was calling. A gruff voice answered *Yeh*. Jazz pressed the cancel button. He sat and thought for a second. It sounded very much like Freddie Link. It was all making sense now. It looked as if Ash had gone to The Pig and Poke, which was straight into the lion's den with Freddie Link there as usual. Freddie would have been ready for him. Jazz didn't trust George at all and knew he would be in cahoots with the likes of Freddie.

He got on the phone to Tom and told him all he knew. Neither of them was sure what to do with the information. If there was a video it seemed to include Freddie Link who did the barge video. It looked like Freddie was the contact for James and that made sense. They would interview Freddie soon. They needed to put a tail on him and see where he went. Ash should be close by.

There was no mention of The Bird Man of Barking and they both knew Freddie would do nothing without his permission. As yet there was no connection between Freddie and The Bird Man on this case. They had connected Ash and the pub. George would be visited again and his memory would be sharpened. Freddie was always in the pub in the evening so a chat with him to shake him up a bit was on the cards.

Tom said a body had been found under the barge and it was being taken to a local mortuary for identification. Jazz mouthed the word *wow* and felt his heart pounding. It was all getting pretty sticky and he wondered if he was out of his depth. Tom was going to give George a little push and make Freddie feel uncomfortable. Jazz was off to fish for bigger fish and see what that brought up. They were both aware that if they didn't find Ash soon they would have to report him missing, and then there would be a full-scale manhunt, which would trample over all the facts. They both agreed the next morning would be the time to talk to DCI Radley. Talking of which, DCI Radley had also rung Tom and asked about the body under the barge so Tom would be burning the midnight oil getting the report ready for tomorrow.

CHAPTER THIRTY
Birds of a feather

God! Jazz needed a drink. He had gone most of the day on empty and he needed just a little Dutch courage and a big drink. He took himself off to a quiet corner of the car park and sat in his car, drinking out of his flask the clear and burningly gorgeous life-giving liquid that is vodka. He so loved the taste and the feeling it gave him. His body, taut with stress and emotion, collapsed into a relaxed mode. He could think more clearly with a drink, he told himself.

After three more drinks, he felt warm and relaxed. He could think now. His mind was forever on Ash; he had to get closer to what had happened. He wanted to go and speak to Peter Daly. Actually, what he really wanted to do was just find Ash and stuff Peter Daly. Just as he was contemplating perhaps another drink to make an even number of four, his phone went. It was Mad Pete, speaking urgently and quickly. 'Be ready for a phone call from The Bird Man. He wants to speak to you directly.' Mad Pete saw this as trouble. The Bird Man never spoke on the phone directly with anyone. It was his way of keeping out of trouble and ensuring a link to him was never made. 'What have you done, Mr Singh? I think you're in deep trouble.

Jazz felt that rumble of anxiety rising; it felt as if The Bird Man was always one step ahead of him and knew everything he did. Full of bravado, he had thought that he could take on The Bird Man and see him charged and arrested. Now he had a sinking feeling that perhaps he had taken on too much. He had got carried away with knowledge that was dangerous to possess.

The phone went again minutes later. It was The Bird Man and there were no pleasantries. 'Git yourself over to my place now. I expect you here in twenty minutes max with an explanation.' Any other villain and Jazz would have put them in their place. He was not at the bidding of villains and he would have marshalled a battalion of officers to back him up. But this was The Bird Man and he would have information on Ash. He knew everything that happened in his town. Jazz was also very sure that if you got in The Bird Man's way, whether you were a politician, police officer, banker, or millionaire, there would be no hiding place; he would get you.

There were hair-raising stories about The Bird Man. Okay, stories got exaggerated but it didn't do to underestimate him. Many, many people had gone missing over the years, attributed to The Bird Man culling his area, but no bodies had been found. It was reckoned that quite a few got fed to pigs; there were many pig farms around the Suffolk/Essex borders. That seemed very possible but how many bodies could you feed to pigs without someone noticing? There was talk of the old myth about mincing up bodies at a slaughterhouse but that was just something out of films. That would be far too dramatic and would mean more people than necessary knowing about the murders. For The Bird Man to keep his nose clean he had to have just a very few safe people he used. Villains gossip and if he had been doing half the things gossiped about, half the East End would have known about it. If nothing else, the Bird Man was clever and knew what he was doing. He had a whole fucking team of police watching him and they couldn't lay anything on him. He was not stupid.

There was only one thing that might get The Bird Man and that was his ego. He fancied himself as a Kray; even Capone appealed to him, although Capone was American and they did things different there. He really thought he was the Godfather of London. He would help the odd little old lady with some money for furniture or heating and they loved him. He gave out tobacco to various old men in the park, and was known to have provided a play area for deprived kids that he wanted called *The Barry Bentall Park*. That told Jazz a lot. This man wanted to leave a legend.

In the past, Jazz had tried to tell the team working on The Bird Man that his Achilles heel was his ego but they wouldn't listen to this upstart of a detective who had a reputation for getting into dangerous situations and taking his team with him.

He was on his way to see The Bird Man when his phone went. It was Peter with an update on the barges and he gave Jazz the information he needed. Suddenly Jazz felt that he had some negotiation powers and his meeting with The Bird Man was going to be interesting.

The Bird Man's home looked empty and there was no car in the drive. He rang the bell and almost immediately the door opened. He was shown into the lounge by a big silent guy: a seven-foot giant with shoulders nearly as wide. Jazz nodded his thanks and gave a timid smile as the giant left him. He was left alone to wait. The room was so plush and the chairs so expensively covered in white leather that he didn't think he should sit down. The longer he waited the more his confidence drained away. By the time The Bird Man came into the room he was rethinking whether this was a good idea. He hadn't told anyone where he was so no one would know if he disappeared. It was a frightening thought but there wasn't time to ponder on it. The Bird Man was speaking.

'You have been bothering people and I want to know why.'

Jazz didn't know how to answer that one. *Bothering people* sounded like he was knocking on their doors and running away. If he messed around with The Bird Man he would be in trouble but by the same token he wasn't sure whether to show his hand yet. He was desperate to know where Ash was.

CHAPTER THIRTY-ONE
You show me yours

Barry Bentall

Barry Bentall, The Bird Man of Barking as he was known, was rattled. He wasn't going to let this piece of shit of a Detective Sergeant know that. Detective Sergeant Jaswinder Singh, standing tall and looking loose, was seriously rattled but he wasn't going to let this fucking bastard of a villain know that. Both men wanted to know something and both were busy thinking how they could find out what they needed to without compromising themselves.

The Bird Man was in a very difficult position. He knew where DC Ashiv Kumar was and he knew he had to do something with him soon. Someone from his team, someone trusted and not known to other members of his team, had gone to see that DC Kumar was safe and well and being fed. They knew he'd had a McDonald's at some stage because they found the wrappings, and there was also a water bottle, now empty. DC Kumar was taken to the toilet and given more water and some fish and chips. The Bird Man thought he had been very generous indeed and that he'd made the detective very comfortable.

He was still trying to work out whether he was going to set him free as a miracle or to top him and get rid of him. He had to weigh up the advantages and disadvantages. For the moment he had some time. He had heard about DS Singh *fannying around* asking questions he shouldn't ask and mentioning Ashiv Kumar's name. DS Singh was like a little fly that kept buzzing near his face; he wanted to swat him and get rid of him but knew he would never be able to do that. Singh was such a fucking prima donna that if he went missing for more than a few hours everyone would know about it. So here he was just putting the screws on and seeing if he could get DS Singh to squirm a little and tell him something that would make his decision easier.

He was going to be a little accommodating too and see what this little shit was made of. It could be that he could frighten him and make him go away. Barry Bentall knew everything. He knew his nickname was The Bird Man of Barking and he revelled in it. He knew there was a team of officers dedicated to watching him and trying to bring him down and he loved it. Notoriety was something to be embraced and enjoyed, and he was loved by the public for it, too. He made sure he did a few good things for the elderly and the young in his town. They used to say that they were safe on the streets while The Bird Man of Barking had control. It wasn't true – crime happened – but Barry lapped up the compliments.

Jaswinder Singh
He was desperate to ask about Ash. The Bird Man of Barking knew everything that happened in his town,

especially when Freddie Link was involved. By the same token Jazz wondered if Ash was somewhere sinister. What if he'd just decided to take off and had left his phone behind? What if all of this was just a load of over-the-top hysterical behaviour because of what happened last time? Jazz was absolutely beside himself, not knowing what to do to find out. He promised himself that when he got hold of Ash he would knock his block off and kick him down every staircase he could find.

He was desperate for a drink. He wanted to sit with The Bird Man, have a drink, and just discuss what was happening in a friendly sort of way. He nearly giggled at such a ridiculous thought. The Bird Man was never friendly with anyone. There was murder in his eyes. The thought made Jazz shiver and he thought of Ash and knew what he would have to do.

Discussions and Decisions

The Bird Man had seen enough. Jazz looked washed out and ready to talk. As he had the last time, he took Jazz to the back door and out into his bird shed. It was his preferred area to talk in. There were no prying eyes and no one to overhear what was said. The only other way into the shed was through the birdcage area, and the birds would become disturbed and fly and squawk if someone tried to enter that way. They were the best alarm system. It was the perfect place for a confidential chat.

Jazz was now not up for messing around. 'I'm looking for DC Ashiv Kumar and I think you know where he is.' He stared intently at The Bird Man. It was a tense moment but it was broken with a smile and a shrug from The Bird Man. 'I don't know why I would know where he is, Jazz.' Jazz caught the personal use of his name and he knew immediately that The Bird Man knew exactly where Ash was. It was in his way of answering and in his stance. Jazz felt the cold stone of fear sinking into his stomach. *Please God, let Ash be alive and okay*, was the mantra going through his head. The Bird Man saw the effect of his words and he smiled. He had Jazz just where he wanted him.

'What the fuck are you doing besmirching my name, Singh?' was the next barb thrown at Jazz.

Jazz looked up and laughed. He couldn't help it. 'Besmirched?' he repeated.

For a moment The Bird Man was angry: *who was this fucking bastard talking to?* Then, fed up with the games and knowing Singh could do nothing with anything he told him, he got two beers out of the small fridge in the corner and handed one to Jazz. They sucked the beers for a moment and declared a truce.

Jazz started with James Kent and Peter Daly. He told The Bird Man he knew he had organized the murders of both John Carpenter and Johnny Peters and he suspected he was also responsible for the murder of Barry Jessop. The Bird Man took a swig of his beer and said pointedly, 'So what! They were all lower than the shit on my shoes. The courts did nothing to put these bastards away. Perhaps when help was asked for it was given.'

Feeling cocky and almost not caring, Jazz retorted, 'What are you, fucking Superman? Or just a fucking villain doing it for money?'

The Bird Man was not happy and moved to give Jazz a slap for his disrespect. He stopped short as Jazz flinched and ducked.

The laugh from The Bird Man started in his feet and worked its way up to his belly and chest. The booming laugh shocked Jazz more than the near slap. 'You're such a tosspot, Singh. Watch your step, otherwise you'll get a slap that will send you into the next room.'

It felt a near thing and Jazz tried to calm down and stop shaking. The Bird Man was a frightening figure; his hands were enormous. One swipe from them and Jazz would be knocked across the room. He needed to stay calm and respectful to find out where Ash was now.

The Bird Man had made up his mind. DC Kumar was going to be topped. He couldn't be doing with such a disrespectful, offensive and bloody nuisance of a detective. He figured that to hand Kumar over to Singh would cause him all sorts of problems. There would be questions to answer and this Singh had no respect for who he was. He didn't need this in his life. The officers watching him were respectful, and kept their distance. But Singh was too-off-the-wall and he didn't want him messing things up.

It would be easy to get rid of the detective. He could be topped and buried within hours and no one would ever find him. Then life could go back to some sort of normality. He couldn't be bothered with it all. Singh's attitude had sealed Kumar's fate. Freddie Link was responsible for taking the detective and he had now disappeared so, hand on heart, The Bird Man could say he knew nothing that could help.

Jazz started again. 'It is my job to solve murders.' The Bird Man laughed at this but said nothing. Jazz gave him a look of *what's so funny*, but The Bird Man didn't respond, so Jazz continued. 'I worked on the case of the murder of Laura Kent and so I have a vested interest in finding out who killed John Carpenter.'

The Bird Man interjected. 'I'll buy that reason.'

Jazz nodded and continued. 'So my colleague had the murder of Barry Jessop to solve and it was another strange murder – will you agree with that?'

The Bird Man, following all this, just said 'Yep!'

'I know you did the murders,' said Jazz. 'I can't prove it, but I would like to know why.'

The Bird Man was relaxed now that he had made his mind up. He had always been so careful not to give the police anything on him and to have one of his premises used in this way would tie him into Kumar's kidnapping. Freddie got what he deserved but now he had to sort this mess out. A phone call later would get it sorted. For now he sat back and parried with this little bit of shit who thought he was so clever.

CHAPTER THIRTY-TWO
Does the worm turn?

Jazz was feeling uncomfortable. This was too nice and too sweet. The Bird Man should be spitting nails at his accusations but he had this Mona Lisa smile which was fucking annoying, and it felt as if Jazz was going to be sent on his way. He needed to bring The Bird Man back to a point where they could talk. It felt as if he had lost Ash and he just couldn't let that happen. For a moment panic took over and then, in one of those blinding flashes, he knew what he had to do.

All the while The Bird Man leaned back, watching Jazz's discomfort and enjoying it. It was going to be uncomfortable – the truth always was – but Jazz had to bite the bullet. He owed it to Ash.

He looked up at The Bird Man and said, 'I am the biggest prick of the first order of pricks. I am an idiot, I waltz into things I know nothing about and fumble around. I think I am a lucky bugger, I often get it right but I know I cause mayhem on the way. I let Ash, that's DC Kumar, down. I was supposed to puppy-walk him through his start as a Detective Constable, but again I seem to have let him down.'

The Bird Man listened to this piece of self-righteous

shit and his response was, 'So you have lost another one, have you, Singh? Seems like you do this a lot. No wonder you are the laughing stock of the Metropolitan Police.' He laughed.

Jazz hadn't expected sympathy but it was a fucking spiky response and he didn't like it. But he had to keep sweet. 'Don't know if I am a laughing stock, more a piss head with a problem.'

The Bird Man laughed; he liked that.

Now was the time to play for something of interest. 'You have got me summed up, Mr Bentall, and quite honestly I have no power here as far as the Metropolitan Police are concerned. You are *hands off* but I expect you know that.'

The Bird Man just looked and said nothing. Of course he knew; he knew everything that went on in his town.

'I have spoken to the team watching you and said things to them to look at regarding you but they just tell me to *fuck off*. They don't trust me at all. Not many do but I am a good detective when I get going.'

The Bird Man laughed again. Jazz thought this was going quite well.

'I can't prove you had anything to do with the three murders. They were so creative and unusual we just couldn't figure out why they had been killed in that way. I've spoken to James Kent who gave me the clue that he had not only organized John Carpenter's death but that he'd stated how he was to be killed and wanted a video of it as well. That is true hatred and revenge. The same goes for Barry Jessop. No self-respecting gangster is going to bother to torture and kill someone in quite that way. There are much easier ways of doing it.'

The Bird Man nodded in agreement.

'Then there's Johnny Peters. How bloody creative can anyone get in nearly drowning him and, just as he's about to drown, the tide turns and he thinks he's saved, only to have a bloody great fucking barge motor over his head, drowning and burying him at the same time. That was all on video too. It was fucking brilliant in a terrible way. We haven't figured out who would have commissioned his murder. Peter Daly was obviously responsible for commissioning Barry Jessop.'

The Bird Man sat motionless, just listening.

'I can't prove any of this. I'm never going to be able to prove it. James Kent will never say whom he spoke to and who organized John Carpenter's death. He thinks that person is a knight in shining armour and he's never going to reveal anything. His alibi is rock solid so nothing to work on there. The same I think goes for Peter Daly. To hear from you what happened can go no further and I would just like to know how it worked.'

'Why the fuck would I talk to you about anything?' asked The Bird Man brusquely. Jazz wasn't handling this right. Those questions should come later. He needed to go on another tack. He needed to find Ash first. He needed reassurance he was still alive. He was totally convinced Ash was being held somewhere, or worse, but he wasn't going there.

'Look, I need to find Ash, my DC. I owe it to him to keep him safe. If I am a prick of the first order then Ash is my best student. I know he has *fannied* around upsetting everyone.' With an ironic smile, Jazz added, 'I don't know where he got that from!'

The Bird Man laughed at that.

'Look,' said Jazz in a placatory way, trying to get on the best side of The Bird Man, 'can you please help me to find Ash. He's a good family man with two genius children, or so he says. He loves his family and he doesn't deserve to die. If he's being held anywhere, I know it will be difficult to let him go because he might have seen someone's face, but I can keep him quiet. I promise on all that is holy and on the khanda that I will get him to look on this as a blip and we can all move on.'

The Bird Man didn't look moved by this plea.

'You're the Godfather of London, Mr Bentall. You can do anything you want and I know you can help me.' Jazz was clutching at straws now but it seemed to have a slight effect. The Bird Man liked the *Godfather of London* inference. Jazz knew he would. But it wasn't getting him anywhere with Ash. There was no sign that he could or would help. Jazz tried to put himself in The Bird Man's place and he offered sympathy for the choices he had to make. 'Perhaps,' he offered hesitantly, 'it's sometimes easier to get rid of someone than return him.' He looked at The Bird Man pointedly and The Bird Man looked back.

Jazz was beginning to sweat. He had to use his ace card and he didn't want to but nothing else was working. The Bird Man was getting bored and looked ready to tell him to leave. 'I think there is a trade-off here,' was Jazz's opening gambit.

The Bird Man raised his eyebrows and laughed at

this stupid fucker. What had he got to trade? Nothing! He was sure of that.

Jazz was on such dodgy ground. He was in The Bird Man of Barking's domain, no one knew he was there, except possibly Tom, and he was about to blackmail The Bird Man. He had to be either mad, stupid or just plain brilliant. He went for the last one, of course. With a rum smile he thought that even at this dangerous time his ego was asking for applause.

'Well?' asked the Bird Man. 'I'm waiting for this revelation.' The sarcasm was very near the top and Jazz thought he was going to wipe the smug smile of The Bird Man's face.

Jazz reminded him that he had been to Paglesham to find the barge that had drowned and buried Johnny Peters all in one go. Whilst there he had talked to a local who'd given him some very interesting information. There was aggregate being taken from the Crossrail project, which was building major new railway connections under Central London and it was brought to Wallasea Island. 'Apparently the RSPB have organized this and since 2008 aggregate has been brought from London to Wallasea to build up the land to take it above sea level, to protect the birdlife there.'

The Bird Man thanked him sarcastically for the history and asked what his point was.

'I made some little enquiries. You own B4, a transport company, and you are well known for your trucks. But very little is known about your barges. You own the barges taking the aggregate up from London to Wallasea. One: it puts you in the frame for the Johnny Peters murder. It was one of your barges that killed him. Two: I just wonder, and no one has thought about this, but I wonder how many bodies might be found on Wallasea Island if searched. A lot of people have gone missing in your part of town and no bodies have ever been found.' He could see that The Bird Man was interested now.

'It has been quite a few years that bodies could have been dumped amongst the aggregate and then spread on Wallasea Island. Who spread the aggregate on Wallasea Island? Well, bless me and all who sail in me... You seem to have the contract for diggers and dumper trucks.' Now The Bird Man was sitting up and taking note. Jazz was enjoying this. He shouldn't but he had nothing to lose now.

He went on. 'I don't care about Wallasea Island and I don't care about your barges, I don't care what might or might not be on Wallasea Island. All I will say is, beware the land gets to be so rich with nutriments that magnificent plants grow there. Someone could ask questions!' Jazz had to laugh at that, but the Bird Man was not laughing. Jazz continued, 'I care about DC Ashiv Kumar. I want him with me in one piece, alive and kicking. That's my negotiation. If not, I will become your biggest pain in the neck. I know no one listens to me and I know I have a bad reputation but believe me, if I shout long and hard enough someone will listen eventually. Now, you don't want that, do you?'

The Bird Man got up and Jazz shrank back a little, wondering what was going to happen.

The Bird Man told him to stay put: he had to go and see a man about a dog. Jazz didn't know if that meant he was going to the toilet, or if he was organizing for Jazz to be topped because he had gone too far. It could have been either. In the meantime he had space to sit and think about what he had just said to The Bird Man of Barking. The bravado and bravery left him for a minute. If nothing else he had seriously pissed him off but that wasn't what he wanted. He wanted Ash back. He patted his jacket and felt for the hip flask in his inside pocket. It was half full of that wonderful clear liquid called vodka. He gave up a prayer of thanks and spent the rest of the time just praying that Ash was safe and that he would be returned. He finished the flask too quickly and wished he had more. He didn't know what to expect when The Bird Man returned.

CHAPTER THIRTY-THREE
Let sleeping dogs lie

Ash tried to sleep. He didn't know what to make of anything. He lived in a deep, painful fear he thought he would never feel. He prayed for strength, he prayed for everything. It didn't seem to help. He'd already said goodbye to his children and his wife and his mother in his head. He had cried at the thought of never seeing his children go to university or never feeling his wife's hair again, silky and soft, smelling of flowers. He would often lie and look at her and touch her hair when she was sleeping. He realized he loved her very much. His mother could be difficult but she loved him and was so proud of him. She made him feel such a clever, brave and important man. He loved her for her confidence in him at times when he didn't have any confidence in himself.

He knew how he had got himself into this situation. He was so ashamed that he'd worked outside the rules as stipulated by the police, and it made him feel useless. What would his mother think of him when they found his body and discovered he hadn't even told his superior what he was doing and had had no back-up? His children wouldn't be proud of him later in life. They would be told their father had been a numpty and he couldn't bear that. His mind wandered and he knew his beautiful wife would be surrounded by single men there to help her through her troubled times as a widow. He wept tears of jealousy and frustration at the thought. He didn't want to die.

He got water and food at regular intervals. But he had nothing to take his mind of his situation and it was torture to him. He wondered if Jazz had noticed he wasn't around. He had no idea what the time was. The fact that he'd had a couple of meals led him to think it was the next day, at least, but he didn't know. They had taken his watch from him, his mobile, wallet and anything they found on him. He hoped the Met Police had undertaken a manhunt for him using helicopters, dogs, horses, all the street police and of course the cars. He reckoned someone would find him soon. He had no idea that his fate hung in the balance with Jazz alone and that he'd made quite a *pig's ear* of trying to find him.

Something different had happened within the last few hours. Instead of someone just coming in with food and dumping it, he was told by a voice through the closed door to turn his back and keep looking at the shuttered window until told otherwise. At first he was very scared. He wondered if he was going to be shot in the back and every instinct in his body wanted to turn around and see his attacker. The voice had made it very clear that if he did turn around it would be the last thing he ever did. So he spent his time keeping control of his urge to turn. He heard noises behind him and then the door close. He was told he could turn around again. When he looked there was fish and chips waiting for him and some water. God, he was so relieved. In fact he cried with the release of tension.

On reflection, after he had eaten, he thought that perhaps that was a good move. Why hide what he looked like if they were going to kill him. Freddie Link had shown himself to Ash but he hadn't seen Freddie Link since. He hoped – no, he had to believe – this was a good sign. Perhaps he wouldn't be killed after all. Perhaps, he thought, he was just kidding himself. Alone in the room with nothing to distract him, his mind was playing huge tricks on him and now he didn't know what to think. He was not a brave man like John Wayne. He was a normal man and not a hero type. He had almost decided to leave the police force if he ever got out of this and lived. He had had enough of danger and he was sure his wife would prefer him to have a 9-5 job. He even thought about opening a corner shop. He knew everyone would take the mickey but he would work hard and there was money to be made there. He spent many hours just trying to visualize a shop that was his and what he would sell. It kept him sane.

Hours later there was a knock at the door and he was told to turn his back and look at the shuttered window again. He did this wondering if it was more food. He didn't think it was long ago since he had his fish and chips but then time meant nothing to him at the moment. He couldn't even see if it was daylight or nighttime outside.

As he sat looking at the window someone entered the room and came up behind him. Just as Ash was about to turn around in terror, as the man had never come so close to him before, a blindfold was put over his eyes and his hands were pulled quickly behind his back and tied. Next he was gagged, as he begged his captor to let him go, saying he wouldn't tell anyone and he knew nothing. It felt like a sack had been put over his head; it was rough and smelt of shit. Before he could think he was jerked upright and told to move.

His captor said nothing; all he could hear was the heavy breathing of the person who was pushing him forward and through an open door. The fear and terror erupted and, mumbling through his gag, he tried to beg his captor to let him go. He knew he was going to be killed. There was no alternative and for a few moments he was consumed by panic. He was held tightly and he did as he was told; he had no power to break away and escape. Reality kicked in and suddenly he just gave up; he had lost his energy and hope. It felt all over and his life was gone. He moved as if in a trance. He was dead meat anyway. He repeated in his head a fervent prayer to God to keep him safe and return him to his family alive. He whimpered as he was led down some stairs, which got him a slap across his head, and he was told to *shut it*.

CHAPTER THIRTY-FOUR
If I can help somebody

The Bird Man of Barking returned. He looked comfortably resigned. Jazz hoped that was a good sign but he waited to see what he said.

Barry Bentall was in control of the situation and he would keep it that way. He told Jazz that he had made enquiries regarding DC Ashiv Kumar and where he might be. He would find out soon what the response was from his contacts. Jazz thought that sounded hopeful.

The Bird Man was about to talk more than he normally would. He was being frank with Jazz and by doing so there was an implicit agreement that the information would stay in this small room. He would put his cards on the table and clear the air. He got another two cans out of his little fridge and they enjoyed the cool sipping of Fosters lager. Jazz enjoyed it trickling down his throat and thanked The Bird Man, saying, 'A lovely drink of amber nectar.' Obviously The Bird Man didn't watch the adverts because the reference went straight over his head. He was busy thinking.

He decided that he would come clean with Jazz as long as Jazz kept away from his business interests. Jazz confirmed he had no interest in delving into anything Barry Bentall did. He reminded Barry that there was a whole team of detectives who were doing that and he wasn't going to give them a hand. They had an understanding now that wouldn't be breached.If it was breached, Barry reminded Jazz darkly, he was a dead man and that was no threat. Jazz knew he meant it and nodded seriously. He was here to get answers for his own satisfaction but more importantly he wanted Ash back, walking and talking.

The Bird Man made himself comfortable and then said abruptly, 'Barry Jessop and Peter Daly. That was the first. The police and courts are an absolute fucking joke! When do you ever dispense justice and protect the innocent?'

Jazz thought that was a tad too much pontificating on The Bird Man's part. He had to answer some of that. 'We caught Barry Jessop, we charged him and we sent him to court. The police did everything they should – it's the bloody courts that are at fault. Don't you think we get upset too when scum we've caught with good evidence to put them away get off on technicalities?'

The Bird Man gave him that. 'Okay, I won't blame the police in the same breath as the courts. Now, can I continue?'

Jazz clocked the sarcasm but decided to keep quiet. He didn't want to upset The Bird Man.

'Apparently good members of the public who felt justice hadn't been seen to be done, and wanted true justice, looked around for an alternative. They were not people to do their own dirty work, more namby-pamby office workers,' said The Bird Man with an ill-disguised disgust. 'They looked for the most powerful person in their area who could get the job done. They asked for the Godfather and they got me.' He said this with a certain amount of pride, which Jazz thought proved the ego of the man.

The Bird Man looked at Jazz. 'The strange thing is, Peter Daly didn't want him to be just murdered, he wanted torture as well. He was very specific in what he wanted doing. Personally I think he watched too many American films but hey, he paid up, and so we did the job that the police and courts should have done. We dispensed justice.'

Jazz thought that sounded a tad too Godfather-like; he wanted to ask if he stuffed handkerchiefs in his mouth to sound authentic, but checked himself quickly.

The Bird Man watched Jazz to make sure he was listening and not taking the mickey. He gave Jazz a look that meant only one thing: danger. Jazz sat up straight and assumed a deferential persona. He knew it took a long time for him to learn lessons, but now wasn't the time to push his luck in any way.

'So,' the Bird Man continued, 'James Kent was an unusual one. He came with Peter Daly to find his *knight in shining armour*. That's what James Kent called me, you know,' he said smugly. 'I never spoke directly to either of them but I got the information via one of my lads. Now Kent also wanted a special killing. He wanted John Carpenter killed specifically and he wanted a video of as much of it as he could. He hated that fucker and I don't blame him. The courts should be shot for letting that bastard escape prison. He didn't escape me, that's for sure! James Kent paid the money and we organized it. We're good at what we do.' The Bird Man said this with a lot of pride.

Jazz could see he truly did see himself as the Godfather. 'What did you charge him?'

'The going rate is £15,000 but I gave them a deal of £10,000. It cost Kent his nest egg but he would have paid more. I do have integrity and wouldn't sting the man. Peter Daly only had so much money left because the bastard Barry Jessop had taken most of it.'

Jazz didn't think The Bird Man had any integrity but he wasn't here to make judgements on his integrity. 'What about Johnny Peters and the barge? Where the fuck did that idea come from?'

The Bird Man was exceptionally proud of this one. He told Jazz that a friend of one of his men had a son who was being groomed by Johnny Peters. 'The mother came to one of my men and told him what she knew and asked for help.' This made The Bird Man exceptionally angry. 'The bastard had just got away with other stuff and he wasn't going to get away with this. I didn't get paid for this one. I did it for free.' He looked hard at Jazz. 'You don't mess with anyone I know. The idea for topping him came from the lads. They had a few drinks and thought the near-drowning and then the barge was a fucking good idea. The barges are mine and Paglesham isn't too far away.'

Pushing his face into Jazz's, he said, 'This is my community, and I do my bit of service for the community.' In the silence that followed Jazz wasn't sure whether The Bird Man of Barking was having a little joke about community service or whether he meant it. The Bird Man was staring at him and Jazz didn't know what to do so he just looked back and sort of nodded. Then the rumble started in The Bird Man's belly and travelled up into his chest and throat, coming out as raucous laughter. 'I got you there *Mr Clever Fucking Clogs*, didn't I?'

Jazz breathed a sigh of relief. So the bastard had got a sense of humour! He gave a little laugh.

The murders were solved, so to speak. Jazz had worked out most of it but he was glad to put them to bed. He didn't know what would be done with them when he got back to the office. He couldn't tell DCI Radley this story of the murders. They would just be put on the back burner. 'Are there going to be any more murders in the near future of this type?' he asked.

The Bird Man shook his head. 'Nothing going on at the moment that I am interested in so all's quiet on the Eastern Front out there.'

Jazz hoped that was true. There was enough going on without these types of murders and the press got all excited and out of control when these murders were reported.

'One more thing,' he asked. 'Who got the video for Johnny Peters' barge killing?'

The Bird Man smiled. 'Apart from You Tube?' It was another joke and the laughter was rumbling in his belly. Without waiting for an answer he added, 'The mother of the boy got a copy. She shared it with the parents of the child he fiddled with before and they have curry evenings and watch the video in slow motion.'

Jazz gulped at someone watching that video so often. There was a lot of hatred out there and he didn't blame the parents at all.

Now the six-million-dollar question. 'Is there any news on DC Ashiv Kumar yet?' He had held off asking but now he needed to know.

The Bird Man smiled and said he would go and ask. He told Jazz to wait. He seemed to be gone for a long time and Jazz was getting very jumpy. He wished he had another flask of vodka on him; he could really do with a drink now. His hands were shaking a little and he held them together in his lap to keep them calm. The Bird Man must help him and he must know something. No one would do anything in his area without his permission and if Ash was dead surely he wouldn't mess around like this. He felt very anxious and wanted to talk to Tom Black but he couldn't use his mobile in The Bird Man's room; it would be disrespectful, and he wanted Ash returned unharmed.

CHAPTER THIRTY-FIVE
The joker in the pack

After what seemed like a long time, The Bird Man came back into the room. He said he had found out some information that might be helpful. DC Ashiv Kumar had been taken by Freddie Link. The Bird Man made it known that he was not happy with this. Freddie had done this off his own back and that was not allowed. DC Kumar had been dumped behind the old B&Q building in Whalebone Lane South. It was a derelict building on a waste ground. Jazz asked if he was alive and The Bird Man shrugged. He said he didn't know. It was nothing to do with him and he'd just made noises to find him.

Jazz jumped up and said he had to go. He thanked The Bird Man respectfully. The Bird Man made him stand still and listen. 'Before you go, Singh, just remember, you leave my fucking business alone. You don't meddle in any of my legit work. What I am doing for Wallasea Island is very important to the little birds out there and the RSPB, so don't balls it up. I have given you what you want and I have found your DC – alive or dead, not sure – but you will have him. So keep your side of the bargain. I'll be watching you very closely and one wrong move and you won't be moving again. You will be very dead.' He whispered the last words and they sounded chilling.

Jazz understood and said so. The Bird Man carried on as Jazz tried to keep his patience. 'You cant prove anything I have said. You can't link me to any of the killings so don't try. If you do, I will come and get you and you will never ask me another question. You will be in your box waiting to burn.'

Jazz was convinced and scared and told The Bird Man he knew the score. He asked if he could go now and find DC Kumar. The Bird Man let go of his jacket, dusted him off, and released him.

Jazz ran outside and dialled Tom Black. When he answered Jazz shouted breathlessly that Tom needed to get a car, an ambulance, and as many officers as he could to B&Q's derelict building beside McDonald's in Whalebone Lane South.

Jazz turned on the blue flashing light and drove fast through red lights, missing old ladies dawdling as they crossed the road. After a few nifty turns, and pressing the horn more than he should, he raced along Longbridge Road through to the Fiddlers and onto Whalebone Lane South. He made it in record time and got there at the same time as Tom Black and the ambulance.

They searched the broken-down B&Q building back and front, inside and out, but there was no sign of Ash. Jazz couldn't believe it; The Bird Man wasn't going to mess him about, not with what he knew. They searched again and again. Out the back of the building there were only weeds and security fencing. To get into the B&Q building they needed to open a lock that held the fencing together. That took no time at all but there was still no sign of Ash. Jazz was sweating buckets but it wasn't sweat in his eyes that was causing the tears. They were tears of frustration. What the fuck was going on. And now the police had been called to help, everyone knew that DC Ashiv Kumar was missing. Perhaps that was no bad thing now, thought Jazz, resigned to his fate. It was his fault and he would take the consequences.

He walked off to his car and sat down away from everyone and called The Bird Man for an update. He wanted to ask, 'What the fuck is going on, you tosspot?' but he couldn't. He needed the bastard to help him. 'Mr Bentall, I am at B&Q Whalebone Lane South and DC Ashiv Kumar is nowhere to be found. Can you help, please?' He thought that adding the please at the end was a nice touch and he hoped it would work for him. The Bird Man said he would ring him back in a few minutes. Jazz sat and waited. He looked in the glove compartment of the car and found his other flask. Giving it a shake, he was relieved to feel the slosh of liquid. He quickly unscrewed the top and gulped a swig. He felt better in moments. Tom came up to the window and Jazz wound it down. Tom caught the blast of vodka as Jazz spoke, but he ignored it; they were so close to getting to Ash and that was more important. Jazz said he was waiting for a call that should tell them what the fuck was going on.

CHAPTER THIRTY-SIX
Traitor's gate

Barry Bentall saw himself as untouchable and as the Godfather of the East End. Villains and straight people alike saw him this way, and he liked it. No one went against him and got away with it. But now something had happened and he didn't know what. His man, Lionel Wood, had taken DC Ashiv Kumar to B&Q and left him there alive. Now DC Kumar wasn't at B&Q and he couldn't contact Lionel Wood. What the fucking hell was going on in his sodding town, he shouted to the muscle men he surrounded himself with, whose job it was to protect him and do his bidding. He sent four of them off to search around the area of B&Q. 'DC Kumar was left alive, so perhaps he's escaped and is wandering the streets. He could have gone into McDonald's, or gone for a piss – anything!' he shouted in exasperation. His men left quickly, knowing what The Bird Man was capable of when he was livid.

Barry Bentall paced up and down. He needed to keep Jazz on his side while he worked out what the fuck had happened.

He rang Jazz back and told him that he was looking into it but now it was in Jazz's best interests to sit back and let him find DC Kumar. He added darkly that he, Barry Bentall, had methods of finding people that the police couldn't use. He would have him ready for pick-up by tomorrow morning.

Jazz was very disappointed and bloody worried. But he dare not upset The Bird Man, who was his only lead, and he knew The Bird Man would have better resources to find out what had happened and to get Ash back. He said he would wait, and went to tell Tom Black. Tom Black wasn't happy either and he bollocked out everyone within earshot. He told the officers to pound the streets, to take their cars and to search the area bit by bit; if a cat had shat on the ground, he shouted, he wanted to know about it. Jazz and Tom went off to look for Ash themselves. They knew that if they went to the police station DCI Radley would make their lives hell, cut off their bollocks and make them go on leave until an enquiry had sorted out where he was going to bury them. There were many haunts that belonged to The Bird Man and they would go and investigate them, just in case they found anything to do with Ash. The call was put out to find Freddie Link. Jazz promised the officer who found Freddie Link in one piece would be up for a commendation. Why any officer would believe Jazz was capable of giving such an award didn't occur to anyone. Everyone wanted to find DC Ashiv Kumar alive.

Tom and Jazz stood and thought. They had dispersed all officers in all directions looking for Ash; that was now covered. Neither wanted to go back to the office. By now Jazz's phone had six text messages and three voicemail messages, all from DCI Radley, telling him to get back to Ilford Police Station before he put Jazz's name on a wanted list. DCI Radley promised to get him dragged through the streets on his arse to explain what the hell he was doing. Jazz deleted the messages and, with a pat on Tom's back, said they should be off to see what they could find out. It was very late. Jazz and Tom were tiring but they had to get a move on. The streets were covered by police looking for Ash. If the silly fucker had wandered off he would be found. For a few seconds Jazz's eyes misted. 'You stupid, tight-assed little fucker, where are you?' he asked no one in particular. He promised himself fervently he would look after him when they found him. But first he would slap him silly for getting into such trouble. 'Please God that I get that chance,' he added. Tom watched and said nothing.

Before they left they got a Big Mac and chips, and a large coffee each. It was all they would get to eat that night and hopefully the coffee would help keep them alert. They got into the car and Jazz drove to a Metro shop en route, saying he needed cigarettes. Tom could see from the car that Jazz not only bought cigarettes but also a bottle of vodka that was put into a carrier bag. He thought for a moment that a drink wasn't a bad idea – he could do with something to perk him up – but of course he wouldn't drink on duty. Knowing Jazz's drinking habits, he knew he would have to keep a watchful eye on him. Jazz paid for the cigarettes and drink and went to the toilet, where he filled up his two flasks and took a hasty swig from the bottle. The smooth firewater made him gasp and then he enjoyed the pleasure as it settled on its journey down his throat to explode his senses. The after-effect made him feel warm and comfortable and invincible: a dangerous combination, if taken in excess.

Mad Pete

The first and only person in the know whom Jazz would contact was Mad Pete. He seemed to pick up every bit of information in the area like a hoover. He picked up crap, dirt, and gossip, but he also picked up little gems of information. He might know what was going on. He wasn't answering his phone, which was a sign that he was scared of something. They drove at speed to Gascoigne Estate. Tom waited in the car and watched out for scumbags who might try and take the wheels or break into the car, while Jazz made his way up to Mad Pete's flat. He knocked many times but there was no response. He knelt down and shouted through the letter box that *if Pete didn't fucking open the door now he would kick the bastard's door down and then kick him in the arse so hard his tonsils would say hello to his testicles.* A reluctant Mad Pete mumbled from the other side of the door that *it was late and he was in bed.* With another threat from Jazz he mumbled *all right, he would open up.* Jazz waited impatiently as the one hundred and one bolts were undone. He was getting madder and madder, telling Mad Pete to *hurry up, as he was wasting valuable time.*

Once inside he told Mad Pete that DC Ashiv Kumar was missing, that Freddie Link had him and that Ash was supposed to be left at the derelict B&Q building in Dagenham but he wasn't there. It looked like The Bird Man didn't know where he was either. Jazz looked at the miscreant before him, all greasy-haired, wearing a filthy T-shirt and jeans with indescribable stains, slouching in front of him. Why on earth had he thought he would know anything. Mad Pete didn't look as if he had the energy to move, let alone listen at doors for gossip.

Jazz frowned and said, 'I thought you said you were in bed? Do you go to bed in your clothes, for God's sake?' Mad Pete just shuffled in response. Jazz gave up getting an answer to that and asked what was going on at the moment with DC Kumar; what had he heard?

As usual Mad Pete started with, 'I know nuffink, Mr Singh. Why do you always ask me these things? I'll get killed if I talk about things to you.' That told Jazz he knew something. He hoped it was something to do with Ash.

'What the fuck is going on, Mad Pete? I need to know. Ash hasn't done you any harm. He's a nice guy, he needs our help. Just tell me what you know and I will, as always, protect you, you know that. What is happening out there?'

Mad Pete started with a whine. 'I ain't never any problem to no one. I don't know why I am always in the wrong place at the wrong time. I was on my rounds. I was in the Cherry Tree Pub just dropping off a little something for someone and there was this fella in the pub I didn't know but he was giving it large and waltzing around. I just hid in the toilets cos I could see he was trouble and I didn't like the look of what was going on. Someone called him Vinnie – not Vinnie Jones the actor, Mr Singh, but Vinnie James. The only Vinnie

James I know of comes from the South London gang run by Eddie Grimshaw and his Grimshaw Boys. They are a vicious lot. Eddie Grimshaw rules from the Thamesmead Estate through Kidbrooke to Eltham. It's tough there; no one moves in that place without guns and knives and it's full of psychopaths. That's why I hid in the toilet. I left when it was safe and went to The Pig and Poke. I was taking a little smack for Freddie Link but he wasn't there, nor was George.'

'So, what does that mean?' asked Jazz.

'I dunno, Mr Singh. After a while I left,' Mad Pete said, but Jazz knew he was lying. *God, why has it always got to be such a long, hard, fucking difficult road getting information out of Mad Pete*, he asked himself. He got up and slapped Mad Pete around the head. Mad Pete grabbed his head and moaned that he didn't deserve it. 'Tell me the truth, otherwise there is trouble,' Jazz threatened him.

Mad Pete knew he would never get away with staying quiet, and it was getting a bit dodgy being so close to so many dangerous people. He got a bottle of Coke and offered Jazz a swig, which was readily declined with the comment, 'No thanks, I haven't had a tetanus update yet.' Mad Pete gave him a look and swigged from the bottle. Jazz took out one of his hip flasks and took a swig from that. Mad Pete was about to say something catty like *so you have a bad habit too* but he caught the warning glint in Jazz's eye and backed off.

'Freddie Link and George bundled someone out of the pub the back way late that night. Now I come to think of it, it could have been your DC Kumar. I watched and guess what? When I looked outside I saw Vinnie James was watching from his car. When Freddie Link and George and the fella they grabbed left in the car, Vinnie James followed them. That's all I know, Mr Singh. I thought it looked strange.'

Jazz asked why he hadn't told him about seeing what was surely DC Kumar and Mad Pete shrugged his shoulders; he said that he didn't know there was anything wrong and maybe it wasn't him. That was a lie too, but Jazz let it go for the moment. 'Vinnie James from South London followed Freddie Link and George. Why?' He turned to Mad Pete and asked incredulously, 'How the fuck are you always in the right place at the right time? I suppose no one saw you either, did they?'

Proudly, Mad Pete said, 'No, Mr Singh, I am invisible. It's just a talent of mine.'

Jazz thought they might not have seen him but, boy, they should have been able to smell him. He sniffed at Mad Pete. ''Bout time you took a bath, don't you think?'

Mad Pete, affronted by such a comment, said, 'That's not necessary, Mr Singh. No one else complains.'

This made Jazz laugh but his face turned sour when he remembered that Mad Pete maybe knew about Ash and hadn't told him. He had to ask the right question to get an answer. He didn't want Mad Pete to go into one of his druggy fits so sorting him out would wait for now. 'Do you know anything else? Do you know where they took the person who must have been DC Kumar?'

Mad Pete shook his head.

'Okay,' thought Jazz: another question. 'Do you know where someone would be kept? Does The Bird Man have safe houses locally?'

Mad Pete said the only one he knew was a place above his storage unit in Bow. It was on the Industrial Estate there and it was a quiet place to keep someone. Again Jazz looked at him. 'How the fuck do you know this, when the Met Police haven't got a clue about this place?'

Mad Pete looked smug. 'I'm brilliant, that's why.'

Jazz gave him a playful slap but told Mad Pete in no uncertain terms, 'You ain't as clever as you think. Don't leave out information in future. If anything has happened to DC Kumar I will hold you responsible.' Mad Pete protested how unfair that was but Jazz just told him, 'Life isn't fair, arse-wipe! Remember that in future.'

He made his way to the car where Tom was sitting, bored and almost nodding off. He told him about Vinnie James and the storage unit. Tom put out a search for Vinnie James and made it urgent. They talked it through and wondered why Vinnie James was in the East End of London. There hadn't been any intelligence that he was in the area. It was quite brazen of him to be in East London, and Jazz wondered aloud why Freddie Link wasn't aware of him being there, and why he hadn't fronted up to him. *What the fuck was going on*?

They made their way to Bow which took a very short time. By now it was 1 a.m. and although there was traffic on the road they passed it easily with the blue light on. Jazz was getting very tired but the adrenalin was keeping him going. They received an update from officers to say there was no sighting of DC Kumar. Another call confirmed that no one had seen Freddie Link.

They got a call to say that George had been found in the local morgue. He had been killed by a runaway car in an area that had no CCTV and the car hadn't stopped. They both knew that was a big coincidence. Again, they asked what the hell was going on. If Freddie Link was missing and George was dead, they knew The Bird Man was behind it. As he said, *nothing happened in his town without his permission.* But the rub was DC Ashiv Kumar was missing and The Bird Man didn't know where he was. Jazz was beginning to go into a deep depression. It was after midnight and he had a meeting at 1 p.m. with DCI Radley; he wanted to go there with DC Ashiv Kumar and tell Radley how they had made a big arrest. At the moment it felt *chance would be a fine thing!* He needed to find Ash and there was only going to be one way to do that. He was going to work with The Bird Man.

CHAPTER THIRTY-SEVEN
Help cometh

The Bird Man was beside himself with fury and frustration. Something had gone very wrong in his town. Where was Lionel Wood, for God's sake? He promised he would do something creative with him when he found him. His men reported in every ten minutes as requested but they had nothing to tell.

Jazz had a number for The Bird Man on his phone. He just looked up incoming calls and The Bird Man had rung him. He dialled the number, which startled The Bird Man, who wondered where the hell Jazz had got his number. The Bird Man wasn't at ease with being in this position. Jazz told him that Vinnie James was in the area and that he had followed Freddie Link and George when they took DC Kumar. He added that he hadn't got a clue where Vinnie James was.

The Bird Man put the phone down and thought for a second. His roar of *Get me Ian Long now!* rang through the room. It took thirty minutes for Ian Long to appear. Although He had dressed quickly, there was no sense of rush about him. He walked into the room surrounded by an aura of calm, dressed immaculately in a dark suit. His demeanour was sophisticated and his appearance was that of a male model: tall, straight, slim, with a light elegant walk. Some had wondered if he was gay but Ian Long never gave anyone the opportunity of asking such a personal question. He had a cruel look with thin lips, piercing light-blue eyes, and jet black hair, which was dramatically slicked back in a forties style with a sharp widow's peak. He smoked long black cigarettes and viewed from a distance he looked upper class, even like a foreign prince. Then he would open his mouth and all would be revealed. 'I presume this is fucking urgent, guv?' He was Hackney-born and bred, and he was born without a conscience; any self-respecting psychiatrist would have him diagnosed as a psychopath.

'I need you to find Vinnie James from the South London mob. He's pinched a DC Ashiv Kumar from me. I was going to give him back alive and kicking to the police and he's been stolen. I want to know where, why, and how, and I want to ask him in person. I want this fucking DC to be found alive so I can give him back to the police and get on with my sodding work. This is all pissing me off and I want it done.'

Ian Long understood and said he would be back soon. He was used sparingly, as The Bird Man of Barking's Exocet missile. He was paid huge amounts of money for his services. Ordinary killings or little threats were dealt with by his lads but anything that required that extra-special expertise and skill was given to Ian Long. He was feared by many and was commissioned to work for The Bird Man only in London. They had a history from the early days and The Bird Man was intelligent enough to know that if he didn't pay Ian

Long a good retainer, he could be on the receiving end of Long's skills.

Ian Long knew everything there was to know about the gangs in London. He had studied them, been approached by them, and killed some of them. Many gangs would like to see him topped but he was too clever for them and kept a low profile when it suited him. The police had no idea of who he was and he intended to keep it that way. He was an ice cold killer and took no prisoners. He was greatly feared by those in the know in London. He was perfect for finding Vinnie James and hopefully DC Kumar.

The Bird Man knew DC Kumar had to have been kidnapped by Vinnie James. He wanted to know what had stirred up Eddie Grimshaw to have the nerve to send someone to his area, and the audacity to pinch a Police Detective from under their noses. Someone was going to pay dearly for this dishonour. It was an unwritten rule that South and East had their own manors and each would never intrude without permission. It was all about respect but it was also all about keeping turf wars to a minimum. Both were businessmen and both didn't want the mess and time and loss of money that turf wars created. The Metropolitan Police was the bane of their lives and they kept them as far away from them as possible. Any fights going on would bring them more to the attention of the police and that wasn't going to happen. For years they had made sure that any work was carved up so that South and East didn't overlap. It had worked well and there had been a relative calm between them.

Now the Bird Man knew it would get sorted. Ian Long would never let him down and soon he would know what the fucking hell was going on. He relaxed a little for the first time that day. He rang Jazz and told him all was good. He told Jazz to wait and he would come back to him in a short time with his DC Kumar. The Birdman was tired now. London should be sleeping at this hour but whilst they slept things were happening out there that would have repercussions later.

CHAPTER THIRTY-EIGHT
The baying hound

When you took on Ian Long, you didn't have to wait for the action. Long didn't mess around. He left The Bird Man and went straight to South London in his black Mercedes-Benz S 600 Guard limo. It looked immaculate and classy, but was discreet enough not to come to the attention of either police or scumbags.

Its armour resisted military-standard small-arms projectiles and provided protection against fragments from hand grenades and other explosive devices. Additional safety features included run-flat tyres, a self-sealing fuel tank and a fire-extinguishing system. When buying cars, Ian Long didn't deal with salesmen; he went straight to the top and spoke only to a director. He was told quite proudly that the Mercedes-Benz S600 Guard was the car of choice for up and coming dictators of small African countries. He told the Director that if it was good enough for those bastards, it would serve his needs.

The car had cost him *an arm and a leg* but it was so worth it, and besides he could afford it. Once inside his car nothing could touch him. The smell of leather, the feel of the steering wheel, the car purred. He loved his

Mercedes-Benz and took pride in the elegant lines and the luxury and safety it afforded. It was a mans' car and he was a mans' man. He relaxed back into a seat that could have been moulded for his shape only.

Before he got to the Blackwall tunnel he made a few phone calls and got the information he needed. He knew the gang Vinnie James belonged to. Mr Eddie Grimshaw was the boss.

Eddie had a family name of Grimshaw that used to resonate with a good, wholesome honest business history. Many years ago the Grimshaws were big in the Midlands, near Barnsley. When Eddie's great-grandfather came to London in the 1930s as the black sheep of the family, the South London dynasty started. They started in the scrap yards and made a fortune during the Second World War when metals were needed. They were used car salesmen and in their spare time they funded bank raids and attacks on Securicor vans. They were proud to be known as the first gang to rip out an ATM machine, affectionately known as a *hole in the wall machine*, from a bank in Greenwich High Street and they took the money. They were a hard, tough gang in an area that was lawless but such was their reputation, no one would touch them in South London.

Ian Long arrived in a short time in a street on the Thames Mead Estate. Sitting in his car, he felt inside his jacket to where his holster snuggled neatly. It held his Glock 22 handgun. It was his preferred weapon: light, comfortable to hold, and accurate, and with a fifteen-round clip and one up the spout he was always ready for action. He was in good company; it was the gun issued to American police and allegedly to MI5 personnel in England. Ian Long was a professional and only the best would do. He was paid a small fortune for his talent and his brains.

He looked in his mirrors before getting out of his car. The street was empty and quiet. Most were sleeping at this unearthly hour. He locked his car and quickly went on his way.

Vinnie James was asleep in an armchair in a flat in a high-rise block on the Thames Mead Estate. The TV was on and all that could be heard was pre- recorded laughter at some antics going on in a programme not worthy of daytime TV. The lights in the room were dim and all that could be seen was the flashing light from the TV onto Vinnie's sleeping face. It was peaceful for the moment.

Ian Long stood outside the door and listened to Vinnie's snoring. He had no time for words. It was like a whirlwind. The door was knocked down, a punch to the face stunned Vinnie, and his arms were pulled behind him and handcuffs smartly put on. Then his feet were tied. In a matter of what felt like seconds, Vinnie James went from comfortably snoozing to being punched, thrown on the floor and trussed up like a turkey. It took Ian a matter of moments to find out that DC Ashiv Kumar was in another room, waiting to be processed by the Grim Brothers who were arriving first thing in the morning. This information caused Vinnie James to lose one ear and three front teeth. He literally didn't know what had hit him and the pain left him breathless and frightened. He had never experienced anyone as coldly focused as this man. He knew he would do whatever he had to do to get information, and Vinnie James was not that brave.

DC Kumar was awake and, hearing the commotion, lay shaking with fear. He had gone from ice-cold certainty that he would be killed to being led to a car and brought to this place. He didn't know where he was and he still had the sack over his head so he could see nothing; he just knew he was still alive and being kept for something. His nerves were shot and it was just the adrenalin of it all that had kept him a fraction above going raving mad.

Ian Long grabbed DC Kumar, kicked Vinnie James into a standing position, and shuffled them both down to the lift and out to his car. He put them in the back seat and checked they couldn't move. He blindfolded Vinnie James and gagged him quickly. Once inside his car with the doors locked, he knew they were safe and no one could get to them. Relaxing, he put some music on; he had a CD of Bill Withers which was his favourite. Mindful of police looking out for drunk drivers at this hour of the morning, Ian Long drove carefully and legally back to East London and to The Bird Man of Barking. His mission had been accomplished with little fuss or trouble. Daylight would bring its own problems but for now he had done his job.

CHAPTER THIRTY-NINE
Dog tired

Jazz, tired by now and not able to do anything else, dropped Tom Black at his home in Chadwell Heath and went home for a couple of hours sleep. He crawled quietly into De Vere Gardens. The house was dark and quiet. He checked his watch and saw it was 3 a.m. He knew he wouldn't get long. He took an urgent swig of vodka from the bottle and settled down on his bed. No time to get undressed: he fell immediately asleep.

Something was annoying him in his sleep. It was a bleep, a buzz or something, and it lived on the periphery of his dream of a stormy sea, where he was being tossed about in a small boat. He was urgently trying to reach someone shouting for help but every time he rowed towards the person a wave pushed him further away. He was stressed and frustrated, and all he could hear was a sodding bleep. Suddenly he woke up and looked towards the noise. His phone was buzzing and bleeping. It was the alarm clock on his phone telling him it was 7.30 a.m. and time to get up. He phoned Tom and told him he would be with him in half an hour. With that he brushed his teeth, brushed himself down trying to pull out the creases he had caused by sleeping in his clothes, and took himself off to Tom's pad.

He reminded Tom that he had a meeting with DCI Radley at 1 p.m. and he badly needed news of Ash. Tom looked at the man in front of him, bedraggled, tired, worried and worn down by the guilt of being responsible for Ash being in this position. It was difficult to be upbeat, but Tom tried cajoling Jazz into a more optimistic way; he was too far down the path of the damned, however, to appreciate any help. Jazz checked his phone for any messages but at that moment there were none.

Tom checked his phone and he had a message to ring the station. One of his men had updated news on Vinnie James. He left Jazz to make a cup of coffee for them both while he went into another room to ring in. His men had found out where Vinnie James lived and sent surveillance there this morning. They had been in place since 6 a.m. and reported nothing until just now. The Brothers Grim, all three of them, appeared about 8 a.m. and after a short while all hell seemed to let loose. They ran out of the flats, looked around, jumped into their car and took off like bats out of hell. Just then three large and suspicious-looking men had appeared in a big van and walked into the flats. The officers were waiting to see what happened next. No one had seen Vinnie James or Ashiv Kumar.

Tom, head bowed in thought, went back to Jazz with the news. It was worrying and Jazz urgently asked why no one had gone to the flat and seen what had happened there. He was almost ready to get up and leave and had hold of his coat. 'Where the fuck are you going?' Tom asked, startled to see Jazz get up and ready to go. Jazz answered that at least if he was in South London he could look around, get some help, search the flat, threaten some *scrot* for information, and find Ash. Tom stopped him and told him to stop being so fucking stupid. He was getting angry now. 'What are you, bloody Superman? Just remember, Jaswinder Singh, you are an arsehole of a Detective Sergeant in the Metropolitan Police Force and that is all. One wrong move could get Ash killed if we screw this up.' He mumbled under his breath, 'If he's not dead already,' and Jazz gave him a look of resignation.

Tom took a deep breath and then a sip of his coffee. Again, he said that they needed to speak to The Bird Man to see what he knew. He said that his money was on The Bird Man getting Ash back. It would be in his interests. 'Something rotten has happened in our town and Ashiv Kumar has got in the middle of it, the stupid fucking bastard!'

Jazz agreed and took out his hip flask for a deep swig.

'I bet that's not orange juice!' Tom muttered. Jazz smiled for the first time and said he needed it today. Tom nodded; there was nothing to add.

He put a friendly arm around Jazz and patted him on the back. 'Come on, you silly sod of a Sikh, let's ring The Bird Man and see what he's come up with. Then we can decide what our next move is going to be.'

CHAPTER FORTY
You know it makes sense

The Bird Man was woken by one of his men. He had told all six of them that as soon as a message, telephone call or the man himself arrived, they were to wake him immediately and it didn't matter what time it was. At 4.30 a.m. Ian Long arrived at the safe house The Bird Man had in Becton. In his possession he had an alive and kicking DC Kumar and a Vinnie James slightly damaged and softened up ready for interrogation.

First things first. The Bird Man wanted to talk to Vinnie James. He wanted Ian Long to stay and assist him. DC Kumar was put in a spare room and left there, trembling and crying. He still couldn't see with the sack over his head and he said he needed to pee. One of the men took him to the toilet and suggested he must have a tiddler if he needed to look for it; with a light slap around the head he was told the sack stayed where it was. By now Ash was getting thirsty, hungry, and had a roaring headache. He kept going from hot to cold; one minute he was thinking he was being taken to be killed and the next he was put in a room and suddenly felt comparatively safe. He was not made of strong stuff and he babbled more and more.

Vinnie James knew he was in trouble. The blindfold was off and in front of him was Barry Bentall, The Bird Man of Barking, looking none too pleased. Beside him was the maniac he'd encountered in his flat and that one scared him nearly as much as The Bird Man. He knew The Bird Man's reputation. Vinnie James had always been a bit of a show-off. Eddie Grimshaw quite liked him and had known him for many years and trusted him. The Brothers Grim thought he was an arsehole and past his sell-by date, but their dad still ruled the roost and they didn't dare touch him.

In truth, Vinnie James was all hot air. He ran errands for Eddie Grimshaw and did his bidding. He wasn't a clever man; he just thought he was. Eddie Grimshaw had sent Vinnie to East London to sort out the rumours he was hearing. He heard that The Bird Man of Barking was calling himself *THE GODFATHER* and that pissed him off big-time. There had always been a bit of fairly friendly rivalry between the two men. Jealousy was not something either would say was an appropriate description but in essence each wanted to be the biggest, the best, the most feared, the richest, the smartest, the most everything. The Bird Man calling himself THE GODFATHER was just a tad too much for Eddie Grimshaw to stomach. Vinnie was to check out what was happening. Eddie had heard about the Barge Murder and knew it was The Bird Man. They kept tabs on each other. The fact that Vinnie was in the right place at the right time was very fortunate.

Someone had told Vinnie about the other murders and how DC Ashiv Kumar was causing trouble for Freddie Link. He watched and saw how Freddie Link had taken the detective and was bundling him into a car and taking him somewhere. Now he knew that was a very naughty thing to do; he smiled as he tutted. You just didn't mess about with a Metropolitan Detective; it was too much of a pain in the neck. Kill them, yes, but don't keep them prisoner. He thought Freddie Link was a total dipstick. But then he thought he could use this. The Bird Man of Barking was a bighead and anything that happened in his town was down to him, everyone knew that.

He waited and watched. He saw Lionel Wood, another numpty in his book, coming out with DC Kumar with a sack over his head. He got out of his car and shot Lionel – well, that might have been a bit extreme but he was on the enemy's territory and he didn't want Lionel causing any problems with his getaway. He bundled a quivering DC Kumar into his car and had it away to his flat.

On the way to Thames Mead, Vinnie phoned Eddie Grimshaw who was interested in what Vinnie had done – until, that is, he heard how he had shot Lionel Wood. His anger knew no bounds. He knew the pinching of DC Kumar was a cheeky little bit of duplicity – but killing Lionel Wood, a smalltime numpty but nevertheless a man from The Bird Man of Barking's gang, would not be forgiven. Eddie told Vinnie to go to his flat, keep DC Kumar secure and wait for his sons to arrive in the morning. They were going to sort this mess out. Vinnie was a little worried but not worried enough to stop him having a few beers and snoozing in his chair watching TV. The Brothers Grim could be a bit unruly but he always got on with them. Their dad, Eddie, liked him and kept him safe. He had no worries.

Unbeknown to Vinnie, Eddie had spoken to his sons and said that, in order to stop a full-scale war erupting between South and East, Vinnie had to go. What were they were going to do with a fucking Detective Constable on their manor? They would have to work on that one. The first thought was to top him and get rid of him. He was nothing but a dangerous nuisance to them. DC Kumar would have been proud to know that he was turning out to be like a piece of shit on the bottom of your shoe; however much you tried to get rid of it, it stuck and caused problems.

If Vinnie only knew he was between a rock and a hard place, and both wanted to kill him! Not for one moment did he Vinnie consider Eddie would get rid of him and he'd never thought The Bird Man would call out Ian Long. Everyone knew of Ian Long but he was used for special reasons, and Vinnie never thought he was worth an Ian Long callout. He'd totally misjudged that one.

With the help of Ian Long, Vinnie told all and more to The Bird Man of Barking. By the end of the interrogation Vinnie, bloodied and in pain, left The Bird Man with a massive problem. He knew the fucker Eddie Grimshaw and his shitty sons were causing him headaches, and something needed to be done. The pillock of a detective was safe and blubbering in the next room and would be sorted soon. Ian Long left knowing his bank account was about to be increased by a decent sum of money and he went home, wherever that was. No one knew exactly where he lived; he preferred it that way.

The Bird Man, furious and frustrated, sat down and thought for a moment. He told one of his men to watch Vinnie and went into another room to make a phone call. Calm now, he rang Eddie Grimshaw. The introductions were congenial; both men were respectful and friendly. They made some small talk and moaned about the brainless buggers that they had to work with. They skirted the issues for a while and then The Bird Man told Eddie that shooting Lionel Wood was not necessary. Vinnie James shot dead Lionel Wood and stole a Detective Constable and someone had to pay for that. Eddie feigned surprise and shock at such happenings and argued that Vinnie wouldn't do such a thing. They both knew that each of them was playing games.

Eddie countered that The Bird Man was getting a bit big for his boots these days, with all the Godfather talk. The Bird Man smiled to himself; he knew that had got to Eddie and that pleased him. He asked Eddie which Godfather act was he referring to and Eddie talked about the Barge Murder of Johnny Peters. Again The Bird Man smiled to himself. It felt good to know his works were known in the South of London. He told Eddie that he had Vinnie and he had the detective back. What should he do with Vinnie? Of course Eddie said to give him back to him and he would sort him out. The Bird Man didn't want that. He had a much better idea.

He was going to get rid of Vinnie in retaliation for Lionel Wood. He would tell the police that Vinnie was responsible for videoing the Barge Murder and he could make that stick. He traded with Eddie that, on the back of Vinnie getting the blame for the Barge Murder, Eddie would be known by locals and anyone of importance as the 'Godfather' who'd arranged it. The Bird Man wanted to be generous to Eddie and give him some kudos. He added it was his gift to Eddie (which sounded just like a Godfather saying). There was no need for any further misunderstandings between them and no bad blood. Eddie argued sufficiently to show loyalty to one of his boys, but he was going to top Vinnie anyway so why not let Barry Bentall do it. After arguing halfheartedly for a while, Eddie caved in and said it would be a just and honourable solution to the little problem. Each had lost one of their boys. They agreed Eddie would call off his sons and The Bird Man would call off his boys and Ian Long.

All was settled. A turf war may have been averted for the time being, but both would be on their guard for quite some time. Neither wanted to start a gang war. It was going to be tense in East and South London, and everyone would be warned not to fart in the wrong place.

The Bird Man rang Tommy, the hitman who got rid of Freddie Link. 'Tommy, I want you here now, and bring Freddie's huge ring with you.' Tommy argued that he never took nothing from Freddie when he topped him. The Bird Man said calmly, 'Oh yes you did, Tommy. I know you. If you don't get your arse here in under ten minutes I am going to fucking break your neck, comprendi?'

Tommy comprendi-ed well and was on his way with the ring.

Half an hour later The Bird Man arranged for Tommy to take Vinnie off his manor and top him. He said he was to be subtle; Tommy could be a bit messy sometimes and he wanted just a body with an assassin's bullet in him. This would be poignant and apt – so one to the chest and one in the head. He gave instructions to put Freddie's ring on Vinnie's finger when topped. Tommy had specific instructions to leave the body of Vinnie in Rainham marshes. Far enough away from The Bird Man's manor but close enough to call in the Metropolitan Police. He didn't want Vinnie found too quickly; he wanted to announce it to the police and let the bastards find him.

All that was left now was to get rid of the fucking pain in the neck of a detective. He thought again about killing him but decided to present him to Jazz in return for his keeping schtum on his business projects in Wallasea. He ordered his men to take DC Kumar to Parsloes Park and get him there by 11 a.m. on the dot: not a minute earlier or later. Ash was being moved again and this was very frightening. He didn't want to go; he felt safe where he was. He thought they would kill him if he got moved. He had been moved so many times and each time had roused in him a heart-stopping, panic-stricken fear of being killed. Getting him out of the room and down to the car was difficult. The stupid bastard kept kicking and making noises. He was sure that this time they were going to kill him. One of the Bird Man's men got a kick in the groin and considered topping him there and then, but The Bird Man would not have liked that.

CHAPTER FORTY-ONE
Pieces of the puzzle

Having sorted everything out, The Bird Man sat and drank a hot tea given to him. He asked for a couple of biscuits. He needed a few moments of thought about the next step. He smiled to himself. He was a clever bastard and he would make that snot-nosed DS Singh dance to his tune now. He finished his tea and biscuits, got up and went to his car. His driver, always on duty, gave a quick look around to make sure no one was about and opened the car door as soon as he saw The Bird Man leave the building. The move into the car was slick and quick; you could never be too careful, it was the driver's job to ensure The Bird Man's safety, and he took his job very seriously indeed.

It was 9.30 a.m. and The Bird Man sat in his car. With everything in place he rang Jazz. He told him to come to his office in Barking by 10 a.m. and no later. He had the news he was waiting for. Jazz asked urgently if he had got Ash Kumar and whether he was alive, but The Bird Man had already put the phone down; he wasn't going to answer that question. Jazz and Tom jumped into their car and, hitting the blue light and sirens, made their way to The Bird Man's office on the Riverside Industrial Estate in record time.

The Bird Man wouldn't talk in front of Tom Black. One of his henchmen put his bulk in front of Tom and suggested he might like to go back to the car and wait. Tom wasn't going to argue; he said good luck to Jazz and that he would wait for him in the car. With a nod, Jazz walked forward to the warehouse that was the office of Barry Bentall, The Bird Man of Barking and B4 Transport Managing Director extraordinaire. His haulage fleet was impressive. The trucks and trailers were lined up in a row, gleaming green with 'B4 Transport' in big red letters on the sides of the trailers. There had to be at least twenty of them lined up and ready to go. Jazz was escorted to the entrance that also had big 'B4 Transport' lettering above the door.

Barry Bentall sat in his huge revolving leather armchair. The outside looked like a warehouse but the room that was his office was done out in light oak and tastefully decorated as befitting a Managing Director. Jazz looked and thought ruefully that crime for slime balls definitely paid! Barry Bentall gestured to the small chair in front of his desk and Jazz sat down meekly. He just wanted Ash back and, with fingers crossed, he asked the question.

Barry Bentall, MD of one of the largest transport companies in Great Britain, currently known as The Bird Man of Barking, and as The Godfather in the East End by all criminals and some members of the public, the bane of the Metropolitan Police, sat smugly looking at this lump of shit before him.

He moved slightly in his chair, causing a creaking and groaning of the finest leather. Jazz waited expectantly.

'I've sorted everything and you are just going to listen,' said The Bird Man. 'Remember this, you owe me big time. I'm not only giving you back a live DC Kumar – which makes a bloody change for your record…'

Jazz squirmed at this but sat upright at the good news.

'But,' continued The Bird Man, 'I am also going to solve the Barge Murder for you. I will tell you the name of the person who did it and where you can find him.'

Jazz said nothing but wondered what the fuck The Bird Man could tell him. He already knew it was The Bird Man himself who'd organized the murder of Johnny Peters, and that Freddie Link was there and responsible. The Metropolitan Police were still looking for Freddie who seemed to have disappeared.

Again, Barry Bentall moved in his chair. He was tired; it had been a long night. He had to get this finished now. 'First things first. You listen good. The person who organized the killing of Johnny Peters, the paedophile, was Vinnie James. I have found out that he used my barge and tried to implicate me. You will know it is Vinnie because he wears the distinctive ring you saw in the video.'

Jazz said that he knew that belonged to Freddie Link.

'Nah, nah, Freddie didn't have such a ring. It always belonged to Vinnie James. When you see Vinnie you will clock the ring on his finger. Vinnie's South London gang got a bit naughty and tried to place me and my boys as the killers. That ain't working. You will find Vinnie in Rainham. He was a naughty boy and pissed off someone and they topped him. He is on Rainham marshes. When you leave here get someone to find him.'

Jazz saw the game and knew what had happened. He would go along with it. It would be a result for him and Tom in the statistics and would clear one murder on the manor. It kept The Bird Man out of it.

'Now I come to that piss head of a fucking bollocking pain in the arse of a Detective Constable of yours. He has got right up my nose. He has been everywhere tonight and it took a lot of work and money on my part to get him back. I worked hard for you, Singh, getting him back alive. I want you to remember that. It makes a bloody change for you to have a live one back; they're usually stiff by the time you find them.' Barry Bentall started the rumble in his belly and by the time it reached his throat and came out as a low laugh, Jazz had digested what he said and sat back with relief.

'So where is he?' asked Jazz.

'Not so fast. I need something from you first before I tell you.' The Bird Man wanted something back for all his hard work. Never mind it was his man who started it and kidnapped DC Kumar. He had, after all, commissioned his Exocet missile of a man, Ian Long, to find him and get him back. He would keep Jazz's job for him and get him a bit of praise for still having a detective on his team alive and kicking, but also he had found the killer of the Barge Murder. Apart from that The Bird Man had lost sleep getting all this done and he wasn't going to lose any more.

Jazz interrupted. Although it was hard to say – he didn't want to jeopardise the possibility of getting Ash back safely – he had to say it. In a pious tone he said, 'I wont do anything illegal for you. I will not be your puppet or a grass. I am a police officer and I am honest.'

The Bird Man looked at him for a second in surprise and then let out a loud bellowing spray of laughter that went on and on. Jazz found this quite disconcerting and didn't know why The Bird Man had found what he'd said so funny. The Bird Man wiped his eyes, blew his nose and, between bubbles of laughter that just wouldn't go away, he tried to pull himself together. 'God! I needed that. That's the funniest thing I've heard for ages.'

Put out and quite aggrieved, Jazz asked, 'What the hell is so funny?' It never occurred to him that everyone knew he worked in a way that was close to the edge. He got results and put the villains away. He certainly would never go over the side and be a villain's pet.

The Bird Man told him to shut up and listen. Jazz raised his eyebrows in surprise but agreed to do what The Bird Man said. It was a promise – after he had found Ash, of course. He said he would come back later with the result. The Bird Man, satisfied by this, told Jazz to get to Parsloes Park at 11 a.m. sharp, and wait. DC Kumar would be deposited there for him to collect.

With many thanks Jazz looked at his watch. It was seven minutes to eleven and it was going to be touch and go to get there in time. He raced out of The Bird Man's office and shouted to Tom to fire up the Batmobile – they were off to get Ash in Parsloes Park. With no further ado, catchy sayings or *what part of Parsloes Park*, Tom Black screeched the car into hyperspeed and put on the blue lights and the siren. They were going to get there in time if it killed them.

It was a quiet time for Parsloes Park. The kids were in school – okay, some of the kids were in school – and for some it was still early. The sight of the five Panda police cars screeching to a halt in Parsloes Avenue and three motorbike police turning up, with four police on bicycles scouring the park, was a bit of a surprise for most residents. A small crowd started to gather as things got more interesting. All the Panda cars had their blue lights flashing and then a car arrived with siren going full blast and a flashing blue light. Jazz and Tom jumped out of their car and checked their watches. It was 11 a.m. and they had made it. They looked around, not knowing what to do first or where to go.

On the other side of the park a car had pulled up and something had been thrown from the rear door. Jazz was the first to run forward. It was a long way to the other side but he ran like the wind. An officer on a bike was already there and he was looking at someone in a sack writhing on the ground. Muffled words were coming from the sack. Jazz pushed the officer out of the way and pulled the sack off the person's head. He looked hard: yes, it was Ash.

Jazz pulled off the gag and rubbed Ash's cheeks, which must have been stiff and sore.

'Ash, Ash, thank God you're safe! You have no idea what everyone has been through to get to you.' Jazz was emotional. The shock of seeing Ash looking so pathetic but alive made him realize how much this man must have had to cope with. Ash was crying. He kept saying he'd thought he was going to be killed and he couldn't believe he was alive.

Jazz untied Ash's hands and feet and rubbed them. The poor man must have been tied up for days. An ambulance was called and it took Ash away. Jazz told Tom he would go to the hospital later but in the meantime, they needed to go to Rainham Marshes and find Vinnie James. Together with a couple of vans full of officers they made their way to Rainham. It didn't take them long to find Vinnie James' body. It had been dumped close to the road.

'Get out of my fucking way, you prick!' The dulcet tones rang out across the marshes, directed at some poor young officer.

'Bloody hell, Jenny, how did you get here so fast?' Jazz was glad to have her there.

'Someone has to sodding well get here before you ruin the evidence,' was Jenny's loving response. Jazz always felt better when she was around. He knew she would get everything done quickly and he knew she was sweet on him so he would get the results quickly. She was the best Scenes of Crime Officer (SOCO) in the Met and nothing got past her. 'Is there anything you can tell me straight away?' he asked.

'Yes. He's bloody dead! Will that do for now?'

Jazz had to smile; he nodded and said he would leave her to it for now.

CHAPTER FORTY-TWO
Did they live happily ever after?

Jazz felt like a *blue-arsed fly*, rushing here, there and everywhere, watching the time and getting where he had to be. It was now noon and he was on his way for a quick chat with Ash. He had to be in DCI Radley's office at 1 p.m. but he needed to get things straight before he went in to that meeting. His job, his life, his reason to get up in the morning – all this was on the line and he knew it.

Ash had been put in a room on his own. Jazz was relieved to hear that this was only because Ash was traumatized, tired and dehydrated. He sat on the end of the bed looking at Ash, who was napping but opened his eyes when Jazz sat down. Having to say what he needed to quickly and then leave, Jazz smiled and, before Ash had a chance to say anything, went into his tirade about what had happened, what Ash had done and how they'd found him. He finished the tirade by giving a story that Ash could tell everyone and anyone, and that Jazz was going to tell DCI Radley in about half an hour at his meeting. Ash just stared at him. Jazz wasn't sure if he was taking it all in but he needed to let him know the plan.

'The way I see it,' Jazz started, looking at Ash to make sure he was paying full attention, 'is that you were on an undercover covert operation for me and Tom Black. Okay so far?'

Still, Ash stared intently at him. It was a bit disconcerting but Jazz had only a few more minutes before he had to leave. 'That's exactly what I'm going to say to DCI Radley. Apart from the fact you were a fucking dickhead to have gone alone to The Pig and Poke and talk about murders and implicate The Bird Man, I need to cover your arse and mine with DCI Radley, who is going to sack both of us for all the havoc caused by your stupidity.' Getting no response, he asked again, 'Okay so far?' Still no response, just a stare, so Jazz had to carry on. 'What we have is the person who killed Johnny Peters, the paedophile. Unfortunately he was murdered contract-kill style but it was definitely him on the video, so you and I have solved that case. Okay with you?' he repeated for the third time. The silence was deafening. Jazz had to leave if he was to get to his meeting in any sort of respectable time, but he couldn't leave Ash like this, looking like a zombie.

'Ash, are you okay? I've gone on here about everything but you look like shit.' Still getting no response, Jazz calmed down and thought *fuck it, DCI Radley can wait*. He started again. 'Ash, I was so worried about you. Tom and I and half of the Barking and Dagenham Police Force have been on the hunt for you. There has been some serious wheeling and dealing going on in the background to get you back. Not only did Freddie Link kidnap you but for Christ's sake! You got kidnapped again by Vinnie James and taken to South London.'

For a moment there was a flicker of interest in Ash's eyes. He stirred. 'Why the fuck did that happen? I was blindfolded with that putrid sack over my head, I didn't know what the fuck was going on. I thought I was being taken to be killed so many times, I was getting used to it.'

His laughter was shaky and a tad manic, Jazz thought. He placed a hand on Ash's shoulder. 'We got you back alive because The Bird Man used his connections. For a start I found out something on The Bird Man, which is between him and me, and that got his interest and his co-operation in finding you. Ash, I owe him big time now and he's going to make me pay, but it was worth it.' He caught a warning look from Ash and shook his head. 'No, no, nothing illegal, but something odd, and I have to do it. I got you back alive and that's all that matters.' He looked at Ash, so pathetic and glum, and felt a pang of remorse. 'Ash, I'm so sorry. I've let you down.' But something occurred to him that made him sit up straight. Cheekily he added, 'But hey!! You're alive. I didn't get you killed this time – that's got to be a bonus.'

Ash looked at him and suddenly leaned back onto his pillow and started to laugh. When, finally, he quieted down, he said, 'You're a fucking bastard to work for, DS Singh, and I'm not sure I'm up for it anymore.'

Jazz was taken aback by this upfront comment, but he wasn't going to have any of that. 'You need to think on this when you feel better, Ash. I think we've got to know each other now and it would be a pity if you left.

Yes, there have been some mistakes made.' When Ash laughed Jazz realized just how stupid that statement was. There had been huge rollercoaster fucking tsunami-sized mistakes made by both of them. He added, 'Look, Ash, we can start again. For the moment you have to forget about the *babe in the wood* murder and the *Sicilian* murder. We can't do anything about those. You were on the right tack but the clients will never talk and the murderers will never be found. We've got one of the murderers. The Barge Murder is solved and we have got the guy with the ring but unfortunately he is dead. He was Vinnie James, the bastard who kidnapped you from Freddie Link and took you to South London.'

Ash began to argue the point of who the murderer was but Jazz told him to just go with the result.

He asked Ash to remember who they were dealing with. The Bird Man was powerful and untouchable and the Met Police had a *hands off* policy. Only the special team put together to watch The Bird Man had any power over what happened to him. He did promise Ash that one day, when he wasn't looking, he would get The Bird Man and put him away.

Ash, looking at this jumped-up DS Jaswinder Singh, actually believed him. If anyone could do it, he could. He flouted every rule in the book, hung onto evidence like a mad dog with a bone and usually got his villain. Yes, Ash believed him.

Jazz thought Ash looked a bit more alert. His wife, mother and children would be visiting soon and he suggested that Ash build a good, exciting and brave story to tell them; if he were Ash, he'd do that.

Ash laughed again. Typical! Mind you, he thought, maybe a heroic tale would make his wife fancy him more, and make his mother prouder and his children in awe of him. He'd work on that while he waited. He smiled to himself, feeling a bit better. Did he want a working life with DS Singh? It seemed to be a bloody, dangerous and frantic ride. Did he really want it? At this precise moment, the answer was no, he didn't want it or need it.

Jazz left with a promise to be back later after his grilling with DCI Radley. By now he was tired, hungry, thirsty and not looking forward to the meeting. He had a lot of blagging to do and a lot of temper to deflect. In the meantime, he bought a bottle of vodka and filled his flasks. He took a few swigs to relax himself. He told himself he deserved a drink after what he had dealt with, and he needed to keep everything clear in his mind to explain it to DCI Radley. A few more swigs made him feel confident. He shouldn't have been driving but it wasn't far to go. He popped a couple of spearmint chewing gum strips in his mouth to clear his breath and it made his growling stomach feel better. He would get a McDonald's later.

His meeting with DCI Radley went fairly well – if being told he was to stay in the office for the next few days and write everything up in a neat and expansive way was a good thing. He was also teetering on the edge of being suspended for not keeping control of his team, and for being so bloody stupid as to lose Ash and causing half the Met Police in Barking and Dagenham to be pulled off other work to find him. Jazz did point out that the police hadn't found Ash; it was he, Jaswinder Singh, who'd found him and got him back. That caused a tirade of home truths Jazz could have done without.

He left DCI Radley's office after a full hour of tirades, justifications and explanations, exhausted and a tad depressed. What the fuck was he doing and what had he done? Had he even achieved anything? He realized he had taken on The Bird Man of Barking and he liked to think it was a draw but perhaps he had lost. Tom was about to be hauled into DCI Radley's office for explanations and tirades. Jazz wished him luck and said it was his fault, not Tom's. At least they had solved the Barge Murder, which had now gone viral on You Tube. DCI Radley was spitting mad about this. Apparently it had had a million hits before it was taken off. The press was baying at the door, and as DCI Radley was now the expert in dealing with the press, he put on his dress suit and gave a statement. At least now he could say the murder was solved due to brilliant police work and the murderer had been found dead.

As an aside, Jazz suggested to DCI Radley that it might be a good idea for officers to look at the other two murders, those of John Carpenter and Barry Jessop, to see if there was any connection with Vinnie James. He suggested the murders were unusual and quite pertinent to their crimes. It could be, he suggested, that Vinnie James had taken it on himself to be a knight in shining armour. James Kent had referred to the person who killed John Carpenter as a knight in shining armour. Vinnie was very capable of killing these people. DCI

Radley paused for thought and nodded; yes, it might be a good idea and it would clear up the murders. Jazz felt good: another plan had come together. He was a tad too cocky but he could also be right. DCI Radley was desperate to solve these murders and get the press off his back so it was worth an investigation. Jazz said that Tom Black was investigating these to which DCI Radley told him in no uncertain terms to keep away from Tom Black and his team and let them do their job. He didn't need Jazz interfering.

Jazz left to go home. He'd had enough for now and he wanted to sleep, eat and have a drink. He had lots to think about. It was only 3 p.m. but he wanted to visit Ash again later, after his family had left. He got his McDonald's, another bottle of vodka (no sense in running out), and took himself home. It was strange going home during the day; the house looked different in daylight.

Mrs Chodda was out and the house was quiet. He could smell the curry she'd had been cooking for tonight and envied the domesticity of the Choddas' lives. Suddenly he wished he had someone to come home to. Someone who would ask what sort of day he had, someone who cared. He felt a little low but he knew that was because he was tired and needed a drink. He would feel better later. He had eaten most of the Big Mac before he got home but he sat with a glass of vodka and orange, and some cold chips. He wondered why the chips got cold so quickly but it was food and he was used to cold chips.

He slept until 8 p.m. and woke feeling better.

It was late, but he was the police, so visiting the hospital at 9 p.m. received only a few grumbles from staff. Ash was bedded down for a good night's sleep and had just turned off the TV in his room. Hospital life started and ended early, so 9 p.m. was like midnight to patients. Ash woke from a gentle slumber as Jazz entered the room, bouncy and full of life. 'I'm never going to feel better if you keep doing this,' was all Jazz got for a hello. He wanted Ash to think again about working with him. Okay, he conceded, he hadn't given him much time but he needed Ash to work with him.

Ash sat up. He hadn't expected to hear that he was useful to work with. All he had got from Jazz up to now was how he was a *useless prick and a dickhead*. He nearly agreed with some of that – but what the hell was Jazz going on about now?

Jazz had thought about Ash and their teamwork. He said that he himself was good at what he did, but that he had no sense of correct procedures, and he couldn't even write. Ash laughed at such an exaggeration but he listened. What Jazz was trying to say in his own way was that there was a good partnership here. Ash was brilliant at finding out information, trawling through the internet, reading and writing reports, formulating plans, and placating other members of staff and other teams of officers. Jazz needed that; he didn't want to and couldn't do any of the above. He figured that between them they could be awesome and solve every crime. He cited the work Ash did in finding out where James Kent and Barry Jessop had been. No one else would have found that out because no one except Ash read such mind-blowingly boring reports. Ash wasn't sure that was quite a compliment but Jazz assured him it was. Getting carried away with it all Jazz thought that together they would be like Sherlock Holmes and Dr Watson. Of course, Jazz would be Sherlock Holmes but Dr Watson was the mainstay in the duo. By now Ash was laughing again. This man was mad! Upbeat, brilliant but definitely mad.

Ash had talked with his family who were so proud of him. They didn't know what had gone on for real but the story he'd told them of undercover work scared, thrilled and excited them. His wife adored him and his mother fought for prime position beside the bed next to her heroic son. His children talked excitedly about Daddy being like 007, which he quite liked.

He thought about his career in the Police Force. It would take him a long time to get over being kidnapped and he'd been promised treatment at Goring for the Post Traumatic Stress he was experiencing. He still didn't know what he would do with his career, but if he was working in the office doing background work, he would like that. For the time being he just wanted to stay safe and keep taking the tablets that staved off the terror he felt when he tried to sleep and the nightmares started. Jazz said he would keep in touch and maybe even visit him in Goring in Sussex where police personnel went for treatment. Ash hoped he wouldn't visit him. For the time being he just wanted to be left alone and get on with getting better; Jazz would be no help with that.

Jazz left him at 11 p.m., confident that after Ash got treatment they would be back working together. Ash was alive and uninjured. Sure, his mind was a bit scrambled at the moment, but Jazz knew that one. It would pass with treatment. He went home knowing that Ash would make a good decision and would continue working with him in the future.

Tom had his meeting with DCI Radley and came off a lot lighter than Jazz. He rang Jazz and told him that all he'd got was a slapped wrist. Jazz liked working with Tom but he was told that wasn't going to happen again. Apparently Jazz was a bad influence on Tom Black, which made Tom laugh. But hey, he suggested, they should just get on with their work and see where it took them. Tom had more fun working with Jazz than he ever did with his team and he wasn't going to let that be taken away from him. His parting words were that DCI Radley could fucking shove his ideas up his arse and that he and Jazz would bloody well solve crime together. He added he was Batman and Jazz was Robin. Jazz said it was the wrong way round and they decided to argue about that one later.

Jazz awoke the next morning with a lot on his mind. He went into Ilford Police Station to start work on the report. God, it was going to be awful to write with so much to write about, and so much that mustn't be made public. The other teams were on form with, *Ash was a jammy git, still alive in your company but only just by all accounts.* Jazz was told that there had been a book set up on how long Ash would survive and to date someone had won a bit of it because they had bet on near-death scrapes.

The book was ongoing, and more money had been put into it by those who had seen what had happened to date to Ash. Someone suggested that instead of a nickname of *The Jazz Singer* he should be called *The Grim Reaper*. Actually Jazz laughed at that; they could never know that it was true because Vinnie James was part of the Eddie Grimshaw gang and his sons were the Brothers Grim. He was going to get his leg pulled continually for quite some time. Not all of it was in jest; some thought Jazz was a bad officer who put the lives of others at risk. No one wanted to work with him except Tom Black and he had been warned off.

Jazz had a job to do for The Bird Man as promised, but before he did that he needed a cup of tea and a 999 breakfast to see him on his way. That would set him up for the day and help take the nasty taste out of his mouth for helping The Bird Man. At least Milly would be pleased to see him.

In the canteen Milly, as usual, dropped everything to serve him. His 999 breakfast took precedence over all other ordered breakfasts and came to him in minutes. He gave Milly a grateful kiss on the cheek, and cockily blew a kiss to the group of officers who'd been made to wait and were now shouting abuse in his direction. He didn't make his life any easier with that attitude but he really didn't care.

CHAPTER FORTY-THREE
Chirpy chirpy cheep cheep

Jazz had made the call earlier. He rang a Mr Ernest Blower from Maidstone, Kent. He said that he was Mr Blower's greatest fan and, as a Senior Police Officer in the Metropolitan Police, he would like to buy his latest addition from him. Mr Ernest Blower was a belligerent and tetchy man who upset everyone he came into contact with. He had no time for people, he told Jazz. The only people he liked a bit were the police.

He had the greatest respect for the police because they'd helped him enormously when his house was broken into many years ago. They'd given him good advice on installing safety features. Mr Blower lived alone and was a confirmed bachelor. The police were the first and last people to enter his home for many years and he liked it that way.

When he had outbuildings put up in his extensive garden he called the police to ask for help in what he should do to stop anyone breaking into them, and a very nice police officer had come around and introduced himself as a Community Police Officer dealing with home security. They'd had a cup of tea together, and the officer was very helpful and kind. Thus Mr Blower was very pro-police and said he would do anything to help them if he could.

Jazz made an appointment to visit Mr Blower that afternoon. He wanted to get this done as quickly as possible. It felt strange and wrong, but he'd promised The Bird Man he would do it.

Mr Blower lived frugally in a bungalow on the edge of a common. He had a large sideway which had a big fence across it. The roofs of the outhouses on the other side of the fence were just visible. Mr Blower let Jazz into a sparsely furnished lounge. It had a dark old-fashioned look to it, like something you would have seen after the Second World War. The furniture was plain but functional, with a dull multi-coloured carpet that had seen better days. The armchairs all faced the tiled fireplace that held a gas fire. Mr Blower made a cup of tea for each of them and brought it into the room and put it on the table. Jazz reckoned Mr Blower wasn't as old as he looked. He looked about sixty but his skin belied that fact; perhaps he was no more than forty-five. He wore a small droopy moustache and he obviously cut his own hair with the dog clippers Jazz saw on the sideboard. He nearly giggled when he thought that dog clippers were apt, because this man had a hangdog expression.

He tried to make small talk and chatted about the weather, but Mr Blower wasn't used to chitchat. Although he professed to like the police he was getting decidedly agitated and aggravated by this officer wasting his time. With no sociable manners and bursting with annoyance, he asked, 'What do you want, man? I have things to do and I need to get on.'

Jazz was used to being affable and getting his way by chatting and being sociable, but he had to change tack very quickly because he couldn't afford to lose Mr Blower's interest or goodwill.

He explained that he knew of Mr Blower as an experienced shower of budgerigars, and that he had consistently had the Best Show in the National and World Show. Jazz explained that his dear old dad was an amateur keeper of budgerigars and, although he didn't show them, he prized them beyond belief. Mr Blower nearly smiled at this. He understood the love of budgerigars. He loved his birds and would sit in the shed with them just listening to them sing and chirp. He told Jazz he had over three hundred birds in his sheds outside if Jazz cared to look at them. Enthusiastically, Jazz said he would love to.

The sheds took up most of the garden. Mr Blower explained he had his aviaries but he also had his breeding cages and the cages where he reared the chicks, and then he noted them on cards and tagged them. Yes, it was a fulltime job and he had a small disability pension, but his inheritance allowed him to indulge in his hobby.

Having now got the measure of Mr Blower Jazz reckoned he knew what his disability was: his lack of personality and social behaviour. Mr Blower was used to living alone so it never occurred to him that you don't burp and fart as you discuss, in company, the finer points of keeping birds.

Now, to the point of Jazz coming here – which Jazz needed to handle very delicately and carefully. 'Mr Blower, I have come to you to ask a very special favour.

My dear old Dad, who will turn seventy next week, has always longed for a potential winner amongst his budgerigars. He doesn't want to show them, just love and adore them. My dad was a police officer for forty years and he served his country and district well – I would love to give him a potential winner as a birthday present.'

He looked at Mr Blower to see what response he was getting and noted he was getting nothing back. Undaunted, he continued. 'Mr Blower, you are the best in the land for breeding beautiful and magnificent budgerigars. I couldn't go to anyone else. I'll pay whatever it takes to own one of your beautiful birds. I want to make my dad happy. I don't know how much longer I'll have him and I want the memory of his face when I give him this wonderful present.' He was surprised to see tears glistening in Mr Blower's eyes.

Mr Blower, wiping away a tear, seemed quite overwhelmed by such a love for birds; he asked which bird Jazz would like for his dad. Jazz asked if it was possible to have one of the chicks from last year's winner. He almost winced at asking such a huge thing. It was common sense that a chick from a winner would be very expensive. But Mr Blower was very amenable. He said he had bred several batches and had a few rather good-quality birds with beautiful spots, and the potential to be winners. 'I have a male and female from two different winners that your father might be interested to breed from. They are, of course, not my best birds – they are for the next competition – but they come from the best stock.'

Jazz, amazed that he'd been offered two, was very grateful indeed. He asked how much the chicks would be and Mr Blower said very warmly he was happy to help the police, so it would be a gift from him. He put the birds in two boxes and Jazz thanked him again and went on his way. God, he thought, he was the dog's bollocks as far as The Bird Man was concerned. He'd got what he wanted and another bird to boot!

He went straight to The Bird Man's house. He was expected; The Bird Man knew where Jazz had been and was waiting impatiently for him. Jazz presented the two boxes and The Bird Man scuttled away like a child with a new toy. Jazz had never seen this side of the bastard before. Almost singing as he took the boxes, The Bird Man said he would be back in a moment. Jazz waited in the little shed for what must have been nearly an hour. He was beginning to wonder if he should have gone when the door burst open, startling him.

The Bird Man was very pleased indeed. The birds were wonderful, and good stock. The fact that Jazz had been given a male and a female was unheard of. 'You don't give breeding pairs away like that,' Jazz was told. How had he done it? When Jazz had told his story, The Bird Man laughed and suggested that perhaps he could find an opening for Jazz in his organization. He could do with someone who could work outside the box. Jazz declined the invitation.

He was curious, though. He asked The Bird Man why he hadn't gone to get the birds himself. He was powerful enough to scare most people into giving him what he wanted. The Bird Man explained that Mr Ernest

Blower was a cantankerous old bastard who was very strange and lived alone. He wasn't clever enough to be frightened of anyone. In fact, if he thought he could piss someone off he would do it for the hell of it. He didn't have any associates or friends and was unapproachable. He knew The Bird Man of Barking wanted one of his chicks and he'd done everything in his power to make sure he never got one of them.

In fact, when approached the first time by The Bird Man and asked if he would sell one of his prize chicks, Mr Blower had gone out of his way to be as belligerent and unhelpful as he could. The Bird Man could have had him maimed and his birds taken, but he was in the legitimate area of showing budgerigars and he didn't want to ruin his reputation. Everyone in those circles knew everyone else's business and he didn't want to get into any of that by sorting out Mr Blower. He proudly said he had a good reputation in the budgerigar showing world.

He reminded Jazz that he had been told about Mr Blower's deference to police and to use it. He was impressed Jazz had used it so well. He'd repaid his debt with interest. Jazz turned as he left, and said that one day they would lock horns again and this time he would win. The Bird Man laughed and told him he was kidding himself. He shouted down the path, 'Try and keep this DC alive for a bit longer.' Jazz flinched but didn't turn around.

It was getting late now and he didn't want to go straight home. He went to the Gudwara. He felt at peace there. The eating area was known as 'Langar'. Every

Sikh was expected to perform 'Sewa', a selfless serving of others in the community. Deepak had instilled this in Jazz as a Sikh. There were three different parts of Sewa:

Tan: physical service, e.g. working in the langar and helping to look after the gudwara
Man: mental service, e.g. studying the Guru Granth Sahib Ji and teaching it to others
Dhan: material service to other people, e.g. giving money to charities or giving time to help people who are in need

Jazz wasn't sure what he was doing here but he wanted to do something. Coming to the Gudwara and helping in the langar made him feel better and of use. Deepak wasn't there but he picked up a tea towel and started to dry up in the kitchen. Others there just nodded hello and got on with it. Some were washing up, and others serving the food as people arrived for worship and then came into the langar to eat, or just came to sit and eat and talk. The gossiping aunties were sitting on the floor of the langar and cutting up onions by the sackful for the next dal dish (which is lentil curry, to the uninitiated).

Jazz felt at peace to be doing something good. Today hadn't felt right. He'd conned Mr Blower with a story that wasn't true to get a good breeding bird for The Bird Man. This was the only way he could think of to make some sort of amends. Whilst he was at it, he should probably do something to make amends for how he'd got Ash into so much trouble. Okay, he argued with himself, the idiot got himself into trouble – but Jazz should have watched him. Nevertheless, Ash was alive and going to be all right.

Jazz stayed at the Gudwara for an hour and left to go home feeling a bit more like a Sikh, having done something selfless.

He got home and went quietly up to his room. He had picked up a pizza. He could have eaten at the Gudwara but what they had there would have made him sick; he didn't like dal. He watched a bit of cricket that was being played in Australia, while drinking a few glasses of vodka and orange. For the first time in what felt like an age, he was relaxed and enjoying being off-duty and doing his own thing. Life had been hectic and he was glad of a bit of empty time. Tomorrow he should find out if his plan had worked.

CHAPTER FORTY-FOUR
Retributions and regrets

He had to go and talk to that shit head Mad Pete. There were going to be lots of things to sort out with that two-faced rat. One: was he in cohorts with the South London Gang? He was too much in the right place at the right time and there had been talk of someone blabbing to Eddie Grimshaw about the Barge Murder. He knew Mad Pete was a slime ball but he was his slime ball, and he wanted to make sure he never talked about his work to anyone. But that would have to wait. There was something else he needed to check. He rang Mad Pete and said he was on his way and he had better stay put in his flat until he arrived.

Mad Pete was waiting for him. He said he had to go out soon, that he had work to do. Jazz bit his tongue. He knew Mad Pete's 'work', as he called it, was supplying drugs and fencing mobile phones and iPads and anything small and electronic. He didn't want to think about that now. He'd brought coffees and two breakfasts from McDonald's. They sat and ate in silence, enjoying the sausage and egg McMuffins.

'I've got some news for you, Mr Singh,' said Mad Pete.

'I thought you might have.' Jazz had been expecting this and he waited comfortably.

'I just heard from my contacts that Bam Bam committed suicide last night in prison,' said Mad Pete. In response to Jazz's *really!* he looked sharply at Jazz. 'You knew that, didn't you, Mr Singh. I can tell.'

Jazz said nothing. He just asked how it happened.

Incredulously Mad Pete answered, 'Well, it's strange, Mr Singh. Bam Bam dived head first from the top floor of the wing onto the cheese grater about thirty to forty feet below.' *(A cheese grater is a wire mess netting fastened tightly across from balcony to balcony that stops missiles thrown from above hitting anyone on the ground. It usually sits about fifteen feet above the ground floor).* Mad Pete went on, 'He must have meant it because if he had fallen on his back or stomach he would have bounced and although a bit messy he would have lived. But the silly bleeder landed head first and that just mashed him up.'

Jazz asked why they thought it was suicide and Mad Pete said because there was no one with him at the time; although there were cameras, they went off in a power cut for a short while and it was during the cut that this happened.

Mad Pete was thinking, which was something he shouldn't do. 'Mr Singh, has this got anything to do with the Triads I contacted for you? It just seems such a coincidence.' Jazz shrugged and said that coincidences do happen. He reminded Mad Pete that there were questions he would ask him in the near future about his association with Eddie Grimshaw in South London. He said pointedly that Mad Pete should remember coincidences can happen at any time.

Mad Pete nodded furiously and said he was good for anything Mr Singh needed, no worries. It was enough to keep Mad Pete where he should be: frightened, nervous of Mr Singh, and deferential, just the way Jazz liked him.

As for The Bird Man of Barking, he was going to keep an eye on all the aggregate being taken by barge to Wallasea Island in Essex to protect the birds for the RSPB project. Jazz knew The Bird Man had buried a lot of bodies over the years in that aggregate, and The Bird Man knew that Jazz had worked it out. It made Jazz smile to knowing that The Bird Man would always be on tenterhooks, wondering if Jazz was going to do anything. It put him in the firing line to be topped but The Bird Man would have known Jazz would put that information somewhere safe in case he was got rid of. They would live in an uneasy relationship and that suited Jazz down to the ground. One day he was going to get The Bird Man banged up and there would be no mistakes on that one. He could wait.

Everything was going well. He had waited for the right time and now Bam Bam was dead. He had a confidential word with the Triad. He'd given them an idea of what Bam Bam had done to them, stirring it well with lots of suggestions of disrespect and grassing them up. You didn't mess with the Triad, and it seemed to have had the desired effect. The meeting had been strange; he had talked and they had listened, looking inscrutable. He had left hoping his words had sunk in and had made them mad enough to do something about Bam Bam. They were never going to tell him what they thought or what they would do, but Jazz knew they wouldn't let such disrespect go unpunished. Bam Bam was dead. It had made Jazz's day. The bastard had got what he deserved and he raised his flask to the memory of DC Tony Sepple.

CHAPTER FORTY-FIVE
I'll tell you a story

He spent the day in Ilford Police Station trying to put together the patchwork of what had happened over the last few days. It wasn't easy but with the help of his trusty flask and a little imagination he wove a very convincing story that ended with a murderer being found. He bigged up Ash's part in the story, making him into a hero, which he hoped Ash would live up to.

He still got the jibes of 'cop killer', and they were back to the old chestnut of *They seek him here, they seek him there, they can't find that bloody Sikh anywhere.* But his back was broad and strong and he lived with the jibes and even laughed at some of them.

He was Jaswinder Singh, the Jazz Singer, and this was his manor and he was going to stay put and sod the lot of them!

CHAPTER FORTY-SIX
Later

That night he went home relaxed, knowing Ash had been returned to his family intact and was being made a fuss of. He would start his treatment at Goring by Sea in a week's time. Bam Bam was dead, so all was well with the world.

Jazz had the weekend off and planned to sleep most of it. He got his fish and chips and was going to eat them in front of the rest of the test match in Australia, along with a good few vodkas, as he didn't have to get up in the morning.

As he put the key in the door of De Vere Gardens, Mrs Chodda opened her kitchen door. For a moment his heart stopped. He really, really didn't want to meet another marriageable woman and her mother – not tonight. Mrs Chodda smiled and said she just wanted to say good evening. She hadn't seen him for a while. Endearingly incorrectly, she said that *their footbridges hadn't crossed recently.* Jazz smiled and said, 'I think you mean our paths haven't crossed recently.' They both laughed at her English. Jazz asked her falteringly, not wanting to seem that interested, 'How is your niece these days? I haven't seen her for a while.' Mrs Chodda noted the interest immediately. 'Oh, you mean Amrit. She has gone back to India.' She saw Jazz's face fall, although he recovered quickly. She smiled knowingly and said, 'She has gone to a family wedding. She will be back in one month's time.'

Jazz tried to hide his smile but she noted it instantly.

Mrs Chodda had never considered Amrit to be a suitable wife for Jaswinder; after all, she was a divorced woman with a son, rather than a good young virgin. But now she saw the interest, she would work on her plans. Jazz might think he was clever but Mrs Chodda was streets ahead of him. He should enjoy his success for the moment; he would have to face his biggest challenge soon. Mrs Chodda was on his case.

Jazz thanked Mrs Chodda and kissed her unexpectedly on the cheek. Going up the stairs, he suddenly felt pretty good. *So her name is Amrit! What a fabulous name,* he thought. A month wasn't long. He reckoned he could sleep for a month given half a chance. The thought wasn't that funny but he started laughing and just couldn't stop. Perhaps he would buy her a welcome home present. He would think on that one. For now he would sit back and enjoy a drink and some thoughts about a pretty, feisty girl who was in India.